sleeper

sleeper

NICK WILKSHIRE

jesperson
publishing
2 0 0 4

Jesperson Publishing
100 Water Street
P. O. Box 2188
St. John's, NL
A1C 6E6

www.jespersonpublishing.nf.net

Library and Archives Canada Cataloguing in Publication

Wilkshire, Nicholas, 1968-
    Sleeper : a novel / Nicholas Wilkshire.

ISBN 1-894377-09-5

I. Title.

PS8645.I44S5 2004   C813'.6   C2004-903649-1

©2004 Nicholas Wilkshire

Interior Design/Layout: Rhonda Molloy
Cover Design:

Editors: Jocelyne Thomas, Tamara Reynish
Cover Photos: Stephen J. Tizzard

Printed in Canada.

For Tanya, who shares my dreams.

And for Matthew, Kate and Ben, who make them real.

"*The presumption of innocence is a hallowed principle lying at the very heart of criminal law… It ensures that until the State proves an accused's guilt beyond all reasonable doubt, he or she is innocent. This is essential in a society committed to fairness and social justice. The presumption of innocence confirms our faith in humankind; it reflects our belief that individuals are decent and law-abiding members of the community until proven otherwise.*"

Dickson, C.J., in R. v. Oakes [1986] 1 S.C.R. 103, at pp. 119-120.

chapter one
—may

The cold air smothered virtually every sound in its blanket of dampness, save for the dull, dual-toned moan of the foghorn every few minutes. The month of May in St. John's could be beautiful, but it also brought its fair share of the dreaded combination of rain, drizzle and fog.

"Where are you going?" the young woman asked with a laugh, as her boyfriend disappeared into the mist off to their left. It was one-thirty in the morning and the two university students were walking back to their apartments from George Street, where they had guzzled their cab fare. Having made the steep climb up New Gower Street and beyond, they had crested the hill that cradles St. John's harbour and were now making their way across Bannerman Park, a well-treed expanse that includes an open common, an outdoor pool, a playground and a softball diamond. But in these conditions, all they could make out was the path in front of them, and even that was a challenge.

"Mother nature calls," he replied, and she heard the rustle of bushes as he prepared to relieve himself.

"Hurry up will you," she said impatiently, looking into the surrounding mist. Other than the distant sound of a car passing on Rennie's Mill Road, the park was deathly silent. "This place is giving me the creeps."

"Oh relax," came the young man's reply as he finished up.

"I'm coming now anyway…Jeez," he stopped abruptly and burst out laughing.

"What's so funny?" the girl was moving towards his voice now.

"There's a guy asleep in the bushes over here. I almost whizzed on him, look."

Groping her way through the fog in the direction of her companion's voice, she came upon his smiling face as he stood over a long pair of legs protruding from the bush.

"Looks like he had a few too many," the young man laughed, bending down for a closer look.

"What are you doing?" the girl was annoyed now. "Leave him alone," she said, and began walking back to the path.

"Hang on. I just want to make sure he's okay."

The young man pulled back the bushes but couldn't see anything in the faint light, so he began pulling on the man's legs.

"You weigh a ton skipper; how are you feel…"

He froze as the man's torso and head came into view.

"Jesus!" he yelled, jumping back as he caught sight of a thick black gash across the man's throat and his blood-soaked raincoat.

"What is it?" came the girl's startled voice from the path. But before she heard a reply, her companion emerged from the fog and grabbed her by the arm.

"What's the matter?" she said as he dragged her towards the nearest streetlight. She had never seen such a look of terror on his face.

"Poor bastard," Inspector Pat Gushue said, looking over the body from inside the plastic tent they had hastily erected after cordoning off the area. The glare from the floodlights picked up every cruel detail of the morbid face.

"Don't shed too many tears, Pat," said his partner with a grin. "He was a lawyer after all."

"Let me see that," Gushue ordered, slipping on a plastic glove and taking the business card Detective Steve Carew had just plucked from the dead man's wallet.

"Stuart Bruce, Q.C. of Bruce, Atkinson. King Street, Toronto. Well, well."

"Probably made more than all of us here put together," Carew remarked.

"Probably so, but it's not going to do him any good now is it? A little respect for the dead, okay Steve?"

"Whatever...," Carew shook his head, returning to the wallet.

"So," Gushue said, returning the card. "We have a Mr. Stuart Bruce of Toronto, Ontario. A white male in...I'd say his fifties..."

"He's fifty-two," Carew interrupted, pointing to a laminated birth certificate.

"That's great, he's fifty-two. Thanks, but what I want to know is what he's doing lying in the middle of Bannerman Park with his throat slit open."

"Well, there's no cash here...," Carew said.

"Credit cards?"

"Nope."

"He looks like the Platinum Card type, so I'd say someone must have cleaned him out," Gushue said with a frown.

"There's a room key, too—the Fairmont," Carew added. "Maybe he was out for a stroll and bumped into the wrong guy."

"You can say that again. What about..."

Gushue's next question was interrupted by a yell from across the park. The two detectives and a couple of the others at the scene ran off in the direction of the call. After a short sprint, they came upon two constables, one of whom was putting handcuffs on a ragged-looking man sitting on the ground.

"What's all this?" Gushue asked, breathing heavily.

"We found him passed out sir," one of the young constables said excitedly.

"This was on the ground next to him," he added, and thrust a plastic bag under Gushue's nose. It contained a knife with what appeared to be blood on the blade.

"Good work boys," Gushue said, kneeling and putting the bag in the face of the cuffed man, as Carew stood over them with a flashlight.

"What's this then...," he began, holding up the bag, but then broke off his interrogation and stood up abruptly, pulling a face. "Christ, he smells like a distillery."

The man muttered something inaudible.

"What?" Gushue said.

"Didn't…do nothin'," the man said groggily.

"We'll see about that," Gushue replied. He turned to Carew and drew him aside.

"Ride with him back to HQ and set him up in the bullpen," Gushue said, referring to the interrogation room. And whatever you do, keep him up. I'll finish handing off the crime scene to forensics and I'll be right behind you."

"Alright Sarge."

"And keep this low-key for now," he added, turning to the two young constables to ensure they got the message. "Loose lips sink ships. The last thing we need is a bunch of questions from the press right now."

As Gushue headed back towards the crime scene, he saw the head of the forensics unit arriving with reinforcements and a van-load of equipment. They would make sure no stone was left unturned. After directing them to the spot where the two young constables were standing and giving some instructions, he looked at his watch. It was three o'clock in the morning, and with any luck, he'd have a confession by breakfast and the whole thing in the bag by the time it hit the morning news. He hurried off to his car.

chapter two

The sun was shining as David Hall sped down Springdale Street, hoping to catch the left-turn arrow at the bottom of the hill, past the growing line of waiting traffic coming off the harbour arterial from the West end and Mount Pearl. The streets were still glistening with last night's rain, but they would soon be dry if the blue sky held. As he glanced up, David decided it probably would, despite the bank of clouds hovering beyond the South Side Hills. He navigated his way east along Duckworth Street and turned up a steep hill across from the Courthouse, tucking his little compact into the last available parking spot. He fed the meter and walked briskly back down to Duckworth, angling his way between the grid-locked cars towards his office, just a hundred yards past the Court of Appeal.

"Morning Debbie," he said with a smile as he passed the reception area on his way to the stairs.

"Morning Dave," she replied before picking up her ringing phone.

As he bounded up the stairs and reached the second floor, he was hit by a heavy mass of warm air.

"Let me guess. They didn't fix the heating."

"You got it," his secretary, Joanne, said with a frown. "That furnace has a mind of its own. We're all going to cook in here today."

He hung his raglan on the coat rack behind the door and switched on his computer, noticing his flashing phone in passing. The messages could wait for five minutes.

"How was Billy?" his secretary called out from her desk.

"Don't ask," he laughed. He had been in an examination for discovery all of the previous afternoon with William Baker— affectionately known as Billy—a personal injury client whose file had been kicked around the firm for years and had been on and off David's desk for the past two. Every few weeks, like clockwork, he would show up downstairs demanding to see his lawyer and ranting about the poor treatment he was receiving. But his bark was much worse than his bite, and he always settled down after a few soothing words from David and a cup of coffee. The fact was his file was the biggest dog in the firm, and the defendant's insurance company had said long ago that they would only pay out the claim when hell froze over. But Billy took a very active interest in his case, and though there was rarely anything new to report, he would still show up for his regular visit.

"I'll be lucky if I can get a case of beer for him after yesterday."

"Why, what happened yesterday?"

"Turns out old Bill's got a list of medical visits a mile long that he somehow forgot to mention to me," he said, shaking his head.

"But he's not settling for less than a hundred grand," Joanne said mockingly.

"Of course not."

David poured himself a coffee from the grimy pot.

"Morning Tina, morning Renee," he said to the other two secretaries on the other side of the stairs. "Where is everybody?" he asked, motioning to the two darkened offices.

"Laura's in court and Phil's not in yet," said the younger one, Renee.

"The slacker!" he laughed, sipping his coffee.

"Hear about the murder?" Renee asked.

"What murder?" He raised his eyebrows. He had slept in and missed the morning news.

"You didn't hear? A lawyer was found dead in Bannerman Park."

"Who?" David asked quickly.

"Good to see you're up on current events," Phil Morgan said sarcastically as he reached the top of the stairs. "He was from Toronto."

"And he's dead?"

"As a doornail," Phil said, pouring his own coffee.

"He was mugged or something, I heard," Renee offered.

"I don't think anyone knows for sure," Phil said.

David whistled, following Phil into his office and taking a seat as the latter settled in his chair and switched on his computer.

"I wonder what he was doing wandering around Bannerman Park in the middle of the night?" David asked, putting his feet up on the desk.

"I don't know. Lousy night for a walk though."

"What was he doing in town?"

"He was here for a discovery. Big insurance claim, I think," Phil said.

"What are the odds of coming to St. John's for a discovery and getting off'ed. I can't believe it."

"Well they said on the news that they've got someone in custody so I guess we'll find out soon enough what really happened."

They theorized about the murder for a while and then moved on to their usual topics.

"So, how was the weekend? Get any sleep?" Phil asked with a smile. Engaged to an accountant, and with no immediate plans for children, he couldn't resist teasing his friend about life with a baby, which he knew was anything but restful.

"Yeah, not too bad. How about you?"

"Arts and Culture Centre on Friday night…," Phil began.

"The hypnotist?" David said mockingly.

"Very funny. A pianist, actually."

"Even better. And you say I'm whipped."

Phil laughed at this, rather than pretending he wouldn't rather have been bar-hopping on George Street. Phil was David's only true friend at the firm and the only one he trusted without reservation. They were both second-year associates, so they were very low on the office totem pole, just above the sole first-year and the half-dozen articled clerks who were crammed into the musty old library on the ground floor. Whether by design or not, the firm's hierarchy was reflected in its physical layout. The third floor was home to the firm's partners and four of its associates, ranging in seniority from three to five years' call to the Bar. The five partners were all in their forties, including Bill McGrath, the man who had founded the firm and who continued to rule it with an iron fist.

McGrath had made his name in the criminal courts and then set up the firm with one other partner, who had since moved out of the province. The firm's focus had shifted over the years to a mixture of family law and personal injury litigation, with the latter being the firm's main money-maker. It had remained a street-based practice, and the lawyers ended up taking on almost anything that came through the door. The implications of this client-base were most significant for the junior lawyers, for whom spending a morning before two levels of courts and the afternoon before a third was a routine occurrence. Also, like most of the firms its size, McGrath & Co. operated on the trickle-down principle that kept the juicy files on the third floor. By the time one made its way through all the lawyers up there and ended up with David or Phil, the chances of making any money off it were slim indeed. The only ones worse off were the articled clerks, though their billings weren't scrutinized as closely. The associates' true motto was that if you wanted to succeed, you had to make the firm money. But by the time you had appeared on behalf of all of the partners for the routine court matters and researched the un-winnable cases to death, there was little left over for the financially-viable files, if you were lucky enough to have any.

Still, this was the expected state of affairs in the St. John's legal community, like many others across the country, and the two young men didn't complain often. They had both joined the firm not because of prestige or money, though their salaries were adequate, but because they knew that of all the local law firms, McGrath & Co. would offer them the most in court experience. David had his sights set on a career as a criminal lawyer, while Phil preferred family law; and in their brief careers at the firm, they had both benefited from plenty of time on their feet in their respective courts.

"So what do you think this meeting's all about?" Phil asked, referring to the associates' meeting that had been called for one o'clock that afternoon.

"Billings probably, and how we're all underachieving," David replied.

Phil nodded.

"You mean the usual pep talk."

"What's on your plate this week?" David asked, sipping his coffee.

"Laura's got a custody trial starting tomorrow that I'm supposed to sit in on," he said, referring to the firm's senior family lawyer. "Should be good for a week. Other than that, I've just got the usual stuff. A first appearance this morning on an impaired…"

"I can do that for you if you want. I'm down there on a peace bond at nine-thirty."

On any given morning, the firm had a handful of lawyers in various different courts and they often traded off assignments to save time.

"Great, thanks. That'll give me time to try and finish this quieting of titles application before tomorrow. If I don't finish it soon I swear it's going to be the end of me."

"Yuck." David said, holding his nose. The only thing worse than family law in his mind was real estate, especially when it involved untitled land in some outport in the middle of nowhere.

"How many hours have you spent on that barker already?"

"I don't want to know," Phil said, shaking his head. "But whatever it is, it's worth a hundred times what we'll get paid for it. I don't know why we have these files anyway."

"It's all politics. McGrath's probably representing the guy's brother on a big P.I. file or something," David said, looking at his watch. "Well, I'd better get going. See you at one."

"Yeah, I can hardly wait."

chapter three

"So did you hear who they picked up near the body with a knife in his hand?" Kelly Lane said as she entered the third floor boardroom and dropped a thin file on the table. The associates looked at her expectantly and she savoured her power over them for as long as she could.

"Tom Fitzgerald," she said finally.

"Who's that?" asked Ron James, the most senior associate.

"McGrath acted for him in a personal injury action a long time ago, then got him off on an assault charge about five years back."

"You're kidding. So he's going to take the case?"

"He's thinking about it," Lane grinned.

"That's going to be a hell of a case…," one of the other associates said with a whistle.

"I thought he was jammed up with trials set for the winter?"

Phil remarked, looking at David across the table, who shrugged his shoulders.

"Half of those'll be settled by then," Lane said with an air of authority.

Kelly Lane was the most junior partner at the firm and held the unofficial position of liaison between the partners and the associates and clerks. She presented herself to the incoming clerks as the sort of friendly, easygoing colleague they could come to with their concerns, and she was always the first to suggest a trip to George Street on a Friday afternoon. But by the time you had spent a summer or two at the firm you realized that she was by far the most ruthless of the partners, and she could not be trusted. Most of the associates had learned that lesson the hard way at one time or another and avoided her as much as possible. This was harder for David than most, since a large part of Lane's practice was criminal law.

"Everybody here?" Lane said, calling the meeting to order. "We had a partner's meeting on the weekend and I just wanted to bring you all up to speed on some of the major issues."

Lane went down through the agenda, from the growing list of accounts receivable to client complaints. Then she got into billings. Phil nodded at David, who tried to conceal a grin. For this segment of the agenda, Lane adopted her gravest facial expression.

"The partners are concerned about some of the numbers, and I think it's fair to say there's room for improvement all around."

She waited for this to sink in before proceeding.

"Now, what we're looking for at this point is your input on what we can do to make things easier for you."

"You could start by giving us some decent files." Phil whispered to Maddy Beckett, one of the third-year associates who spent most of her time doing family law.

"What was that Phil?" Lane didn't appreciate the interruption. She was running the show here, not some little second-year associate.

"Nothing, Kelly. I was just saying it's a little warm in here."

"Oh. Yeah, the office manager's got a call in to the repairman about the furnace. It keeps cutting in when it's not supposed to. Anyway, as I was saying, we're interested in hearing from you on how you think we can all improve things. We're not looking at letting anybody go right now but with those receivables up there, we have to keep a close eye on the bottom line."

Lane heard a few suggestions from some of the other associates and scribbled some notes.

"Anything else?" she said, then continued with other matters, ending the meeting twenty minutes later with the announcement of the summer barbeque in a month's time.

"Lane's such a weasel," Phil said, as he and David sat in the latter's office after the meeting.

"Keep your voice down," David said, putting his finger to his lip. "She's probably got all of our offices wired."

They both had a laugh at Lane's expense.

"All that crap about receivables," Phil sneered. "Give me a break. Everyone knows it's the partners who advance all the money to their own personal injury clients. Our unpaid accounts don't add up to anything by comparison."

"Makes you wonder why they're even asking for suggestions, doesn't it?" David said, putting his hands behind his head.

"You mean they're getting ready to cut somebody loose?"

"Or maybe they're just trying to scare us into working harder, who knows. We wouldn't be the first to go anyway, we're too useful. We go to court for them, do their research and we work for cheap."

"Yeah, I'd be worried if I was in Ron's shoes," Phil said, referring to the firm's senior associate. Ron James was beginning to look isolated, not having found his niche in his time at the firm, and the rumour mill had it that his days were numbered if he didn't find one soon.

"He hates it here anyway. Probably be happy as hell if they let him go."

"So do you think McGrath will take the murder case?" Phil asked, changing topics.

"I don't know. When's the last time he did a criminal trial?"

"Before our time. Still, it's like riding a bike, I guess."

They were interrupted by David's phone.

"Hang on a sec," he said, picking up the outside line.

"David Hall…Oh hi. What? Oh shit…hang on, I'll be right there."

"What is it?" Phil asked as David got up.

"My roof's leaking," he said, looking out the window. He hadn't even noticed the rain that had been falling steadily for the past twenty minutes.

"There's a piece of flashing that gets bent out of shape by the wind, and causes the water to run into a crack…" He reached for his overcoat.

"Anything I can do?" Phil said, following him out by Joanne's desk.

"No, it's no big deal. Jo, I'm at the law library if anyone asks—about half an hour."

"Might want to take your briefcase," Phil said with a grin as he looked at his watch. "Looks more studious."

chapter four

"Hello Tom," Bill McGrath said as he was led into the interview room at the Royal Newfoundland Constabulary's headquarters at Fort Townsend. His face still sporting a tan from a recent vacation and his athletic frame draped in an expensive blue suit, McGrath looked every bit the part of the successful trial lawyer. But more important than looks, or even the formidable legal mind behind them, it was McGrath's natural ease with people that was the source of his real power. His balanced mix of confidence and good-natured flattery had a way of instantly putting friends at ease and foes off-balance. And when it came time to do battle on a file, there wasn't an insurance lawyer in town who didn't think twice before risking his client's policy limits to McGrath's fearless, gloves-off courtroom style. This was why he had built a client base that was the envy of the St. John's bar, and why most of his insurance cases never got past the courthouse steps. And though he hadn't done much criminal work in recent years, his instincts were not about to let him turn down such a high profile case.

"How's it goin'?" Fitzgerald said, unenthusiastically.

"I'm more worried about you right now," McGrath said, appraising him gravely.

"Yeah."

"This is Kelly Lane. She's one of my partners."

"Hi Tom. Can I call you Tom?"

Fitzgerald shrugged.

"So, Tom," McGrath began, sitting down. "We know the police version of what happened. Why don't we start by you telling us yours?"

Fitzgerald gave them a drawn-out explanation of the evening of the murder, beginning in a rough and tumble bar called Duffy's at the east end of the harbour. He had been having a hard time lately, Fitzgerald explained, what with his being unemployed and on the outs with his girlfriend. He had been drowning his sorrows most nights for the past few weeks. His memory of leaving the bar was spotty, but he vaguely remembered walking in Bannerman Park.

"When was that?" Lane interrupted.

"Dunno. It was late I guess. Not many people around."

"Go on," McGrath prompted him gently.

"Like I said, I was in the park and I was lyin' on the ground. Then it started to rain. All I can remember is thinking I've got to get out of the rain or I'll be soaked. So I got up and walked over to this big tree and sat down against it. And that's it. The next thing I know some friggin' cop is shakin' me and wavin' a knife in my face, saying I killed somebody."

"You didn't see anyone before you blacked out?"

"No."

"And the knife wasn't yours?" Lane asked.

"Fuck no, I'm tellin' you it wasn't me," Fitzgerald said irritably.

"Alright Tom, we believe you. We just need all the information we can get right now," McGrath said soothingly. "Did you give a statement to the police?"

"No. That prick Gushue wouldn't give up though. Kept tellin' me if I didn't sign the confession, he'd make sure I got a life sentence."

"Good, Tom, that's good. They're just trying to pressure you because they know they haven't got enough evidence." McGrath gave him a reassuring smile. "Were you talking to anyone at Duffy's?"

"Yeah, lots of people."

"Can you give us names?" Lane held her pen at the ready.

"Johnny Walsh and Edgar Lawrence mostly. And I was talkin' to Jimmy, the owner."

"Is that Jimmy Duffy?" Lane looked up from her notes.

"Take a wild guess," Fitzgerald said sarcastically as Lane smiled falsely and went on writing.

McGrath continued the interview, asking about everything from Fitzgerald's criminal record, to his medical and employment history, to his drinking habits, to what he was wearing that night. After an hour, he had all he was going to get for the time being.

"And you're sure you don't remember seeing anyone in the park that night, or anything unusual?"

Fitzgerald shook his head.

"Alright Tom. That's good for now," McGrath said.

"You gonna take the case?"

"Sure I will, Tom. Is there anything you need? Do you want me to call anyone?"

"My missus. Tell her to come see me. I'm allowed visitors right?"

"Yes, but they're going to transfer you to the Pen tonight. She'll probably have to wait until tomorrow."

They concluded the interview and McGrath and Lane were shown out.

"What do you think?" Lane asked as they made their way to her car.

"It's not good so far, but it never is. My main problem is timing, though. The trial's bound to be in the spring and I've got that damned Cole trial set for April 4th."

"Oh yeah," Lane nodded as they got in and she started the engine. She knew full well the importance of the Cole trial. It was a personal injury file that McGrath had opened more than seven years before. Every lawyer at the firm had worked on it in one way or another. Tina Cole had been a teenaged girl at the time of the accident. The car she was riding in had been hit head-on by a truck in the middle of a winter storm. The young girl had suffered a brain injury and paralysis from the waist down, which meant the stakes were very high for all concerned. Liability had been disputed hotly from the start by all of the half dozen insurers involved, and that alone would keep the case in court for weeks or even months, before they even got to an assessment of damages. There was a whole corner of the firm's filing room dedicated to the boxes of transcripts, medical and accident reconstruction reports, and other documents that had accumulated over the years. As they drove back down over the hill to Duckworth Street in silence, Lane knew without a doubt that her boss would have to pass on Fitzgerald's trial. There was no way around it.

"I can help you out with the Cole file," she said reassuringly. "I've already done a lot of the leg work…"

"Hmm," McGrath muttered, looking out the window as Lane kept her little smile well concealed.

chapter five

"Will you be careful," Elizabeth Hall scolded, seeing David toss their nine-month old baby boy once more above his outstretched arms.

"Ah come on, look at him. He loves it."

Ben Hall cackled with delight and showed off his two new teeth.

"Just don't drop him, that's all," she said with a smile, kissing both of them on the cheek.

"Time to go to Mama, Ben," David said, passing the pyjama-clad infant to her and resuming his hurried breakfast of a toasted bagel and coffee.

"Are you in court this morning?"

"Yeah, just a couple of first appearances in provincial court—no monkey suit," he replied, referring to the official black and grey garments required for all matters in the Supreme Court of Newfoundland.

"Well I got the coffee stains out of your court shirt, so you might as well take it with you anyway. It's in the hall closet."

"Thanks hon," he kissed her on the cheek. "See ya Ben."

He waved at the little boy, who was busy chewing on his fingers.

"Don't forget dinner tonight," she called after him as he went through the door into the warm morning air.

"I won't," he called back, shaking his head. How could he?

David loved Elizabeth with all of his heart, but her family was a different story. They had come from different worlds, and he often wondered how they hadn't been torn apart by their differences. While David's upbringing had been middle-class and suburban, hers had been sheltered and privileged. Her father came from a long line of Newfoundland doctors, while her mother traced her roots back to the wealthy fishing admirals of the colonial era. And they had made no effort at concealing their disappointment over their daughter's interest in David, from when the couple had first met in University, to their marriage upon his return from law school. As for Elizabeth, though she loved her parents, when it came right down to it she didn't care what they thought. She preferred to follow her heart, and that made David love her all the more.

This evening would be the usual formal, stuffy dinner at the Furlong's grand old house on Circular Road. He despised these occasions but he knew they were mandatory. At least it would be just the four of them. If he had to listen to Liz's only sister, Janet, and her husband, Sean, talking about the colour schemes for their new house, he was afraid he might go crazy. Sean Taylor liked to think of himself as part of the St. John's aristocracy. In fact, while his grandfather had built a successful business, Sean's father was rumoured to have squandered most of the family money through reckless spending and unwise investments. Given every advantage, Sean had struggled through part of an undergraduate degree before abandoning it, along with the hopes of any further academic endeavours. And despite his father's maneuverings on his behalf, Sean had wasted several choice opportunities before turning up on the doorstep of the family business. Even if the rumours about his father's mismanagement were unfounded, David knew Sean was sure to fritter away whatever was left of the family money if he ever took over the reins, as evidenced by his recent insistence on buying a grandiose home in an exclusive new subdivision bounded by a golf course. It was fond thoughts of this inevitable future that allowed David to smile calmly whenever his obnoxious brother-in-law put down David and Elizabeth's modest house in the lowly downtown core, or their second-hand car.

Reaching the office, David climbed the stairs two at a time and greeted Joanne as he passed her desk.

"Mr. McGrath wants to see you right away," she said.

David stopped in to switch on his computer and take off his jacket before heading upstairs. He peeked around the open door into McGrath's office. He was sitting behind his desk, going through the morning mail and drinking a coffee.

"Come on in David," McGrath said with his customary smile, waving him in.

"Good morning," he replied, taking an empty seat.

McGrath asked David about his work and made some small talk before getting to the point.

"As you know, Tom Fitzgerald has been a client of mine for some time."

"The murder suspect. Yes, I heard you might be taking the case," David paused, awaiting confirmation.

"Well, I've thought about it, and I've decided I just can't. The Cole case has to take priority. I can't do both at once and expect to do either one justice."

David nodded, wondering where he fit into this.

"But I want this firm to represent him. So I've asked Kelly to take the case and I want you to help her out."

"Sure…I'd love to," David said excitedly. He couldn't imagine Lane had asked for his help so it must have been McGrath's idea, which made it all the more rewarding. His first murder trial!

"Now it's going to eat up a lot of your time, but it's a great way to get your feet wet. I've always thought it's never too early to throw a young trial lawyer into the fire."

David nodded eagerly.

"That's how Kelly saw her first murder trial, as my co-chair."

David knew the story well, though from Lane's version you'd swear it was McGrath who had ridden her coattails, and not the other way around.

"What's the defence?" David asked.

"Good question. From the initial interview there's not much to go on. But I'm sure you'll think of something…," he smiled. "Anyway, I haven't told him I can't take it yet, so I want you to come along with Kelly and me to the Pen this morning. Ten o'clock."

McGrath gave David a brief smile to indicate he was dismissed.

"Thanks again Bill. I won't let you down," David said, turning to leave.

"I know you won't."

chapter six

The fog hung low around Her Majesty's Penitentiary, the grey stone building that housed Newfoundland's prisoners—at least those serving sentences of less than two years. McGrath parked his SUV by the entrance gates and the three lawyers got out. David looked at the dreary old building and thanked his lucky stars he had ended up on the right side of these walls. They made their way inside and went through the admission procedure at the guardhouse.

"Follow me," said a burly guard, who led them out through a door and across a covered walkway to the main building. As they entered the main cellblock and the heavy doors slammed behind them one by one, the awful stench of stale smoke and body odour permeated the humid air. They were led to the older wing of the building, to a little room with a high arched window covered in bars and Plexiglas. It looked like something from the Dark Ages, except for the lime green paint on the walls.

"Have a seat," the guard said, motioning to the simple wooden table and chairs.

"What a hole…," David remarked, after the guard had left the room.

McGrath laughed.

"It's not the Fairmont, is it?"

"First time in the Pen, Dave?" Lane grinned.

"First time in this wing," he replied, holding his nose. "And why is it so hot in here?"

"They must have done something wrong," McGrath replied with a smile. "The guards sometimes crank up the heat as punishment when the inmates misbehave."

They sat down and a few minutes later, Fitzgerald was led in and seated on the other side of the table by a guard.

"How are you, Tom?" McGrath asked as the guard left.

"Been better…"

"Did your girlfriend come by?" Lane asked.

"Yeah, she was here."

"Good, good," McGrath smiled. "Do you need anything?"

"Naw."

"Alright then, let's get started. I've done a lot of thinking about this and there's no way around it. I can't take the case."

Fitzgerald looked at him blankly.

"I've got another trial scheduled for the spring, when yours is likely to take place. It's a file I've had for seven years. There's just no way I can take your case on as well, so…"

"So what am I supposed to…"

"Hang on Tom. I'm not leaving you out in the cold. Kelly here is an experienced criminal lawyer," McGrath said, motioning to Lane, "and she's got the time and energy to put into your case. I know she's up to it, so I've assigned her to the file…with your permission of course."

"Yeah, I guess," Fitzgerald muttered. "I don't know any other lawyers…"

None of the three on the other side of the table mentioned that any number of criminal lawyers in the city would be happy to take on a high profile murder case like this one on Legal Aid's tab, if not for free.

"And this is David Hall, who'll be helping out as well," McGrath carried on.

"Hello, Tom," David said.

"How'm I supposed to pay you guys?" Fitzgerald asked.

"Don't worry about that Tom," McGrath said smoothly. "We'll get you Legal Aid funding, and if that's not enough, you can let us worry about the rest. Kelly's got a retainer agreement here," he nodded to Lane, who handed him two copies of the document.

"Whatever," Fitzgerald said as Lane handed him a pen.

"There," McGrath took back one of the signed agreements and handed it to Lane. "Now, we need to discuss how you're going to plead."

"I told you I never did nothin'…"

"I know Tom, but we need to tell you what your options are anyway," Lane interjected.

Fitzgerald let out a sigh.

"You think I did it, don't you…"

"It doesn't matter what we think Tom. It's what the Crown can prove to the jury that matters," Lane said matter-of-factly.

"Hmph," Fitzgerald grunted. He looked at David for a moment. "What about you. You think I did it?"

David considered the question for a moment as they all looked at him.

"No, Tom, as a matter of fact I don't."

chapter seven

"Oh there you are," Elizabeth's father said as his wife escorted David and Elizabeth into the large sitting room.

"It's my fault," David said apologetically. "I was working late."

"For what they pay you!" Sean Taylor said in mock indignation from the other side of the room.

"Hello Sean," David said, biting his tongue. "Hello Janet."

"Actually, David's got exciting news," Elizabeth said proudly. "He's going to be representing Tom Fitzgerald."

"Who?" Sean asked.

"The murderer?" Elizabeth's father asked incredulously.

"Alleged murderer," David said quietly, accepting a glass of wine from Elizabeth's mother.

"Well congratulations, that's very exciting," she said.

"Hmm," Lloyd Furlong muttered with distaste, "I hope you're not going to help him get off on a technicality. That's all we need, another murderer on the loose."

"David's job is to defend him to the best of his ability, Dad," Elizabeth smiled, patting David on the arm. He was beginning to wish she hadn't brought it up.

"It's not safe to walk the streets of St. John's anymore," Elizabeth's father said gruffly.

"Don't be so dramatic Lloyd," his wife scolded him.

Although in the beginning Sylvia Furlong had been cool towards David, she had grown to like him, and had become his only ally in the family apart from Elizabeth.

"The system is designed to let two adversaries present each side of the accused's case before a jury of his peers, and let it decide his fate," she said, summarizing the criminal justice system with remarkable accuracy. "It's not up to us to decide."

"Oh come on, Sylvia," Lloyd Furlong said dismissively. It was clear he had little time for the principle of presumed innocence. "Everyone in this room knows he did it, including you, David, if you're honest with yourself."

"I really don't think he's guilty," David replied.

"What's it like rubbing shoulders with a scumbag like that? Must make your skin crawl," Sean said, not wanting to miss out on a chance to increase his father-in-law's disgust for David.

"I feel sorry for him. He's one of these guys who never had a chance."

"So you think that makes what he did alright?" his brother-in-law said quickly, trying to bait him.

"Like I said, I don't think he did anything," David replied calmly, "other than drink too much, and if that's a crime then half of St. John's should be locked up."

Elizabeth let out a giggle.

"Well they must have confidence in you down at that firm, if they're prepared to give you such a big case," Sylvia Furlong said with an encouraging nod.

"Well, I'm assisting Kelly Lane actually."

"Oh, Lane. Now, she's a good lawyer," Elizabeth's father said. "How is she?"

"She's doing well," David said, trying to avoid eye contact with Elizabeth. She knew David's dislike for Lane and the way she sucked up to people like Elizabeth's father.

"She represented the medical association last year. I bet she's a fine criminal lawyer," Elizabeth's father continued. "You're lucky to get the chance to work for her."

"With her, Dad," Elizabeth corrected him.

"Carrying her briefcase and getting her coffee?" Sean said with a malicious grin.

David just chuckled, rather than being drawn into a verbal sparring match with Sean over the dinner table. He knew it would upset Elizabeth and Sean wasn't worth that.

They were soon seated around the massive mahogany table in the formal dining room, laid out with fine linen and silverware.

"So when is the trial?" Elizabeth's father asked, taking a sip of the choice Burgundy he had selected to accompany the roast beef.

"The preliminary inquiry is probably going to be in October. The trial won't be until some time in the new year, probably the spring."

"You're going to have a hard time getting away in the fall then," Elizabeth's father mused. The Furlong family spent three weeks in their condo in Sarasota every fall. Much to David's relief, he and Elizabeth had missed the trip the previous year because of Ben's arrival, but there had been constant hints that they were expected to spend at least a week or two there each fall from now on.

"Liz and Ben can always come if you're too busy…," Elizabeth's sister Janet said, throwing in her two cents.

"We're not going without David," Elizabeth said.

"Why not, you're just sitting around at home," said her father. "You need a vacation more than anyone—cooped up in that little house." He couldn't resist an opportunity to slight their modest home.

"I'm not cooped up Daddy—I chose to be at home with Ben, remember?" Elizabeth brushed off her father's concern with a laugh while David concentrated on chewing. "Besides, he might be able to get away after the preliminary hearing if it doesn't run too long, right honey?"

"I'm sure we'll work something out," David said, doing his best to be diplomatic.

"What is it with your stay-at-home obsession anyway? Haven't you heard of daycare?" Janet said, smugly.

"Ben's better off with me than in any daycare. You'll realize that if you ever have your own children," Elizabeth said, an edge to her voice. Janet knew she was no match for her spirited younger sister and she changed topics immediately to landscaping—her latest medium for spending large amounts of money unnecessarily.

"I heard a great lawyer joke this morning…," Sean piped up from the other side of the table, as David reached for his wine.

chapter**eight**
–october

David shuffled awkwardly through the autumn leaves that blew along Duckworth Street, struggling with an oversized briefcase stuffed with court documents. Over the past four weeks, he had read every page, but despite this preparation and the countless hours of other research he had done, he couldn't help feeling nervous and a little overwhelmed by the importance of this morning's proceedings. As he passed the Courthouse, he turned into an alley that led, by way of steeply descending groups of steps, down to Water Street and the Provincial Courts. He darted through the morning traffic and entered Atlantic Place and made his way to the escalators. Setting the heavy briefcase down for the ride and loosening his overcoat, he went through the case in his head again. Though Lane would be conducting the preliminary inquiry, she had left much of the prep work to David, who had taken his role very seriously, not only because of the gravity of the crime but because of the man accused of it.

David and Lane had met with Tom Fitzgerald on numerous occasions over the summer, in preparation for the preliminary inquiry, and while it was clear Lane considered him guilty, David had formed his own opinion. There was no doubt that there was a considerable amount of evidence against him, but without an eyewitness to the actual murder, it was all circumstantial. Aside from the question of evidence, there was something about Fitzgerald that convinced David of his innocence. Maybe it was just a gut feeling— nothing more—but he couldn't believe Fitzgerald had done it. And the fact that Lane seemed so convinced of her client's guilt annoyed him, though he knew in the end it really didn't matter. Lane was enough of a professional to know that her job was to put her client's best case forward and let the jury decide his guilt or innocence.

As for the preliminary, neither David nor Lane had any doubt their client would be ordered to stand trial. The only question before the court at this point was whether there was enough evidence to create the possibility for a jury to convict, and the answer was unfortunately clear. They were approaching the exercise more as an opportunity to get a better feel for the Crown's case. As he reached the landing at the top of the escalator and headed through the entrance to the courtrooms, he saw Lane chatting with another lawyer.

"There's my slave," she said with a smile, as she caught sight of David.

"Morning Kelly."

"David, have you met Frank Sullivan?" Lane said, motioning to the grey-haired man to her right. Everyone knew Francis Sullivan, Q.C. He was a senior partner at Bowring, Hallett—the oldest and richest of the St. John's firms—as well as being a Law Society bencher and chair of a number of committees.

"No, I don't think I have, but I've certainly heard a lot about you, Mr. Sullivan. Nice to meet you."

"It's a pleasure, David. You're not wasting any time getting into the big files, are you?" Sullivan said with a grin.

"In the right place at the right time I guess," David smiled.

"Good for you. Might as well get your feet wet early," he said. "Though I hear you've got your work cut out for you on this one."

"That's because nobody's heard our side of the story yet, but they will," Lane said confidently.

"Really? I thought it sounded pretty open and shut," Sullivan said, with a raised eyebrow. "But then murder is hardly my area."

"Well, we'd better run," Lane said, breaking off the discussion. "Why don't you have the tape couriered to me this afternoon," she added.

"Yes," Sullivan nodded. "Call me when you've had a chance to consider my counter offer—and don't say no." He paused as the trace of a grin showed on his face. "Nice to meet you David."

"Likewise," David said.

"Prick," Lane muttered after Sullivan was out of earshot.

"What do you mean?" David asked.

"I've got a pre-trial with him next week on one of my personal injuries—a bad whiplash I was claiming a couple of hundred grand on. He casually tells me this morning he's got a video of my client loading a couch into a van. He's going to cut the shit out of my claim now for sure."

"I take it your client's not supposed to be slinging furniture around?"

"My client's not supposed to be able to lift a pencil—Goddamn surveillance is killing me!"

"That's tough," David said with a whistle as Lane led the way to Courtroom number five.

As they got settled and arranged their documents on the table, the crown attorney, J.P. Gallant, came in with his own stack of papers.

"Hello Kelly."

"J.P. This is David Hall. He's going to be helping me out on this file."

"Yeah, we've met. David's been making me earn my pay," Gallant said with a grin. Just a week prior, David had used a rather creative defence to obtain an acquittal for a client Gallant was prosecuting for assault, and the two had crossed paths before. Gallant had struck David as a very reasonable, but worthy adversary. He knew Tom Fitzgerald would have an uphill battle.

chapter nine

Tom Fitzgerald's preliminary had been running for over a week and so far, things had gone predictably. J.P. Gallant had been thorough in putting more than enough evidence to convict Tom before the court. But Lane had done a reasonably good job of representing her client's interests as well. She had managed to have some of the evidence excluded, and although she had no intention of conducting any intensive cross-examination of the crown witnesses—she was content to be everybody's best friend at this point—she did ask them enough questions to get a feel for their likely reactions when she attacked them before a jury.

As for David, he was enjoying his first murder preliminary, even though he would have preferred to be asking the questions himself and a little part of him wished quietly it would wrap up soon so he could attend to his regular practice. Lane had off-loaded plenty of work at the end of each day and though David was keen to help, it meant he was forced to neglect his day-to-day files, not to mention his family. He had gotten in at 2:00 a.m. that morning, and though she didn't complain, David knew Elizabeth was finding his absence from home difficult as well. Ben had been up half the night with an ear infection and with no help from David, she was facing another trying day.

The judge arrived for the morning session and the small courtroom, which had been filled for most of the hearing with lawyers, family members and reporters, rose out of custom. Lane and David had been eagerly awaiting the appearance of their next witness, and they had spent a great deal of time on his testimony, which was the only potential silver lining in the very grey cloud Gallant had managed to create in the past eight days of the hearing.

A down-and-out drinker with a few minor brushes with the law of his own in the past, Reggie Button was not, by any stretch of the imagination, an ideal witness. But despite his obvious credibility problems, what he did have to say, if accepted, could be a significant blow to the prosecution. For Reggie had shown up at Fort Townsend, the headquarters of the Royal Newfoundland Constabulary, shortly after the start of the preliminary and provided a voluntary statement to the effect that he had seen Tom Fitzgerald on the night of the murder. It turned out that Reggie, who knew Tom Fitzgerald casually from a local bar, had been walking through Bannerman Park at around eleven-thirty and came across Tom Fitzgerald asleep or passed out at the foot of a large maple tree. Since the time of death had been estimated as occurring between eleven-thirty and one a.m., this evidence was crucial.

For David, the evidence was just further confirmation of Tom's innocence, but for Lane it seemed to change everything, evoking a new excitement that David had not seen before. In fact, listening to Lane in the last few days, you would never know she had ever harboured even the slightest doubt about Fitzgerald's innocence. In any case, this new evidence had lit a fire under her and David was pleased to share in Lane's new dedication, whatever her motives.

Lane rose and addressed the judge in a manner that made it clear she enjoyed hearing her own voice, and with an obvious sense of satisfaction she called Button to the stand. She asked the standard introductory questions and then skilfully led Button through the events of the fateful evening, stopping here and there to interject well-placed questions. When she got to his discovery of Tom Fitzgerald in the park, she slowed her witness down deliberately.

"What brought you to Bannerman Park at that late hour, Mr. Button?" she inquired with an appropriately raised eyebrow.

"Well b'y," Button began in a particularly heavy version of the mix of English and Irish dialect spoken to some degree by most Newfoundlanders. "I was on me way home. I couldn't get a cab downtown so I walked up over the hill and decided to keep walking. It was a pretty warm night."

"So you were crossing the park from the Military Road side?" Lane continued to lead him, without any objection from Gallant, who was busy taking notes.

"Right. I was almost at the playground when I seen something under the tree."

"And what did you see Mr. Button?"

"There was a man asleep, so I went closer and I seen it was Tom."

"Tom?" Lane asked, awaiting the rest of the answer.

"Tom Fitzgerald."

"Do you know Mr. Fitzgerald?"

"Yes, I knows 'im from the boarding house I used to be at downtown. And from Duffy's Bar," Button added, clearing his throat.

"And you're sure it was him, under the tree?"

"Oh yeah, I'm sure. I tried callin' his name and shakin' him but he wouldn't wake up."

"Did you notice anything in his hands?" Lane continued innocently. David was waiting for Gallant to object but he seemed content to scribble his notes and let Lane carry on with her leading questions.

"No. He never had nothing in his hands. I'm sure."

"And what time of the night was this?"

"It was about eleven-thirty. Maybe a little later."

"How do you know?"

"Well, I walked up from the East End Club and I asked the bartender before I left what time it was—I wanted to get home before twelve 'cause the pizza place around the corner closes at midnight."

"And what time did the bartender say it was?"

"Eleven-fifteen. It took me about fifteen or twenty minutes to walk up from downtown."

Having extracted from Button the testimony that Fitzgerald had been seen shortly before the time of the murder, already asleep and with no murder weapon in his hands, Lane wrapped things up, thanked Button and took her seat. The judge peered over his glasses at the Crown's table.

"Mr. Gallant?"

"Yes, your Honour," Gallant said as he rose to his feet. Button took a sip of water and braced himself.

"Can you tell the court where you were last night Mr. Button?" Gallant began as Lane and David exchanged puzzled expressions.

"Uh, yeah. I was down to Duffy's for a while," Button said a little sheepishly.

"Were you anywhere else?" Gallant continued.

"I dropped into the Dory after, yeah."

"The Dory is a bar, is it Mr. Button?"

"Yeah."

"I see. What were you drinking at Duffy's and the Dory?"

"I had a coupl'a rums at Duffy's, and a beer or two at the Dory."

"Do you feel that you were drunk, Mr. Button, when you were at the Dory?"

"I dunno, I was feelin' okay I s'pose."

Lane had heard enough, and rose to her feet.

"Can I ask counsel to explain what the relevance of Mr. Button's social life is to this proceeding, your Honour?"

The judge rested his chin on his hand and looked towards Gallant.

"Where are you going with this Mr. Gallant?"

"I only have a few more questions for Mr. Button, your Honour. I'll get straight to the point."

"Very well. Proceed, Mr. Gallant," the judge said, as Lane reluctantly sat back down.

"Do you know the bartender at the Dory, Mr. Button?"

"I knows his name is Gus, but that's about it."

"Did you have a conversation with Gus last night at the Dory Mr. Button?"

Button scratched his eyebrow and considered the question for a moment.

"Uh, yeah. I think I was chattin' with him a bit."

"Do you remember what you were chatting about Mr. Button?"

"Ah, no," Button began scratching his eyebrow more intensely. "Not really. But I knows I was talking to him."

"Very well, Mr. Button. Those are all my questions."

Button looked relieved as the judge told him he was free to go.

"What the fuck was that all about?" Lane whispered in David's ear as Button left the stand.

"I don't know, but I've got a bad feeling…," David whispered back.

"Your Honour, I'd like to ask that the witness remain in the courtroom. And also, that the Crown be permitted to call an additional, unscheduled witness," Gallant asked politely as Button stopped near the door and looked inquiringly at the judge.

"We've had no notice of any other Crown witnesses," Lane said, hopping to her feet.

"Your Honour, this witness only came to my attention this morning, and his testimony relates directly to that of Mr. Button."

"Hmm. Do you have anything to say, Ms. Lane?"

"Well your Honour. We've had no notice…"

"I'm aware of that Ms. Lane, neither have I," the judge said shortly while Lane tried to think of something to add. "But I'm prepared to allow it, unless you can demonstrate prejudice to your client. Mr. Button, please have a seat."

Button sat obediently at the back of the courtroom.

"But your Honour. This is highly irregular…"

"You'll have time to prepare a cross-examination if you wish," the judge said with finality, ignoring Lane's pleas. "Where's your witness, Mr. Gallant?"

Gallant whispered to his assistant, who headed for the door to the courtroom and disappeared through it.

"He'll be here in a moment, your Honour."

"Your Honour, I really don't see...," Lane got up to her feet again.

"Relax Ms. Lane, this is not a trial, and there's no jury here. I'm quite capable of determining whether what the witness has to say is proper. If it is not, I will let Mr. Gallant know. I see no prejudice to the accused in the circumstances."

There was little else for Lane to do than sit back down, as Gallant's assistant returned with a man in his forties. Gallant instructed him briefly and directed him to the witness stand to be sworn in by the clerk.

"Please state your name for the court," Gallant began.

"Gus Tavernor."

"And your occupation, Mr. Tavernor?"

"I'm a bartender at the Dory."

"Were you working last night, Mr. Tavernor?" Gallant inquired innocently, as though he wasn't quite sure himself.

"Yes sir, I was."

Gallant took him through a few more questions to establish the time and the number of people in the bar, and then got straight to the point.

"Do you recognize the gentleman seated in the back of the courtroom, Mr. Tavernor?" Gallant pointed to where Button was seated, looking anxious.

"Yes, that's Reggie Button, I was talking to him last night at the Dory."

Lane and David were on pins and needles, though neither dared to look anywhere than straight at the witness stand.

"And what was the nature of your conversation?"

"Well, Reg...Mr. Button started talking to me about this case, right, and how he knew Tom Fitzgerald," Tavernor looked at Button, who seemed to be shrinking into his seat.

"Go on, Mr. Tavernor," Gallant prodded him.

"Anyway, I think he'd had a few and he was kind of chatty, you know, so I listened to him for a while. He told me he was going to get Tom off the hook and he was going to be a real hero."

"I see. What else did he say?" Gallant glanced towards Lane, who didn't take her eyes off the witness stand.

"He said he was going to be in the newspapers, and he might make some money off it," Tavernor continued.

"Did Mr. Button have anything else to say about his statement to the RNC, or the night of the murder?" Gallant continued.

"Yeah," Tavernor glanced at Button and then back to Gallant. "He said he was nowhere near Bannerman Park that night, but he knew Tom didn't have it in him to…"

"Thank you Mr. Tavernor. Those are all my questions for you."

Gallant sat down as a hush came over the room and all eyes turned to Lane. She rose and addressed the judge in as cheery a voice as she could muster.

"Your Honour, I'd like to request an adjournment to review this witness' testimony."

The judge looked at his watch. "Two o'clock?"

"Thank you, your Honour," Lane said as the court clerk rose.

"All rise," she said, as the judge got up and left through the back door.

"I really didn't know about him until this morning. That's the truth," Gallant said across the gap between the two counsel tables.

"I'm sure you didn't," Lane said with an edge in her voice, as she packed up her briefcase and David followed her out.

chapter ten

"That fucking Gushue!" Lane snarled as she slammed the door to the little conference room.

"The inspector?" David asked.

"He's a tricky bastard. He must have had Button tailed after he gave his statement."

"What do we do now?" David asked quietly.

"How the fuck do I know—Jesus, I can't believe it. So much for our star witness."

"Do we cross?"

"And establish what, that we're even bigger idiots? There's nothing we can do now, other than end this thing."

"Shouldn't we check Tavernor for a criminal record or something."

Lane rubbed her eyes.

"I'm sure Gallant wouldn't have had him on the stand if he had anything that would damage his testimony, but go ahead and check. I've got to get back to the office and stop wasting time on this bullshit case," Lane said with frustration. "Tell Tom we'll be wrapping it up at two."

David looked at the floor as Lane left. It was such a disappointment after the lift they had gotten with Button's emergence just a few short days ago. Now, with no defence to speak of, they were back to trying to prevent the crown from proving its increasingly solid case. He picked up the phone and dialed his office.

"Hi Joanne…I've got to see Tom for a minute and then do a CPIC search at Fort Townsend. Hopefully, I'll be able to check in before we resume here at two. Anything urgent?"

"Your wife wants you to call her, and you've got a half dozen messages from clients. And Phil said he needs to talk to you right… actually, he's here. I'll transfer you in if you like."

"Okay."

"David? Hang on, let me close the door," Phil said, as the receiver hit the desk and David heard the sound of the door closing.

"There."

"What's up Phil?"

"There's a rumour going around that you missed a limitation on the Miller file."

"The Miller file…that's impossible. I issued the statement of claim over a year ago," David said confidently.

"Renee overheard Caines telling McGrath you missed a limitation on that file."

Greg Caines was the partner who had handled a couple of calls on David's personal injury files over the past few weeks.

"I don't know what the hell he's talking about."

"Me neither."

"Shit. I'm stuck for another hour or more…"

"Do you want me to get the file from Joanne and have a look?"

"Yeah, yeah. Can you do that?"

"Sure. It's probably bullshit. I'll call you if I find anything before you get back."

"Alright. Thanks for the heads up," David said, hanging up. He felt his stomach churn a little as he considered the possibilities. The Miller file was the only P.I. he had that was worth anything, though it was still years away from being settled. If he had messed it up, he had a lot to lose, and Caines had made it even worse by going to McGrath. But David had drafted and filed the statement of claim himself—he was sure of it. There had to be some misunderstanding. He tried to put his concerns aside as he headed to the holding cells. He had to discuss the disappointing morning with his client.

chapter eleven
—december

"Still snowing?" Elizabeth asked, as David looked out from behind the living room window into the street.

"It's gotten worse," he said and returned to her side on the couch. "All you can see is the glow of the streetlights. We're going to be buried by tomorrow morning."

"Oh, I love a good blizzard," she said with a laugh as she put her arms around him and pulled him close.

"Looks like we'll be late for the Boxing Day brunch at your sister's." David said innocently.

"David Hall," Elizabeth replied in mock exasperation. "Don't even think about it. There won't be anything that a shovel and some elbow grease won't fix." She jabbed him playfully in the ribs with a finger.

"Easy for you to say."

They had been up at six that morning—Christmas morning—when Ben decided he had slept long enough for his second Christmas, and they had been going ever since. David's parents' place for lunch, then Elizabeth's for dinner. Two huge turkey dinners and sixteen hours later, they were both exhausted and enjoying the quiet while Ben slept peacefully upstairs.

The last few months had been anything but peaceful for either of them. After the Fitzgerald preliminary, David had discovered his error on the Miller file. Although he had in fact preserved the main limitation period by issuing his statement of claim in time, he had failed to name Miller's own insurer in the suit, which was important because Miller's policy included a special insurance rider called SEF. If Miller's claim exceeded the amount of insurance carried by the defendant driver, David's failure to claim under the SEF rider would prevent him from accessing those additional funds. It was impossible to know whether that additional coverage would be necessary at this point, but if it were, Miller would have a negligence claim against David. Even worse, he would have failed his client and embarrassed the firm, which generally did not go over well with McGrath. But as angry as David had been with himself, he was surprised by McGrath's relatively tempered reaction. Other than a warning, which was certainly warranted, he had not dwelt on the matter. Even more surprising, and eye-opening, was the reaction of the other partners, who had been dropping not-so-subtle hints ever since about his limited future at the firm. Most of the other associates, especially Maddie Beckett and Ron James—and of course Phil—had been supportive, and he had tried to put it behind him and get on with his work.

As for Elizabeth, her encouragement had not faltered, though he knew the increasingly long hours were taking their toll. Ben had developed a serious lung infection in early November and she had spent a week at the hospital with him. Unable to free himself from the office for long, David knew he had not been there as much as he should, and the ensuing guilt gnawed at him. Matters had not been helped when he had showed up at the end of visiting hours one night to find Elizabeth's parents comforting their obviously exhausted and stressed-out daughter. Her father had decided to give him a heated lecture about his family responsibilities, which fortunately for David had been cut short by Elizabeth's mother reminding her husband of the hours he himself had put in as a resident when Elizabeth was a baby.

As he lay on the couch in Elizabeth's arms, with the soft Christmas music playing in the background, David thought of poor Tom Fitzgerald, sitting in his dingy cell at the penitentiary. Not much good news had come his way since the end of the preliminary hearing in October. Lane had done little, other than send David to meet with Tom at regular intervals. David had done his best to keep his client's spirits up, but with nothing to offer other than his assurances that they would mount the best defence possible, he found it a frustrating experience. He was developing a good rapport with Tom though, who seemed to enjoy the visits, if for no other reason than to talk with someone from the outside world. And the more Tom talked, the more David was convinced he was innocent. But on the facts, there appeared to be no other explanation. Tom's presence at the scene that night, combined with the knife, and the victim's money and other effects in his possession, seemed insurmountable, especially when there was no plausible motive for anyone else to have done it.

But there were always other possibilities. They would just have to find a forensics expert who could uncover another set of prints on the knife, or some other evidence that would point to the real killer. As for Tom's presence at the scene, they would have to portray it as a case of his being in the wrong place at the wrong time. He remembered reading criminal cases in law school that seemed open and shut on an initial reading, but had ended in acquittals. With hard work, skill and a little luck, a good lawyer could turn a life sentence into an absolute discharge during the course of a trial. It would be up to Lane and David to do so.

"You look deep in thought," Elizabeth said, running her hand through his hair.

"Just thinking about Tom Fitzgerald."

"You still don't think he did it, do you? Even with all that evidence against him."

"Anything's possible, I suppose. I don't know, I just have a feeling about him. I don't think he's capable of it."

"Well you'll have to make sure you win the trial, won't you," she said with a smile.

"I love you," he said, kissing her hand.

"I love you too. Why don't you forget about work for a while and just lie here with me and watch the snow fall."

"That sounds like a good idea," he said, as he closed his eyes. He decided he would not go into the office tomorrow after all. Whatever was waiting for him there could wait another day.

chapter twelve

It was a cold, grey and windy January morning as David drove through the morning traffic on Duckworth Street. He had hit the snooze button several times before Elizabeth had put her foot down and shooed him out of bed. Now, as he passed the courthouse, he glanced up the hill and saw the last of the parking spots were taken. He would never find anything along Duckworth at this hour. He took the next left and found something a block and a half east. Stepping out of the car and into a puddle of icy slush a foot deep, he cursed and fumbled in his pocket for change to feed the meter. As he put in a couple of loonies, the wind whipped a stinging volley of sleet at him, forcing him to shield his face with an arm. After a treacherous descent back to Duckworth Street, he arrived at the office freezing and wet.

"Lovely day," he said sarcastically as he arrived on the second floor and greeted his secretary, Joanne.

"Can I get you a towel?" she replied with a smile, looking at his wet hair and dripping overcoat.

"No need. I've got to change into my court clothes and go right back out. I'm in chambers at ten."

"Don't forget your eleven o'clock," she said as he shook off his coat before entering his office.

"What have I got at eleven?" he called out from behind the door.

"The discovery at Mr. Hanlon's office."

"Oh shit," David swore quietly as he remembered the discovery. He looked at his watch—it was already nine o'clock and he would be lucky to get any time at all after the morning's chambers application to review the file. He would have to wing it. He knew the case well enough and his client's role was minor. But he still hated to be unprepared, especially when he was up against a senior lawyer like Hanlon.

"Can you hold my calls and arrange for a cab out front for ten-to? I'm not walking anywhere in this."

"Sure," she said, appearing at the door. "Do you want this shut?"

"Yes. I need the discovery file first, though."

As he popped a fresh tape into his Dictaphone, Kelly Lane appeared at his door.

"Running a little late this morning?" she said casually.

"Car trouble," David muttered as Joanne arrived with his file. David had overheard Lane discussing Maddie Beckett's habit of coming in late with McGrath, and David didn't need that kind of publicity if he could avoid it.

"Whatever. Listen, I need to sit down with you to discuss the Fitzgerald case this afternoon. Do you have time?" Lane asked, as though she were willing to rearrange her own schedule to accommodate his.

"I should be okay from one o'clock on."

"How about two, then? My office—see you then."

Lane disappeared before David had a chance to ask what the meeting was about. He didn't have the time to get into it now anyway.

So far, David's day had not gone well. First, his routine application for court approval of a minor's settlement had been bounced because of a missing medical report. To make matters worse, he had been the second-most junior lawyer in chambers, which meant he had waited until almost eleven o'clock to be told in none too sympathetic a tone to come back another day when his application was complete.

Rushing out onto Water Street from the lower entrance to the Courthouse, he had been pelted with freezing rain for all of the hundred-yard dash to the office tower where the discovery was being held. Arriving at the 10th floor boardroom still in his court clothes, he found a somewhat hostile room of lawyers tapping their pens and waiting for his arrival. And shortly after the start of his straight-forward discovery, it had quickly become more complicated. David was representing a co-defendant with what, until now, had been a relatively minor role in the lawsuit. But as the plaintiff's lawyer started peppering the first defendant's witness with awkward questions, that witness started blaming David's client for all sorts of things, requiring him to prepare a whole different set of questions on the fly. By the time it was finally over, shortly after two-thirty, David was drained and starving—not to mention late for his meeting with Lane. With no time for lunch, he headed straight back to the office.

Stopping in long enough to throw his coat in his office, and ignoring Joanne's pleas to return some of the pile of phone messages on his desk, he climbed the stairs two at a time to the top floor where Lane was waiting.

"There you are," she said, as David knocked on her open door.

"Sorry I'm late, I had a discovery that went longer..."

"Don't worry about it," Lane said in her falsely friendly manner. "Come on in and close the door behind you."

David did so and took a seat in front of Lane's desk.

"I've decided not to continue with Tom Fitzgerald's defence," she said abruptly, before David had settled in his chair.

"What do you mean?" was all he could manage in reply.

"I mean I'm withdrawing as counsel. Somebody else can take it on. It's a loser."

"But we agreed to represent him, and we've already done the prelimin..."

"And now we're telling him to find someone else to do it for free," Lane said, looking out the window.

"But we can't just dump him now. Apart from anything else, it'll damage his defence for whoever else takes it on."

"Too bad. Don't forget the bottom line here, David. I've been shopping around for forensic experts to take a look at the knife and the autopsy. Do you know how much they cost? And with what happened at the prelim...do I need to say more? Besides, I haven't seen much of a defence shaping up from your research."

David was surprised at this jab, even from Lane. He had considered his work so far to be reasonably good in the circumstances, and Lane hadn't told him she was dissatisfied before now.

"I've been researching what you told me to research," David replied, a little defensively. "But I'll put more effort into it. Surely we can put together a good defence, even without an expert."

Lane tried another tack.

"Look, I know its a tough call, but there's really no other option. The timing won't hurt him because it's long enough after the prelim not to look bad, and long enough before the trial to get somebody else up to speed. Let a firm with deeper pockets hire their own expert. There'll still be plenty of them out there to represent Tom. Besides," Lane paused for effect, "I've already discussed it with McGrath."

So that was that, David thought. He still couldn't believe Lane was going to bail out now.

"Have you talked to Tom yet?" he asked.

"No. I'm going to meet with him today around four. Do you want to come?"

"Yes."

"All right then," Lane said, returning to her seat and looking towards the door to indicate the end of the meeting.

David returned to his office and sat dejectedly in his chair. He couldn't understand why Lane was doing this. Sure it was a tough case to win, but she must have known that going in. What had really changed, to prompt Lane to make such a drastic move? David knew a change of counsel would only hurt Tom's chances, despite what Lane had said, and it wouldn't do much for her reputation as a criminal lawyer either. This consideration alone should have been enough to keep Lane involved, since she prided herself on being an expert in every type of law she practised. As he tried to think of Lane's angle, Joanne appeared at the door.

"You've got about ten urgent phone messages from this morning and you need to have the Parsons statement of defence filed by tomorrow. And…"

"I need to get out of this monkey suit first," he said, referring to the court clothes he had been wearing since that morning. "And if I don't eat something I'm going to fall over. I'll run down to the deli…"

"I wouldn't do that if I were you," Joanne said quickly.

"Why not?"

"Because Billy's downstairs."

"Oh great," David sighed as he considered the unpleasant prospect of having to meet with his most frequent visitor, William Baker.

"That's the third time this week. How many times can I tell him there's nothing new?"

"I said you were in a meeting all afternoon but he's been there for half an hour already."

"Great. I might as well go to the bank and get a loan of five grand myself. I'll tell him his claim is settled and maybe he'll give me some peace."

"I'll run down and get your sandwich," she said with a laugh. "You return some of your calls."

"Thanks, Jo."

chapter thirteen

David looked at his watch and was just about to go up to Lane's office when the phone rang.

"David, Kelly here."

"Ready to go?"

"Sandy double-booked me for this afternoon. I've got a meeting across town in fifteen minutes. Why don't you go on over and meet with Tom and I'll catch up with you there?"

"Oh," David said, pausing. He sensed Lane was holding something back. "Do you want me to tell him myself or shall I wait for you?" he said, beginning to feel annoyed with Lane's attitude towards Tom. The man was charged with murder, after all, and David wondered what sort of meeting could be more important.

"Go ahead, I don't know when I'll make it. Tell him I just don't have the time to devote to it. And make sure he understands he needs to get another lawyer on the file right away."

"Sure," David said, as Lane hung up. This was unbelievable. David had always thought Lane was a bit slippery, but he had never dreamed she was capable of this sort of behaviour.

David's teeth chattered as he brushed the snow out of his hair and turned on the windshield wipers. How he hated January in Newfoundland! He felt the damp cold deep in his bones and he turned up the car's heater, which brought only a rush of cold air. He pulled away from the curb and cautiously descended the slippery side street down to Duckworth. A few minutes later, the fog had cleared from his windshield and he could actually see where he was going without constantly having to wipe it with the back of his gloved hand. It was practically dark out as he made his way along Forest Road, trying to think of how best to break the news to Tom. Pulling up outside the grim walls of the Penitentiary, he decided there was no way to sugarcoat it, he would just have to be honest.

David was overwhelmed by a feeling of depression as he made his way through the damp, foul-smelling building to the meeting room where Tom was waiting.

"Where's Lane?" Tom asked, after David had taken his seat.

"She's going to catch up with us later."

"Whatever. So what's up?"

David took a deep breath.

"I've got some bad news Tom."

"What?"

"Kelly is going to have to withdraw from the case. She can't devote the time necessary to ensure you've got the best defence possible."

"Hmpph," Fitzgerald muttered with a sneer. "She figures she can't win so she's fuckin' off out of it," he said, giving a remarkably accurate summary of the situation.

"It's not that Tom, really..."

"What about you?"

"What about me?" David said, unsure what he meant.

"Are you dumpin' me too?"

"I'm just a junior, Tom. I don't know that it's in your best interest..."

"You think I did it?" Fitzgerald fixed him with a stare.

"No, I don't think you did. But that's not the point."

"What is the point then?"

"Look Tom, other than there being no eyewitness, all the evidence points to your guilt. It's going to be a tough sell to a jury that you didn't do it, no matter what I think."

"So you don't want the case?"

"I'm just saying you need to think about what's best for your defence, and that maybe you need someone with more experience. This is my first murder trial and there are plenty of seasoned defence lawyers who'll take you on."

"What if they don't want to take the case? What if they think Lane knows something they don't?"

David was surprised at how well Fitzgerald understood the implications of Lane's withdrawal at this stage.

"I don't think there'll be a problem finding you alternate counsel," David repeated, not sure what else to say.

"I don't want some big shot asshole who talks to me like an idiot. I already had one of those," Fitzgerald said, looking David in the eye, "And I don't want Legal Aid either."

"So what do you want, Tom?"

"I want you to take the case. Unless you think you can't do it."

"I...I don't know, Tom," David hadn't prepared for this. He just sat there looking across the table at Fitzgerald, who was waiting for a reply.

"I'm just thinking of paying the expert witnesses we'll need...," he said, trying to think of any plausible reason not to take the case.

"My missus has a couple of grand. I'm good for the rest if you can wait a little." Fitzgerald said, mentioning money for the first time.

David sat there thinking. Was it possible to even think of it? There was no doubt that running his own murder trial would be quite an experience, but whether it would be a positive one was less obvious. Apart from anything else, it would require a lot of time away from his regular work, and from home.

"I need to talk to Mr. McGrath."

"He'll let you," Fitzgerald said confidently. "I got respect for him."

"I'll come back tomorrow afternoon, okay?" David said.

"Yup."

"Do you need anything in the meantime?"

"Yeah, I need a doctor," Fitzgerald said with a frown.

"Are you sick?"

"I had a black-out. I used to get 'em, but not in years."

"Did you ask anyone here?"

"Yeah, these fuckers won't do nothin' I ask."

"Alright, I'll have a talk to somebody and make sure you get seen by the prison doctor. Anything else?"

"Nope."

"Alright then, same time tomorrow?"

Tom nodded.

"And Tom, I want you to think about this carefully. It's your life after all."

They shook hands and David left, his mind filling with potential complications. He wondered what McGrath would say, let alone Lane—who would certainly think David had undermined her intentionally—but that was her problem. Most importantly, what would Elizabeth think? He had twenty-four hours to find out.

chapter**fourteen**

Having made it home to Elizabeth and Ben for an hour in the early evening, David had been forced to return to the office to catch up. He had wandered upstairs for some coffee, since they had a slightly better brewer on the third floor, and discovered McGrath's light on. Peeking in through the open door, David found him reclining in his high-backed leather chair reading a letter.

"Bill," David began tentatively. He was not looking forward to the discussion.

"David, come on in. What's up?" he said, tossing the letter onto the desk.

"Do you have a minute? I need to discuss something with you."

"Sure. Have a seat."

"It's about Tom Fitzgerald," David began as McGrath nodded his head.

"That's a shame about having to let him go. Some files you just can't afford to take."

"So you agree with Kelly," David said more as a statement than a question.

"I trust her judgment. Do you disagree?" McGrath asked, tilting his head a little, the way he always did when he became involved in an important exchange.

"I don't think it's right. Not at this stage."

"There are a lot of factors that go into a decision to take a case like this, David. There's your client's fate for starters—you have to be confident that you can represent him well. There's also your reputation as a lawyer to consider, as well as the financial burden a big case can bring with it. It's one thing if you think you've got a shot at winning it, but if that's not the case, you have to wonder why you're doing it."

"And if you think your client's innocent?"

McGrath put his index finger across his top lip and paused for a moment.

"Have you discussed this with Kelly?"

"No, I haven't seen her since the meeting. And now I'm in a bit of an awkward position."

"How so?"

"When I told Tom the news today, he said he wanted me to go on representing him." David paused to gauge McGrath's reaction.

"I told him he was better off to get a more experienced lawyer but he says he wants me to carry on."

"I see," McGrath. "And what did Kelly say?"

"She wasn't there..."

"What do you mean she wasn't there?" McGrath said with surprise.

"She had a meeting she couldn't get out of," David said, making a half-hearted effort at defending Lane.

McGrath shook his head and sat up in his chair, resting his arms on the desk.

"And you think Tom's innocent?" he asked, looking at David intently.

"Yes, I do."

"And what about a defence? You have that all figured out as well?" McGrath said pointedly.

David was caught flat-footed and searched for an answer, but McGrath beat him to it.

"Because without a strong defence, I wouldn't recommend it as a good career move for your first big trial. It's a fine line between trying to build a name and being remembered as the rookie who lost that high profile murder case."

David considered this sobering advice, before making his pitch.

"What if there was a decent defence?"

"Then I'd say you had a hard six months or more ahead of you, but it just might be worth it," McGrath said leaning back again. "If you really want it, that is." McGrath paused. "Do you really want this file?"

"I do."

"Then I suggest you either come up with a good defence, in which case we can talk again, or you don't and you let Tom find himself another lawyer—and soon."

David had to agree with this advice.

"And you need to talk to Kelly first thing tomorrow." McGrath added. "You may not agree with how she's handled this, but you need to discuss it with her face to face."

"I will," David said as he got up to leave.

"Then you need to really think about whether you're ready to take this on. I'm all for you taking on challenges and proving yourself, but this is as big as it gets and what I think doesn't matter. You're the only one who knows whether you're up to it or not."

chapterfifteen

avid stood at his office window and watched Lane make her way down from the firm's parking lot half way up the adjacent hill. He was not looking forward to the impromptu meeting that would be necessary this morning, but there was no avoiding it. David had gone straight home after his meeting with McGrath the previous evening and had a heart to heart with Elizabeth. He had been honest about what taking on the case alone would mean in terms of his time, and hearing his own description, he wondered how she could possibly agree. But she had asked only whether it was something he felt was important to do, and having established that, she offered only encouragement. David knew he would have to make it up to her somehow, and to Ben, but with her support he had felt a surge of excitement and had lain awake half the night thinking of possible defences.

On arriving at the office early, he had sifted through his growing in-tray and deferred everything but dire emergencies and the morning's court appearance. Now, as he heard Lane coming up the stairs, he was anxious to deal with her so he could devote his full attention to persuading McGrath to let him take on Tom's defence.

"Kelly," he called as Lane began to climb the stairs to the third floor.

"David, how are you. I was going to come and see you to ask about the meeting yesterday. I couldn't get away…"

"Can we talk? It's sort of urgent."

"Sure. Come on up."

David followed her upstairs and into her office, where he waited for Lane to finish chatting with her secretary and get her coffee before finally taking her seat behind the desk.

"So what's up?"

David proceeded to tell her about Tom's request, and was about to tell her about his meeting with McGrath the previous evening when he was interrupted by Lane's laughter.

"You can't be serious. You want to take this on alone?" she asked, shaking her head in disbelief. "Jesus, David, you were just supposed to relay the message and get the hell out of there. I thought you understood that."

"I'm just telling you he asked me," David said, angered by Lane's laughter at his expense. "And I'm telling you I want to take the case."

"Oh, is that so? Well why don't you just march on down to McGrath's office and tell him you'd like him to authorize a little disbursement of twenty grand for an expert's fees."

"I've already talked to him, and I don't think the disbursements are that import…"

"When did you talk to him?" Lane said sharply, her expression changing from mirth to pure venom.

"Last night, I was…"

"You little bastard, if you're trying to pull an end run…"

"I'm not trying to pull anything," David said, raising his voice. "I had to discuss it with someone if I'm going to consider Tom's request seriously. You weren't at the meeting and he happened to be here last night…"

"And you just happened to be here too. Well imagine that!"

Lane's secretary poked her head around the door, alerted by the raised voices.

"Do you want me to shut the door?"

"Yes."

"You listen to me you stupid little prick," Lane said, pointing her finger at David. "This case is unwinnable, why the fuck do you think I'm dumping it? I'm trying to protect this firm, and now you've got Tom thinking he's got a chance to keep us on the hook."

"I don't see it that way, Kelly. He just wants…"

"What does he want? A shoulder to cry on? What's the matter with you David, I thought you were smarter than that!"

Lane shook her head again and let out a sigh as she sat back in her chair.

"I'm supposed to meet with him again today…," David began.

"You're not doing a fucking thing until I've talked to McGrath and straightened out whatever bullshit you fed him last night."

There was silence as the two glared at each other.

"I've got work to do. I'll deal with you later," Lane said, standing up.

As David got up and left the office in silence, he passed Lane's secretary, who looked at him with a concerned expression on her face. Maybe she was right, David thought to himself. Maybe he had made a big mistake.

David hadn't had long to feel sorry for himself, as he had a chambers application at ten. Arriving at the courthouse, he spotted Phil Morgan finishing up a chat with a pretty articling clerk at the top of the stairs outside the motions courtroom.

"Hello, stranger. If I'd known you were coming I would have bribed you into covering for me."

"Hi Phil," he said with a somber smile. He had barely seen Phil at the office in recent weeks, between his own hectic schedule and Phil's family law practice, which had him at the Unified Family Court on King's Bridge Road on an increasingly regular basis.

"How are things?"

"Don't ask," David replied. "I think I might be cleaning out my desk in the near future."

"What are you talking about?"

David summarized the events of the last twenty-four hours as Phil listened in disbelief.

"You should just take the case and tell them all to go to hell," Phil said after David was finished. He had been having his own conflicts with the partners lately.

"That's great advice Phil, but I still have to eat, don't I?"

"Oh yeah, Phil grinned. But you could lose a few pounds."

"Very funny."

"So what are you going to do?"

"I need to find something to convince McGrath to let me take it on, and fast—before Lane talks him out of it. I'm supposed to meet with Tom later today but I'm going to have to delay that."

"You're right, you don't have much time. The trial's only a couple of months away. What are you doing here anyway?"

"I've got this stupid probate application…"

"Give it to me. My matter's going to be contested anyway so we'll be last to go."

"You sure?"

"No problem. Give me the docs and get out of here."

"Thanks Phil, I owe you one."

"You're buying the next round."

chapter sixteen

D avid's head was buried in a casebook at the back of the law library when it occurred to him that he had forgotten to call the prison doctor for Tom. He put the book down and called his office from the coffee room at the law library. Getting Joanne, he tracked down the administration's number and after being bounced around for a while he was finally connected to someone who promised to look into it.

"It's very important," David said in his most authoritative voice. "A fall from a blackout can be very dangerous, and I don't have to tell you about the prison's potential liability if you refuse medical treatment. Can I have your name for the record, sir?"

"It's McBride, and I said I'd look into it," the official at the other end said in an annoyed tone.

Satisfied, David hung up and returned to his casebook. He was sure they wouldn't be foolish enough to ignore his request. And it was true after all, that Tom could fall and be seriously hurt. As he resumed his reading, his mind wandered to Tom's blackout. It was curious that there had been no record of anything in his medical history. Then again, Tom had said he hadn't had any blackouts in a long time and David had not seen any of his early medical records. He put the book down as he tried to remember what Tom had said about their recurrence. Had it been recent? A feeling of excitement ran down his spine as he got up and walked briskly towards the stacks of criminal law case reporters and found an index. He looked up a term and was directed to a number of case digests, scribbling notes as he went. Bringing them to the stacks with him, he tracked down the relevant volumes and carried them back to his desk. Double-checking the page number in the citation, he flipped through the first volume and found the case he was after. He skimmed the headnote and then scrambled for the other two cases, finding them both in a matter of minutes and then carrying all three volumes to the photo-copier. He couldn't contain a smile as he hurriedly copied the three cases, shoved them into his briefcase and headed for the door.

Certain that another meeting with Lane would be pointless, David decided to go straight to McGrath, who happened to be in and was willing to spare him a few minutes.

"Kelly came to see me this morning. She's pretty pissed off at you, David."

"Yes, we had a meeting this morning."

"She thinks you're trying to submarine her."

"All I'm trying to do is represent a client who asked for my help, and that's the truth."

"I believe that's true, David, though I can see Kelly's side of it too. But none of that really matters, does it? The real question is whether anything's changed since our discussion yesterday."

"I think it may have."

"And how's that?" McGrath asked, cocking his head inquisitively.

"I think I've found a defence, something I overlooked before."

"And what's that?"

"Automatism," David said confidently.

"Automatism," McGrath repeated, shaking his head. "Do you know how difficult that would be to establish, David?"

David knew the unusual defence was rarely successful. Not unlike temporary insanity, it was based on the idea that the accused had not been in control of his mind or body when the crime was being committed, and that the person was reduced to something like a robot. However, as strange as it sounded when described by his criminal law professor, David recalled him adding that every ten or twenty years a murder case came along in which the defence was successful. What made it truly unique was that if the defence worked, it meant an acquittal and absolute freedom, as opposed to the lengthy term in a psychiatric institution that usually accompanied an insanity plea.

"I know it's rare," he said quickly, "but I think this is a classic case. It's got all of the signs, and Tom's got the medical background to boot."

"What medical background?" McGrath said skeptically.

Having returned to the office from the library, David had breathed a sigh of relief on finding that Lane had not yet repossessed what he had of Tom's file. He had found what he had failed to properly review before—the medical records from Tom's childhood to his early twenties—and he was prepared for McGrath's question. He explained the documented history of episodic blackouts and sleepwalking, beginning in his childhood and in the case of the sleepwalking, lasting for several years, before disappearing again until his late teens. From then, Tom had continued to sleepwalk off and on until his mid-twenties.

"And when's the last record of him sleepwalking before the murder?"

"Several years," David admitted, but carried on quickly. "But what if we could establish that the occurrences were cyclical, or that they could be triggered by any number of events that might have occurred at the time of the murder?"

"Hmm," McGrath stroked his top lip with his index finger. "For the right price, I suppose you could find a quack who would cooperate. The question is, would the jury buy it?"

"All we need is a reasonable doubt."

"You'll never get a local shrink to stake their reputation on a long shot like this."

David hadn't thought of that. And while a local psychiatrist would only be paid fees according to a modest court tariff, if he ended up having to hire someone from the mainland who testified for a living, it would cost a fortune.

"I'll find someone, even if they're still in med school. I'll get them up on the stand and have them recite from a textbook that it's a medical possibility."

McGrath leaned back in his chair and put his feet on the desk. "It'd be a helluva coup if you pulled it off," he said with a chuckle. He paused again and David waited breathlessly for his next words.

"But what if you don't, David, and the jury doesn't buy it? You can't just go back to plugging away at the Crown's case, you'll be stuck."

"I don't think there's much to lose."

"And everything to gain—literally," McGrath said, getting up and walking over to the window that looked out over St. John's harbour. The fog was rolling in through the Narrows as the grey afternoon dulled to black.

"Are you sure you're prepared to go all the way?" he said finally, not looking back.

"I'm sure. I really want this."

"Then take it," he said, turning to face him. "We'll carry the disbursements, but you'd better be prepared to throw everything you've got into it," he added severely.

"Oh I am," David said, showing a cautious smile. "Thank you, Bill. You won't regret this, I promise."

"I hope not," McGrath said, returning to the window as David got up to leave.

"Oh David."

"Yes?"

"I'll have a word with Lane."

"Thank you."

David left quickly, before McGrath changed his mind.

For his part, McGrath lingered at the window for a while, watching a flock of seagulls as they gathered around a little tug making its way into the harbour. He had to admire the kid's pluck. David reminded him of someone else he once knew who was willing to take risks. Not enough of the new generation of up and comers was willing to take risks.

chapter seventeen
—february

David looked up from the case he was reading and rubbed his eyes. He took a break to walk over to his office window and look out at the swirling snow. He had been here all night, and he could only imagine what awaited him when he made his way out to his car. It was probably buried by now. He checked the time—he didn't dare call home, for fear of waking Ben. He hoped Elizabeth was sleeping soundly too.

The past month had been crazy. It was only after he had committed to Tom's case that he fully realized the amount of work it was going to take. He had already spent countless hours poring over the mountain of written material that had accumulated since the previous spring, and he had sent out letters to everyone under the sun that might have a written record in any way related to Tom Fitzgerald. He had gone back as far as Tom's childhood medical records and report cards and made his way slowly and deliberately forward. In fact, he had been amazed at the wealth of information that was available, discovering a lot about Tom's life in this process that he had not anticipated.

An only child, Tom had begun his life in a small house in a working class neighbourhood in the west end of the downtown core. His father had been a bricklayer and Tom's misfortunes had begun at the age of two, when his mother died of pneumonia. Whether from the loss of Tom's mother or not, his father had turned to drink and before long, it was clear that Tom's happy home was gone forever. He had been placed in foster care at the age of four, and though the social services reports gave no clues of anything unseemly going on in the foster home, Tom's medical records painted a very different picture. Within a year of his first placement, strange injuries had begun to appear in his medical records. There were the usual cuts and bruises that most kids suffered, but there were other, more serious injuries for a child of his age. These included two fractures of the same arm within a year, bruised ribs, and a blackened eye. There were explanations for all of these of course. Tom had fallen off his bike, or hit his eye on the doorknob, according to the records. After a while, the explanations got more repetitive, and less plausible, and David began to wonder why no one had done anything to protect him.

Finally, at the age of seven, Tom had been relocated to another foster home and things seemed to have gone better for him. His injuries seemed to disappear, and his report cards showed a dramatic improvement at the social level. David was also a little surprised to find that for grades two through six, Tom was in the top third of his class. His report cards were filled with positive remarks from his teachers, and it seemed that he had managed to come through the troubles in his earlier years intact. But his foster family had left the province after grade six, so at the age of eleven Tom was sent to a new family, one with three older boys. Though there was nothing in any of his files to indicate any type of abuse, his performance at school dropped dramatically, and his file became filled with evidence of anti-social behaviour. Whether it was a failure to get along with the other boys in the foster home, or adjusting to a new school and the pressures of junior high, Tom had effectively withdrawn into a shell, with few friends and little positive influence. He started skipping school, and then got into fights and was expelled on several occasions.

By the age of fifteen, Tom had been in several scrapes with the law and it wasn't long before vandalism and petty theft turned to break and enter, and assault. He had been sent to the Whitbourne detention centre for boys, located about forty-five minutes outside of St. John's. From what David had heard about it, it was a tough place to be. Its effect on Tom had been anything but remedial, and he had been in and out of the facility until he reached the age of majority and ended up in real trouble. A conviction for auto theft at the age of nineteen had landed him in the Penitentiary for a year, and the pattern he had set in his youth of sporadic repeat offences spilled over into his adult life, where he battled alcohol and drugs in between stretches of incarceration. It made for a rather depressing read, in fact, and as David had pieced together this unhappy existence, he couldn't help but feel sorry for his client. It wasn't much of a life, and what he had left was now at stake.

But there was one ray of hope that had emerged from this review, and that was hard evidence dating back to Tom's early teens of the sleepwalking that had prompted David to think of the automatism defence. It had shown up not only in Tom's medical records, but also in some of his monthly foster care assessments. Apparently he had given his foster parents quite a shock one evening when they had awoken to find him sitting in the car in the driveway, with the engine running. He was still in his pyjamas, and when they asked what he was doing, they were even more spooked by his apparent inability to come out of whatever trance he had fallen into. He had been assessed by his family doctor, who thought nothing of it since it was the first such occurrence. But it was not, by far, the last. Tom's records from the Whitbourne facility revealed five documented cases of some form of nocturnal disturbance, discovered by staff during night rounds.

On one such occasion, Tom had been found walking around his bunk, rambling incoherently. On another, he was sitting at a table writing a letter, the contents of which no one could later decipher. In each case, the guards attested to his apparent detachment from reality upon being discovered, after which he had returned to normal. After the fourth incident, the superintendent of the facility arranged for a consultation with a psychiatrist, and this was where David might have caught a real break.

Like most facilities of its size, Whitbourne had an arrangement with a psychiatrist to come in to do consultations from time to time, rather than employ a full time psychiatrist. While they were all no doubt competent, the government rate payable on these consultations usually attracted only people who were just establishing their careers. David was therefore surprised to find that for some reason, fate seemed to have intervened in Tom's case, since his consultation was with none other than Dr. Felix Clark. Even David, who knew very little about the field of psychiatry, recognized Clark's name immediately as that of a nationally renowned psychiatrist. As David recalled, he was pretty sure Clark was a member of the faculty at University of Toronto and had given a lecture at a medico-legal conference when David was in law school in Toronto. How he had ended up seeing Tom Fitzgerald out at Whitbourne was beyond David completely, but he knew one thing for sure—if he could get Clark not only as an expert witness, but as an expert with personal knowledge of Tom's case, the Crown would have a lot of trouble discounting his evidence. But he was getting ahead of himself. First of all, Clark's assessment was very brief and concluded only that Tom had experienced an episode of somnambulism. There were certainly no notes of the assessment in the file, and it was questionable whether they still existed. Secondly, there was no telling whether he would support the theory that Tom had a medical or psychological profile that made automatism a possible defence. And last but not least, Tom wondered what it would cost for an expert of Clark's stature to testify. David had contacted Clark's office but had discovered that he would be out of the country for another week. In the meantime, David had done some research and determined that Clark was by no means a professional witness. His name had appeared several times in a search of Ontario court decisions, but usually as an authoritative author on psychiatry. He had only actually testified in two cases that David could find, and neither was of any relevance to automatism, which was not surprising. Still, David couldn't help feeling a little excited by the possibilities.

It was now after midnight and he had read all that his mind could digest about dissociative states. He decided to do himself a favour and go through his messages for the following morning before he left. As much as he wanted to get home and crawl into a warm bed, there was nothing worse than showing up first thing in the morning and being besieged by emergencies, and this was the way it had been for the past six weeks. From eight-thirty to five, he tried to keep his ever-increasing regular workload under control, and spent nights and weekends devoted entirely to Tom. While the growth his practice was undergoing both in terms of criminal and personal injury files was encouraging in many ways, it was reaching the point where it was becoming unmanageable. And when it became unmanageable, the practice of law was a very dangerous occupation indeed. All it took was a missed limitation period on a civil matter and he and the firm could suddenly become a defendant instead of counsel. And while it was never good to prejudice a client's right to compensation, the stakes were even higher for a slip on a criminal matter, where there was more than money on the line.

David found himself scrambling more and more to meet various deadlines and limitations. And while he genuinely enjoyed working the criminal files, he despised personal injury and took these files on only for business purposes. If he had his way, he would do nothing but criminal law, but as was the case with most criminal lawyers in St. John's, personal injury was an important supplement to the often poorly-paid criminal practice. This was especially so for the juniors, who had to balance the importance of gaining experience on their feet with that of justifying their existence to their senior partners.

In his case, David had continued to enjoy McGrath's blessing on Tom's file, but he knew only too well how quickly that could evaporate if he allowed the rest of his practice to slip. As for Kelly Lane, she had barely spoken to him since their heated meeting, other than to assure David that he was going to damage the firm's reputation by foolishly representing such a sure loser. Phil and some of the other associates had overheard Lane bad-mouthing David to some of the other partners as well, and he had been sensitive to the need to watch his back.

He finished separating the urgent from the routine tasks for the following morning and switched off his computer and the lights. From his dark office, he peered out at the thick, wet snowflakes backlit by a nearby streetlamp. He shuddered as he thought of walking through shin-deep snow and sitting in his cold car. He consoled himself with the knowledge that spring was not far off.

chapter**eighteen**

"Come here often?" Phil Morgan said with a grin as he leaned on the bar next to David.

"Mr. Morgan. How the hell are you? Where's Judy?"

"She's probably found Elizabeth by now."

David nodded. He and Elizabeth rarely made it out to Law Society functions, but they had decided to make an exception this time. They had both needed a night out.

"Well that's good. Then neither of us can get in trouble if we wander off for too long," David said.

"See McGrath yet?" Phil asked. "He's in good spirits."

"No, we just got here. Anyone else from the firm here?"

"I saw Lisa earlier, and Maddie's here somewhere, with her flavour of the month. And don't look now but there's your pal, Kelly."

"Great. Let's get out of here quick."

They made their way back to their wives and were soon joined by Maddie Beckett and her date, and a few other junior lawyers interested in discussing Tom Fitzgerald's case with David.

"So, I heard you're going to do a deal," one of them said, with some authority.

"No way, we're going to trial," David replied with a subtle smile.

"Gallant doesn't think so, at least that's what he told me last week," the young man continued, unfazed.

"Well I don't know why he'd tell you that, but it's not going to happen."

"But seriously, what kind of defence can you possibly hope to put together," chimed in another observer, a clerk with the city's premier criminal law firm, Rogers & Jerome.

"All he needs to do is raise a reasonable doubt," Phil jumped in. "And anything can happen at trial."

They continued the discussion for a while, and then David saw McGrath approaching, his wife in tow.

"Hello David. How are you, Elizabeth?" McGrath was all smiles. "Enjoying yourselves?"

They exchanged pleasantries as another senior member of the bar walked by. David recognized him immediately from the first day of Tom's preliminary, when Lane had first introduced him to Francis Sullivan, Q.C.

"Frank, how are you?" McGrath shook his hand heartily. "Have you met David Hall? He's one of my associates."

"Yes, I believe I have," he said, extending his hand.

David greeted him amicably as McGrath overdid the praise for

David's achievements, and casually mentioned the Fitzgerald trial.

"Yes, I heard," Sullivan said, congratulating David and chatting for a few minutes before excusing himself and moving on.

"That smug bastard has cost me a lot of money over the years," McGrath said with a snarl after Sullivan had left. "You'll see when you have a file with him, he's a smiling knife."

David actually liked Sullivan because he had shafted Lane, but coming from McGrath, the advice was worth bearing in mind.

"Oh, there's the Chief," McGrath said, referring to the Chief Justice of the Supreme Court of Newfoundland. "I'll see you at dinner," he added as he disappeared into the crowd.

"Come on," Elizabeth tugged at David's arm. "I'll buy you a drink."

David paid the babysitter and waved goodbye, stumbling a little as he closed the door.

"Is she gone?" Elizabeth whispered from the living room.

"She's gone," David whispered back.

"Come here," she ordered, grabbing him around the neck and pulling him forcefully to her as their lips locked and their hands roamed. He grabbed her around the waist and slung her over his shoulder, beginning the ascent up the stairs as she giggled.

"Don't drop me!" she said in a hushed warning. "You'll wake Ben."

"Don't worry," he chuckled as they reached the landing, crept past Ben's door and arrived in the bedroom. He laid her gently on the bed and they resumed their kissing and were mostly undressed, gradually making their way to the centre of the bed when they heard it. First it was a muffled cough, followed by a snort and a brief pause.

Then came a low-pitched wail, which slowly grew louder. David buried his face in the crook of Elizabeth's neck and she let out a sigh.

"I'll get him," he said after a moment, getting up and putting his bathrobe on. A moment later, they were all cuddled in their bed, Ben fast asleep again in his mother's arms, and David looking on enviously. He leaned over his sleeping son and gave her a kiss.

"We need a soundproof room," she said with a smile.

"I think you're on to something there. Good night."

"Good night."

David lay his head back on his pillow and closed his eyes. As the combination of fatigue and alcohol kicked in, he felt a wave of relaxation come over him. For some reason, he thought of Tom Fitzgerald, sitting in his damp, foul-smelling cell at the Pen and tried to imagine what it would be like to be in his place right now. He rolled over, put his arm around his wife and son and tried to push the disturbing image out of his mind.

chapter**nineteen**
–march

David held the phone at his ear and, checking his watch, calculated the time difference between St. John's and Toronto once again.

"Dr. Felix Clark please," he asked politely. He had called a half dozen times but Clark had not been in and had failed to return any voice mail messages. This was the first time he had reached a real person.

"May I ask who's calling?" said the woman at the other end.

David explained who he was and why he was calling, and after a few moments, his call was forwarded.

"Felix Clark here," the voice was anything but inviting.

"Good morning Dr. Clark, my name is David Ha..."

"Yes, you told all that to my secretary, what do you want?"

"Well," David was a little taken aback by his abruptness. "I wanted to talk to you about a client of mine that you saw about fifteen years ago. His name is Tom Fitzgerald."

"Where did you say you were calling from?"

"St. John's, Newfou..."

"Oh, I thought she said Saint John. Must have been the fall of...1987, was it?"

"Um," David scrambled for his notes. "Yes, that's right."

"I spent a semester at Memorial University as a visiting lecturer."

"I wondered what your name was doing on his files," David said.

"Yes...so what's he done now?" Clark said without much empathy.

"Well, what makes you think he's done anything?"

"You are a criminal lawyer, are you not?"

"Yes, but...," David tried to counter.

"So let us not waste time. What has he done?"

David sighed and decided to get straight to the point.

"He's been charged with murder."

"Has he indeed? Well I hope you're very good at what you do, Mr. Hall—for his sake."

"I was hoping you might be able to help," David ignored Clark's sarcasm and ploughed ahead.

"How so?"

"Tom had a history of sleepwalking," David began, and described Tom's history as well as the circumstances surrounding the case. When he had finished there was a brief pause at the other end of the phone.

"So, you would like me to place my professional reputation on the line and testify that Mr...."

"Fitzgerald."

"That Mr. Fitzgerald was insane..."

"Not insane," It was David's turn to interrupt. "My belief is that he suffered from non-insane automatism, a defence recognized by..."

"I know what it is, and whether it is recognized in law or not, there is considerable debate in the psychiatric community as to whether it is a valid diagnosis."

"I realize this is an unusual case, but I really feel Tom is incapable of murder, and with his history..."

"Sleepwalking alone doesn't predispose one to a dissociative state such as automatism," Clark said dismissively.

"No, but combined with other factors, such as a blow to the head or a psychological assault, it is consistent with automatism," David had done his research well.

"In any event, Mr. Hall, I really don't know that I..."

"All I'm asking is that you review your files and see if you have any notes of your assessment. In the meantime, I can send you a summary of the Crown's evidence and what I have uncovered in my own research."

"I'm very busy..."

"Please, Dr. Clark, if you could just check your records. You're under no obligation to testify, and I won't subpoena you if you're not going to help my client's case," David paused before he added the last part of the pitch. "He didn't do it, I'm convinced of it. But his trial is in six weeks and if I don't get some answers soon, he will be convicted."

"I will review my files," Clark said, after a brief pause. "But that's it."

"Thank you Dr. Clark. Shall I call you back, say in..."

"I will call you, Mr. Hall. I have your number. Good day."

"Thank you, Dr. Clark," David said, into a dead phone. He put down the receiver and let out a big sigh. So much for his perfect expert witness—he would be lucky if he even bothered to look for Tom's records. He tried to remain positive, but he knew this was a blow to his case. Clark's help had been a long shot, but it had at least been a possibility. Now, he would really be down to a medical school student and a psychiatry textbook to prop up his defence.

David began to wonder whether it was worth pursuing the defence at all, without a credible expert to back it up. He considered returning to Lane's original strategy of attacking the Crown's case, in the hopes of poking enough holes in it that it would sink, or at least founder.

The Crown's forensic report, with which David had been provided a copy after months of delays, emphasized the fact that the fatal wound had been inflicted by a left-handed killer. Since Tom was left-handed, it did not bode well for his defence, but David knew that some of it was more speculation than hard science and that it could be attacked, although again not without expert help. Lane had gotten as far as shopping around for a forensic expert, but nobody with any credentials had been willing to look at it for what David had to spend. One thing was sure—wasting time on trying to build two separate defences at this late stage was not a good idea, and he would have to make a big decision soon. It was time to see Tom again anyway.

chapter twenty

It was 9:00 a.m. and David had lost control of his day already. A settlement offer he had planned on finishing in ten minutes an hour ago, had no end in sight. He had a meeting in fifteen minutes that he had not prepared for and a Small Claims Court trial at eleven. If he survived the morning, he had a meeting with Tom scheduled for three to discuss the potential change in strategy—a meeting he was not looking forward to. He tried to ignore the e-mail messages that were clogging his computer and decided to search for the meeting file, abandoning the letter for the time being.

"David," a voice said abruptly from outside his office. David looked up from the floor where he had been searching through a collection of files. Was that Kelly Lane's voice?

"I'm in here," he called.

"Did you appear for Paul Hiscock yesterday morning?" Lane asked, appearing at the door.

"No," David said, knowing he had not. "Which court?"

"Provincial," Lane said, in a hostile manner.

"Paul Hiscock. That sounds familiar," David said, retrieving his day timer and flipping forward through the pages.

"Well I guess it does, he's McGrath's nephew."

"Is there something wrong Kelly?"

"Oh no, not at all," Lane said sarcastically. "As long as you don't mind explaining to McGrath why his nephew's got a bench warrant out on him because you didn't show up for his first appearance."

"Whoah. Hang on a minute…here it is. Paul Hiscock—first appearance on a DUI set for next Tuesday at ten."

"I gave you that file a month ago…"

"And you told me it was set for the 18th…"

"I told you it was the 11th, and anyway the date's in the file."

The two stared each other down for a moment, before David retrieved the file from the pile on his side table. Flipping it open, he scanned through it, stopping at a brief memo from Lane, indicating the appearance was in fact on the 11th.

"Well, what does it say?"

"You told me the 18th," David replied sharply, avoiding the direct question. "Why else would I have written the 18th in my day timer?"

"I don't know, but I don't think McGrath's going to care when he gets here."

"I take it you've told him already," David said sarcastically.

"Actually I didn't." Lane was quick to say. "He gave me a blast of shit over the phone because he got a call from the cop who processed the warrant. Lucky for you, he gave McGrath the heads up because of a house deal he did for him, otherwise…"

"That's just great," David tossed the file onto his desk.

"McGrath's on his way in. You might want to be around when he gets here, and have a good explanation. He postponed his golf trip to South Carolina to straighten this out. Anyway, I've gotta go. Best of luck to you," Lane said sarcastically as she made for the door. David sank into his chair and let out a sigh.

"And by the way," Lane poked her head around the door. "Don't even think about trying to blame me for this. There's nothing McGrath hates more than a back stabber."

"Thanks for the tip," David said mockingly as Lane disappeared. He tipped his head back and ran his hands through his hair. This was a disaster! McGrath was relatively even-tempered, but David had seen him in a rage before, and it was not a pretty sight. And this was just the type of thing that would set him off.

David shook his head before getting the file again. He reviewed the memo one more time, and there it was, plain as day. Whether Lane had told him the 18th or not, the onus was on David to check the file. He was going to have to face the music, and the timing couldn't have been worse. With Tom's defence on the rocks, he had considered approaching McGrath about having the firm come up with more money for a forensic expert's fees, but he could forget about that now. He would be lucky to hang on to his job long enough to go to trial. He walked over to his window and watched the people strolling down the street in the wintry morning sunshine, apparently oblivious to his misery. He felt like climbing out the window and joining them as he caught sight of McGrath's shiny SUV coming down over the hill. David felt his stomach churn as it stopped in front of the building, and he watched McGrath emerge, looking decidedly angry. David returned to his chair and took a deep breath as he heard the sound of heavy footsteps taking the stairs two at a time. There was nothing else he could do.

chapter twenty-one

David had been here so many times that the smell didn't even bother him anymore. Neither did the jeering of the inmates as he was led to the depressing little meeting room, or the clanging of the metal gates that echoed through the lime green halls. In fact, with the kind of day he had been having on the outside, there was almost something comforting about being confined in here as a visitor. He had survived the morning's "meeting" with McGrath, but barely. When the shouting had stopped, he had been left with a warning— to get his act together, or look for another job. Phil had heard the racket, along with everyone else on the second floor, and he had tried to console David by taking him to lunch.

"He'll get over it," he had said, dismissing the whole thing, but David was not so sure. Apart from damaging his future at the firm, David was annoyed at himself for having made such a stupid mistake. He always double-checked the dates, and how he could have missed that memo was beyond him. He turned his mind to

Tom's case as he heard the sound of approaching footsteps and the jingle of keys in the door.

"Hello Tom," he said, extending his hand. Tom acknowledged him with the usual nod and grunt.

"How are they treating you?"

"Same," Tom replied simply.

David got right to the point.

"I wanted to talk to you about our strategy."

"You mean that robot stuff?" Tom said sarcastically. David had taken great pains to explain the automatism defence in detail, and had used a robot as an analogy for the classic automaton.

"I'm wondering whether we can take the risk…"

"Thought you said it was my only chance."

"I said I thought it was your best chance, but I'm not so sure now."

"Whaddaya mean now? You can't get that shrink?" Tom crossed his arms over his chest.

"It doesn't look good," David sighed. "I spoke to him again, and though he does have some notes from your assessment, he doesn't seem to feel there's enough there to justify his testimony."

"So he won't help me…"

"He didn't say that, exactly."

"What'd he say then?"

"He said that without more evidence, he wasn't prepared to testify that automatism was a reasonable possibility."

"So get him more evidence."

"It doesn't work like that Tom. I can't just make things up."

"Why not. We're making this whole fucking thing up aren't we?" Tom said in a rare burst of emotion. "All I knows is I didn't kill no one. I was drunk, I passed out and I woke up with a knife in my hand. What the fuck do I know about automaticism—or whatever it is."

"I'm not making anything up, Tom. I'm taking the facts as they are— that you were there at the time of the murder, that you were found with the knife in your hand and with the victim's credit cards and cash in your pocket. I'm taking those facts, and I'm taking your statement that you didn't do it, and I'm trying to fit it together into a defence that's going to succeed in court."

"But now we got no expert," Tom said, dejectedly.

"We may not be able to get this expert, who's the only one who would have the additional credibility of having actually treated you—albeit a long time ago."

"So we get somebody else."

"We can try, but with what we've got to offer as a fee, our choices might be very limited. One of the reasons I wanted Clark was because he's not a professional expert, and I was hoping if he took it on, he wouldn't gouge us with a heavy fee." David got up and moved toward the grimy Plexiglas window. "What I came here to do today was to discuss the possibility of returning to the original strategy, of making the Crown prove its case."

"Hmmph," Tom grunted, apparently unimpressed.

"They have a strong case, there's no doubt about it, but it's still all circumstantial. We can take a run at all of it, particularly their conclusion that the killer was left-handed," David said enthusiastically, omitting to mention that the same financial limitation applied to finding a forensic expert.

"And we can use your blood-alcohol level to your advantage, that you were too impaired to have done it. There are a lot of things that could go wrong for the Crown, and don't forget it's him that's got to prove his case, not the other way around. All we need is a reasonable doubt."

"I got a long history of drinkin'. All they gotta do is look at my breathalyser readings to know I can handle my booze."

David had seen the files on his three drunk driving convictions. In two of the cases, his readings had been over two hundred, well in excess of his estimated blood-alcohol at the time of the murder. It was true that arguing incapacity would be a hard sell if he had been able to operate a car with that much booze in his sytem. David regained his seat.

"Look, automatism is a pretty technical defence, and we need to get someone on that stand to convince a jury that it's for real. All I'm saying is if we can't get someone like Clark, then I'm not sure who we're going to be able to get for a couple of thousand dollars."

"I'll tell my missus to get more."

"But she's not going to be able to come up with that kind of money in time," David said, shaking his head. Tom sat there quietly, tapping his left index finger on the table.

"So I'm fucked either way, right?"

"That's not what I'm saying…"

"Do I get to decide or what?"

"Decide what?"

"The defence we use."

"Yeah," David said with a shrug. "I'm trying to help you make the right choice, but it's your call."

"I got a better shot with the robot stuff. Nobody's gonna believe I didn't do it, not with the friggin' knife in my hand and all the rest. As for the expert, get whoever you can."

David considered his client's choice, before nodding his head slowly.

"Okay Tom, that's what we'll do."

"You're not gonna give up on me or nothin', are you? You're my only hope of gettin' out of this shithole you know."

Suddenly, David felt ashamed.

"No Tom, I'll never give up, I can promise you that much."

chapter twenty-two

"So what the hell do I do now?" David asked Phil Morgan over a pint of beer in the corner of a crowded pub, just down the street from the courthouse. The two had recently been making a habit of a Friday afternoon drink to round out the week.

"That's a good question," Phil replied with a shake of his head. "But whatever it is, you'd better do it soon. You've only got a month left before trial."

"How am I supposed to find an expert in that time with what I've got to spend?"

"Don't suppose the firm would kick in a few extra bucks…"

David let out a laugh at the suggestion as Phil nodded his head.

"I guess you're right. Hey, you could always ask your good friend Lane, I'm sure she'd go to bat for you at the next partners' meeting."

They both enjoyed a good laugh at that, then David's face took on a more serious expression.

"I don't know. I'm starting to think this whole automatism thing was a mistake. All I've done is given Tom false hope. And now he won't even consider any other strategy."

"Maybe that's not such a bad thing," Phil said, sipping his beer. "So what if it's a long shot—I mean let's face it, the evidence is pretty damaging to any traditional defence. It's not like you're giving up a great defence to pursue automatism. You haven't got much to lose."

"I guess so," David said, considering the argument.

"As for the expert, this is St. John's, not California; the jury's not expecting you to call Sigmund Freud. All you need is a warm body up on the witness stand to say automatism is a legitimate condition. If you can't get a psychiatrist, get your prof from Psych 101."

"Yeah, but whoever it is, he's going to have to beat whoever Gallant pulls out of the woodwork, and you can be pretty sure it's not going to be his Psych prof."

"Ah," Phil said, waving his hand dismissively, before trying another approach. "Alright, ask yourself one question."

"And what would that be?" David said with a grin.

"If your hot shot expert from Toronto—or anyone else for that matter—had agreed to testify, would you think it was the best defence for Tom?"

"Yeah."

"So why don't you think it is now?"

David hesitated, and took another sip of beer.

"Simple as that," Phil said, slapping his hand on the table. "Now stop whining and beat the bushes for your expert—he's out there somewhere."

"You're full of shit Phil, but thanks for the support anyway."

He raised his mug and tapped it off David's.

"Attaboy. If you ever need inspiration, think what a moron Lane's going to look like when you get Tom acquitted. Did I tell you she didn't know what automatism was?"

"No."

"She had one of the clerks look it up. He told me Lane couldn't even spell it!"

They had a good laugh at Lane's expense and ordered another round from a passing waitress.

"So how are Elizabeth and Ben?"

"Good, they're in Florida with her family. I couldn't make it…"

"Gee, you must be so disappointed you're not there," Phil said sarcastically.

"Yeah. Ben likes the beach though."

"So we're two free men then."

"Why, where's Judy?"

"She's on the west coast working on a big account—her busy time is starting. Even when she gets back in town I'll hardly see her until after the filing deadline. What do you say we hit George Street after this round?" Phil said, looking at his watch. "We can catch the rest of happy hour at the Eclipse. It's a nice night—the deck's probably open."

"That place is a meat market."

"We're still allowed to look, you know."

"I was just making an observation, not an objection," David said, laughing. He would sleep in tomorrow before turning his attention back to Tom. It had been a while since he had been out on a bender with Phil. It felt like too long.

Everything was right in the world. David was swimming in deep relaxation, wallowing in it. He could feel the muscles in his face relax into a broad smile as his body floated contentedly. He was in a bar, or was it on a beach? It didn't matter, as long as this feeling continued. But something was calling him back from his peaceful refuge, invading it with a ring that began faintly and quickly became louder, until it was unavoidable. What on earth was it? David opened his eyes and put his hands on his temples as the rush of pain rose to his head. He tried to shake it free but it gripped his whole skull, and radiated down his neck. It was the phone. He fumbled for it, if only to kill that infernal noise it was emitting.

"Hello?" he said in a raspy voice.

"Sleepin' in?" came a familiar voice.

"Um, Tom?"

"Yeah. I need to see you."

David sat upright and fought off a wave of nausea before collecting his wits.

"What is it Tom? Is something wrong?"

"No, I just need to see you. Somethin' I remembered about the case."

David looked at the clock radio. It was eleven-thirty. He hadn't slept in that long since before Ben was born.

"Okay," he continued groggily. "I'll call down and try to get in to see you first thing Monday, alright?"

"Uh, I'm outta smokes too, I was hopin' you could bring me some today."

"Oh," David thought. So that's why he was calling. What the hell, it was the least he could do.

"I'll see if they'll let me in to see you later this afternoon."

"Thanks."

David hung up and fell back into the pillows. He felt awful, and what was that stink? His bedroom smelled like a brewery and he was still wearing the shirt he had put on yesterday morning. He lay back and pieced together the events of the previous night. First the Eclipse for happy hour, then the Crossroads. He had an awful taste in his mouth, like bitter lemons—had he been drinking tequila? He racked his brain for more details and remembered doing upside-down margaritas. Had Phil been dancing on the bar or was his mind embellishing? No, he had been dancing alright, until he fell off. David lay there for a minute rubbing his eyes, then chuckled as he remembered seeing Phil dusting himself off from behind the bar as a laughing crowd looked on. As he lay there alone with the sunlight streaming in, remembering more, the chuckle progressed into a deep laugh. He wondered how Phil was feeling this morning.

chapter twenty-three

"So Tom," David said, deciding to play along. Tom was ripping the plastic off the cigarettes like a wild man. "What is it you wanted to talk about?"

Tom lit a cigarette and took a long drag of smoke, blowing it out in relief above their heads. It reminded David of bar smoke and he felt his stomach churn. He had been nursing a hangover all day and even now, in the late afternoon, he didn't feel quite right.

"I been thinkin'," Tom began. "I been thinkin' about the night of the murder, and what I was into before."

"What do you mean?" David said, surprised that Tom might actually have something to add after all.

"I think I had a scrap on the way to the park. After the bar I mean."

"You were in a fight?"

"Yeah, I never remembered it before, but I was just lyin' here the other night, going over everything in my head and it came to me. I was around the hotel when some arsehole started mouthin' off, so I gave him a shot, and I think he gave me one too, I'm not too sure."

"By the Fairmont?"

"Yeah."

"And you punched each other?"

"Yeah. I sorta missed his face and got him in the ear—musta got outta the way."

"Did he hit you back?"

"I was pretty drunk. Normally I coulda kicked the shit out of 'im but…"

"He probably didn't have as much to drink as you did," David suggested.

"Yeah, probably. Anyway, I ducked a bit but he stung me pretty good on top of the head. Musta had a ring on or something cause I remember blood comin' from somewhere."

"But there was no blood on you when the cops found you."

"I had a red coat on, and plus it was raining."

David considered the revelation for a moment.

"I don't understand. How could you forget all that for so long and then suddenly remember so clearly?"

"Jesus, I dunno." Tom said, shrugging his shoulders. "Like I said, I was just lying there thinking and I remembered. I guess the booze really fucked me up."

David rubbed his finger over his top lip as he allowed himself to entertain a fleeting feeling of excitement as he considered the possibilities. But there would be no evidence to support Tom's claim.

"I betcha there's somethin' in the doctor's notes about it too. He took enough friggin notes," Tom said, sucking the last of the nicotine out of his cigarette.

"What doctor?"

"The one the cops had there that morning."

"You were examined by a doctor?" David said in surprise.

"Yeah."

"Well, well," David said, shaking his head. "Looks like Mr. Gallant's got some explaining to do, because he didn't give me a copy of any medical assessment from the morning of your arrest."

"So what do you do now?"

"I'll be on the phone first thing Monday morning, demanding a copy of the report, and anything else that's missing from the disclosure package."

David watched as Tom stubbed out his cigarette, then reached for another.

"You don't remember what he looked like do you? The guy you fought with."

"Naw, it was pretty dark. He was a young fella."

"What, early twenties?"

"Yeah, I suppose."

"And there's nothing else you want to tell me?"

"Nope."

"Alright then," David said. They went over a few other aspects of the case and then concluded the meeting.

Walking out of the dreary stone prison into the cool evening air, David's mind was making the counter-arguments over and over. It seemed an unlikely story for starters, and perhaps Tom had just made it up for a pack of smokes. But as strange as it seemed from an objective point of view, David had no reason to think Tom was lying. He couldn't pronounce the defence his lawyer was trying to mount, let alone realize he may have just given it an important boost.

David sat in the waiting room and flipped through a magazine. After his meeting with Tom the previous Saturday, he had called Gallant and demanded to know about the medical examination of his client, and why he had not been provided with the written record of it as part of the Crown's disclosure package.

Gallant had reacted coolly to David's suggestion of wrongdoing on his part, explaining that the RNC had called in a doctor to take some blood tests, the results of which had been provided. There had been no physical examination or written report to disclose, and nothing to get excited about, in Gallant's view. David would be the judge of that, he thought as he looked at his watch. In any case, he had been promised any written notes, and though David had followed up immediately with the doctor's office, Dr. Ted MacDonald had been on vacation in Florida until the day before. Now Thursday, David was barely able to contain his impatience as a tanned man in his forties approached and extended his hand.

"Sorry about the wait, Mr. Hall."

"No problem," David said, following him back to his office.

As they sat in the office, David took MacDonald back through the events of the morning in question. After providing his account, MacDonald produced a copied page from a notebook, and handed it to David.

"This is all I have from that morning," he said, as David read the page.

"R. Par. Lac. What is that?" David asked, referring to a notation in MacDonald's scribbled handwriting.

"Right parietal laceration," MacDonald replied.

David had done enough personal injury law to be familiar with some medical terms, and he quickly confirmed that this was a reference to a head injury.

"Here," MacDonald said, putting his hand on the right side of his head, just above the hairline.

"He had a cut there?"

"There was a small cut and a rather large bump."

"Is that so," David remarked. "But not big enough to do anything about?"

"I really wasn't there to give him a physical examination. I just happened to notice some blood on the top of his head and checked it out."

"And if you had been giving him a physical examination, would you have done anything differently?"

"I'm…I'm not sure."

"I don't understand," David furrowed his brow, sensing he was onto something.

"Well, he was clearly disoriented, but just as clearly drunk, or badly hung over."

"Let's say you were seeing him in your office, or at an emergency department. Would you have ordered any tests, x-rays—anything like that?"

MacDonald pondered the question for a moment.

"I suppose I might have," he acknowledged, after a moment.

David asked a few more questions, thanked MacDonald for his help and headed straight to his office to make some calls.

chapter twenty-four
–april

David scanned the crowded pick-up area outside Pearson International Airport for a cab. Spotting an obliging cabbie, he made his way through the warm spring air and in moments, he was being whisked away from the curb. He breathed a sigh of relief as a rush of air blew into the back seat through his open window. It was a warm day for April, even for southern Ontario, and the fact that he had left rain, drizzle, fog and ten degree weather behind in St. John's this morning made the heat that much more noticeable.

"Where to, sir?"

"Roy Thompson Hall," David said, leaning back into his seat and looking out the window at the incoming planes.

Although he had no desire to live there, he felt at home in Toronto. Having gone to law school at the University of Toronto, he had a lot of good memories of the place, and plenty of friends in the area. Charlie Whalen was a fellow Newfoundlander who had gone to work for a hedge fund around the end of David's law school days, and had made a killing in the stock market. These days, he lived in a trendy condo downtown and what he spent on lunches was probably more than David's salary. But he was still the same guy when it came to old friends, and when David had called, he had been quick to offer him a place to stay for the weekend and a night out on the town.

As they sped towards the Toronto skyline, David tried to focus on how best to accomplish his objective. With the short notice, and the fact that he was flying on his own points, he hadn't exactly had his pick of flight times. It would be six o'clock by the time he got to Charlie's place, but he supposed it was better than nothing. They would have plenty of time to get reacquainted, and fortunately, his meeting with Clark was not until the following afternoon. He went over what he would say once again in his head. Clark had been reluctant to agree to the meeting, but David had practically begged to be given a chance to be heard. He would have only one chance to get Clark on board. If he couldn't, he was running out of options, and more importantly, out of time.

David sipped coffee and waited anxiously at the coffee shop around the corner from Queen's Park. He knew it was only a few minutes after one, but he had visions of Clark not showing up, making his whole trip a waste of time. David also knew that even if he did show today, the odds were against Clark agreeing to testify. He was going over his pitch in his mind one more time when he spotted an immaculately-dressed, grey-haired man in his fifties approaching.

"Dr. Clark?"

"Mr. Hall, I presume?"

"Yes, call me David, please."

"How was your trip?"

"Fine thank you," David replied with a smile as they both sat. "Thank you so much for meeting with me."

"I'm still not sure why you're here, but since you are, it was the least I could do."

"What can I get you?" David asked, waving to a nearby waiter.

"Americano," Clark said as the waiter nodded and left.

"So, Mr. Hall. I assume you are here to convince me to testify on your client's behalf," Clark said with a wry grin.

"Yes, that's true," David prepared for his big pitch. "And I hope that once you hear what I have to say, you'll agree that Tom deserves your help."

"And what is it you have to say?" Clark said, brushing a piece of airborne lint away from the lapel of his tweed blazer. As his coffee arrived, David began his speech with the sad circumstances of Tom's broken childhood—the physical abuse, the string of foster homes, and the bright spots in between that were in such vivid contrast to the rest of his existence. He continued through Tom's unfortunate educational and vocational history. He described in detail every entry of note in Tom's social services file, his report cards and his medical records. David outlined Tom's history of sleepwalking from an early age, up to the time when Clark himself had assessed him, and continuing thereafter to the age of nineteen.

Next, David described Tom's criminal history, going through the date and nature of every offence he had ever committed, noting that with the exception of a couple of assault charges in his early twenties, both of which were relatively minor, his criminal portfolio was restricted to property-related crimes, usually theft. Finally, he reviewed the state of Tom's life at the time of the murder, noting that he had been out of jail for over a year and in a steady relationship with a girlfriend he had been seeing for a number of years. As Clark sipped his coffee, calmly David moved on to the facts of the case against Tom, starting with the established events of that evening, from the point of view of both the accused and the victim. He described the crime scene in detail and all of the evidence that had come to light since the night of the murder, including the forensics reports, the statements and the transcripts from the preliminary inquiry.

When David had finally finished, he paused to allow Clark a moment before responding. The academic pursed his lips, then shook his head.

"I'm sorry. There is just not enough objective evidence to support a dissociative state," he said simply. David nodded his head as he digested the response.

"I know you've worked very hard," Clark said, "and I must say, I was surprised to hear that Tom had been charged with such a brutal crime. I do remember him from my assessment and he didn't strike me as violent then…but people change."

"He hasn't changed Dr. Clark, I assure you. His only crime was being in the wrong place at the wrong time."

"Again, I'm sorry, but…"

"You said you lacked objective evidence," David said, looking at Clark and awaiting confirmation.

"Yes."

"So if you had more objective evidence—more than just sleepwalking that is—and given your impression of Tom's personality, you might be willing to testify?"

"It would depend on the evidence," Clark said, crossing his arms and leaning back in his chair. He would have to say yes to something this lawyer was asking if he wanted to get out of here this afternoon.

"What if there were evidence of Tom suffering a significant blow to the head just before the time of the crime?"

Clark's expression changed slightly upon hearing this.

"Are you saying there is such evidence?"

David proceeded to summarize the story Tom had told him at the Penitentiary the previous weekend.

"And he never mentioned this before?" Clark asked, resting his chin between his thumb and forefinger.

"No. He says he forgot about it—as though it had been wiped from his mind."

"That's what he said?" Clark asked.

"That's what he said. Pretty outlandish I guess," David said.

"Yes, perhaps," Clark said. David could see the wheels turning.

"But the strange thing is," David continued, "the doctor who examined him on the morning after the murder confirms the presence of a large lump on his head," David pointed to the top of his skull, on the right side.

"You're sure it was the right side?"

"Yes, I'm sure," David said with certainty. "Now I'll defer to your judgment, but doesn't a substantial blow to the head, combined with amnesia—supported by hard, objective evidence of course—change things?"

"Do you have a copy of this medical examination?" Clark asked after a brief pause.

"There is no formal report. But I do have a copy of the doctor's notes, as well as my notes of a meeting with him a few days ago," David slid a sheet of paper across the table, and waited with his heart in his throat as Clark skimmed the notes.

"Well?" David could barely stand it.

"I'll need some time to consider this new information."

"Dr. Clark. My client's trial starts in less than a month. Time is the one thing he doesn't have."

Clark let out a sigh.

"When are you going back to St. John's?"

"In about six hours," David replied, looking at his watch.

"I need a few hours. Can you leave me a number where I can reach you?"

"I can call from the airport if you like. Do you have a cell?"

"I don't have one of those abominable things. Here's my office number," Clark said, giving him a card. "I will be there for your call."

"Thank you, Dr. Clark."

"Don't thank me for anything yet."

"I meant for meeting me here today, on a Sunday."

"Oh," he said with a slight smile as they got up to leave. "My pleasure."

chapter twenty-five

After the meeting with Clark, David had walked around downtown for a while, enjoying the warm sunshine. He had met up with Charlie for a late lunch before gathering his things for the ride out to the airport. They had chatted about the old days and shared a lot of laughs, so that by the time they reached the airport, David had almost forgotten about the case. Now, as Charlie honked and pulled away from the curb, it returned to the forefront of his mind. He checked the time and decided to head straight for the nearest pay phone and get it over with. His pulse raced as he waited for what seemed like too many rings before it was finally picked up at the other end.

"Mr. Hall," he said simply.

"Have you had a chance to consider my request?"

"I have."

For God's sake, David thought. Could he just tell him one way or the other.

"And?"

"I must say I'm concerned about certain aspects of this case, Mr. Hall," Clark said severely.

David's heart sank.

"But I am prepared to testify that non-insane automatism could have caused him to act out of character."

There was a pause as David considered Clark's offer.

"Are you prepared to testify that it could have caused him to kill?" David asked anxiously, not wanting to push his luck.

"Yes, I suppose I am."

David felt as light as air as he tried to conceal his relief.

"That's good Dr. Clark. That's very good," was all he could manage. With this huge obstacle out of the way, it occurred to him that another one almost as large was laying in wait.

"Uh, we didn't discuss your fee, Dr. Clark," David's mind was beginning to focus on where he was going to come up with it as he asked the question.

"I'll expect return airfare from Toronto," Clark said in his usual, curt manner.

"But what about your fee…"

"I'm not doing this for compensation Mr. Hall," Clark said as though it were an insult to even ask.

"But your accomoda…"

"I may turn it into a little vacation. It's been too long. Just arrange my travel and I'll look after the rest."

David was still in shock.

"I don't know what to say, Dr. Clark. Thank you."

He hung up the phone and just stood there for a moment, letting the relief and excitement flow through him. He had come here with nothing, and was leaving with the free services of a psychiatrist of national renown to testify in his client's murder trial. He threw his bag over his shoulder and made his way to the check-in counter with a spring in his step. For the first time since he had had the idea to pursue this defence, it seemed as though there was a chance it might actually work.

chapter twenty-six
—may

David paced anxiously from one end of the kitchen to the other. Outside, the sun was shining and the birds were chirping after a brief morning shower. He had been awake since six a.m. and had been experiencing a gradually worsening case of the butterflies ever since. He tiptoed upstairs so as not to wake Ben or Elizabeth, who were enjoying a rare sleep-in. As he took his wallet from the dresser and began to creep back out of their bedroom, he heard the rustle of bedclothes.

"Are you leaving?" Elizabeth said in a hoarse voice.

"Sorry hon, I didn't want to wake you."

"That's alright. Come here," she beckoned. "Good luck," she said softly before kissing him on the cheek. "I know you'll be great."

"Thanks, but I don't feel so great right now," he replied with a smile.

"Jitters are normal. They're a sign of good things to come. Once you get started you'll be fine."

"Say good-bye to Ben for me," he said as he kissed her forehead.

It was almost nine by the time he arrived at the office. He had no intention of trying to do any last minute preparation for the trial, which was due to start in thirty minutes. He had done all the preparation that was humanly possible in the past two weeks and now he just wanted to get it under way. Once at his office, he stopped briefly to check in with Joanne before gathering his gown and oversized briefcase.

"Wish me luck," he said on his way out. "I'll need it."

"Break a leg," she said enthusiastically as he made his way downstairs and out into the morning sunshine for the brief walk down Duckworth Street. On the front steps of the courthouse, a camera crew and some reporters were milling about. As David approached, one of them pointed to him and they sprung into action, shoving microphones and tape recorders in front of him as the television camera rolled.

"Mr. Hall, is it true you intend to raise insanity as a defence?"

"No comment," he said with a smile, as he made his way up the stairs.

"I'm told you included a psychiatrist in your list of expert witnesses. Can you confirm that?"

"Sorry, no comment," he repeated, pulling open the heavy wooden door.

"Can you tell us anything about your defence?" another reporter asked.

David paused, holding the door open for a moment and enjoying the way a hush came over the small group as it hung on his next words.

"No, but you'll know all about it soon enough," he said, disappearing inside. He entered Courtroom number one, located just inside the front doors, to the left. He greeted the court clerk and deposited his overstuffed briefcase on the floor by the defence table.

"Morning David," J.P. Gallant said, coming up behind him with another man.

"J.P.," David replied with a smile.

"This is Inspector Pat Gushue. He's the lead man on the investigation."

"Yes, I know. Morning Inspector."

Gushue nodded.

"Listen, do you mind if Pat sits up front with me for the trial? He'd like to observe…"

"I don't know if that would be appropriate, J.P.," David said with a conciliatory smile. "After all, these tables are reserved for counsel only, and there's lots of room to sit in here," David gestured to the large courtroom, still only half full.

"Don't worry about it J.P.," Gushue said sharply, returning to the spectator's bench behind the counsel table. David had no problem with Gushue personally, but he had heard a senior defence lawyer complain that his client, and to a certain extent the lawyer himself, had been unnerved by such an arrangement in a drug trafficking trial, and David was not about to take a chance. As for Gallant, David both liked and respected him, but he knew it would be better to dismiss any pretence of cooperation beyond the requirements of the rules of court—this was war.

David put on his robe and filled his glass with ice water, then turned his attention to arranging his notes and his book of authorities. He sat and swivelled his chair around to look over the audience. The large and rather imposing courtroom, with its vaulted ceilings and intricate panel work, was used for the bigger trials, and for official ceremonies like the call to the bar of the new lawyers. One of the bailiffs was opening a side window to let a breeze into the rapidly warming room. David noticed that the audience had grown considerably in the last five minutes, composed of police officers, reporters, and a surprising number of lawyers, some in suits and some dressed in their court clothes, apparently hoping to catch the opening of the trial before their matter was heard in another courtroom. As the prospect of addressing the judge and jury in front of far more experienced counsel loomed, David felt his stomach churn and he looked at the large clock on the wall behind the imposing bench. As he did, Tom was brought into the courtroom and escorted to the docket by two husky bailiffs.

"Hello Tom. How do you feel?" David said, approaching the docket.

"Alright I s'pose," Tom said quietly, eyeing the prosecutor's bench and the policemen seated behind it. "Beats the Pen."

"It does, doesn't it," David said, trying to emit a genuine laugh to conceal his nervousness.

"You ready?" Tom said, looking at David.

"Ready as I'll ever be," David patted him on the shoulder. "Now remember what we talked about, Tom. No smiling or frowning, and avoid direct eye contact with the jury, okay?"

"Yup."

As Tom answered, the court clerk rose suddenly.

"All rise!" he said, as a hush came over the courtroom and everyone rose together to greet the judge, who appeared from a small door behind the bench. The clerk went into the usual speech:

"Hear ye, hear ye, hear ye, all those having business before…"

The words blurred into the background as David stood arrow straight and tried to control his rapidly increasing heart rate.

"Good morning gentlemen," Judge Robert Hutton said tersely, as he settled in his chair and everyone else returned to their seats. In his mid-fifties, Hutton had been a criminal lawyer himself, and was known for being a gruff, but fair, trial judge.

With the opening remarks out of the way, the jury was called in and David looked each one over once again, trying to guess who would be the easiest to win over. Jury selection had taken less than two days, and although he had used his challenges wisely and was content that the majority of the group were at least impartial, if not biased in his client's favour, he was still concerned about a couple. As he watched the neatly dressed insurance broker take his seat in the front, he cursed his luck at not having the chance to have him booted. It was too late now.

After the judge had finished his instructions, he looked towards Gallant, who rose calmly and strolled towards the jury box before launching into his opening statement. David sat back and took it in showing no sign of emotion, but experiencing a sinking feeling inside. Gallant laid out the Crown's plans in a deliberate and methodical way. He began with the victim's life story, noting his accomplishments as a lawyer as well as the pro bono and charity work he had done over the years. Next he moved on to the night of the murder, describing everything from the weather that night, to the key points he intended to prove, such as the fact that a knife covered in the victim's blood had been found in possession of the accused. After about twenty minutes of this, Gallant gave a brief description of what the law required the Crown to establish, emphasizing that he intended to prove to the jury beyond any doubt whatsoever that Stuart Bruce's killer was sitting within twenty feet of them. As he thanked them and headed for his seat, David had to admit even he felt swayed by the calm, logical presentation they had all just heard. It made his own upcoming words all the more important, since it would be the only opportunity to plant the seed of doubt in the jurors' minds until after the Crown had closed its case, which would no doubt be weeks away.

As the crowd behind him shifted in their seats and whispered, David waited anxiously for Hutton to finish whatever notes he was taking up on the bench. After what felt like an interminable pause but was less than a minute, Hutton looked at his watch.

"Do you want to take a break Mr. Hall?" he said, although he was really asking whether David intended to be more than thirty minutes, in which case, Hutton had no intention of continuing without a break.

"No M'Lord. I intend to be brief."

"Very well. Proceed, Mr. Hall."

"Thank you M'Lord," David said, standing and moving to the front of his table. He took a deep breath as total silence gripped the courtroom. "Ladies and gentlemen of the jury, what I have to say this morning may surprise you, but I would ask you to indulge me for a few brief minutes and then we can get this trial under way." David felt his hands shaking, so he put them behind his back as he turned towards the prisoner's docket.

"There is no doubt that Mr. Fitzgerald is innocent of murder, I intend to convince you of that," he smiled at Tom and then turned to the jury. "But you will find that I won't argue with much of what the Crown offers as evidence of the crime. For instance, I won't argue with the Crown's assertion that my client was at the scene that fateful night, or that he is left-handed, or even that he caused the victim's death."

As David paused to let this last statement sink in, a buzz whipped through the crowd and some of the jurors raised their eyebrows.

"Now I know you're probably thinking that I intend to argue that Tom is insane, or at least that he was at the time of the crime, but that is not my intention."

As David got into the flow of his speech, and his butterflies vanished, he started using his hands for gestures, and his voice grew louder and more confident.

"On the contrary, the man you see before you today," he gestured back towards Tom, "is as sane as you or I. Which makes what happened to him all the more unimaginably horrible." David paused again for effect and walked right up to the rail of the jury box. "Try to imagine waking up one morning to find a murder weapon in your hand, and a police officer telling you that you had killed another human being. Try for a moment to imagine the confusion, the horror of that realization and you will know how my client felt that cold, damp morning in Bannerman Park. How could that be, you ask? How could someone commit such a heinous act and not know it? How indeed," David pulled on the lapels of his robe as he strolled by the front of the jury box, stopping in the middle and facing them.

"Non-insane automatism," he said clearly and with conviction. "That's how. I'll say it again because it is not a common term. Non-insane automatism."

David leaned on the front rail.

He turned and walked back towards his table, picking up a pile of books.

"I could read off many of the names of conditions found in these books on psychiatry and psychology and you'd probably recognize them all, even have a working knowledge of most of them. Conditions like Paranoia, Hypochondria, Obsessive-Compulsive Disorder, Post-Traumatic Stress Disorder, to name a few. As a society we're comfortable with them because we hear about them so often. And what of non-insane automatism? It doesn't exactly roll off the tongue, does it? It doesn't sound very sexy, does it?" He approached the jurors again, with a book in each hand.

"But you will find in here the same amount of material devoted to it as is devoted to any of those other conditions with the more familiar names. And why is that?" he said, putting the books on the front rail for the jury to see. "Because it is as much a condition as any of the others, with the same objective criteria, arrived at through the same methods of scientific research. But you needn't take it from me. Instead, you will have the benefit of the expert testimony of a nationally renowned psychiatrist in arriving at an inevitable conclusion—that Tom Fitzgerald could not have intended to harm, much less murder the victim, since he had no control over his actions on the night in question."

David took a few steps back and looked through the jury.

"All I ask is that you listen to the evidence that is put before you in this room over the following weeks. If you do, I know that there is only one possible conclusion for you to reach—that Tom Fitzgerald is innocent."

David thanked the jury and returned to his seat, less than five minutes after leaving it. Even Hutton seemed a little dazed by the unusual course his trial had just taken.

"Uh, thank you, Mr. Hall," he said, adjusting his glasses. "Why don't we take a break and resume at eleven?"

"All rise!" came the familiar cry as Hutton disappeared behind the bench, and the jury filed out.

The courtroom was instantly abuzz with chatter.

"You must really be desperate," Gallant said with a chuckle, as David passed in front of the prosecutor to retrieve his books.

chapter twenty-seven

David took his place on the couch next to Elizabeth, and they both watched Ben playing with some building blocks on the living room floor. The first day of trial had gone remarkably well. With his opening address out of the way, David was feeling much more comfortable. Gallant had spent the rest of the day taking the lead investigator, Pat Gushue, through the crime scene. Since most of it was routine, David had been content to take notes of areas he might like to pursue when his opportunity to cross-examine arose, probably late tomorrow. They had adjourned at five and he had stopped by the office to find Joanne had everything under control. He sipped his coffee and chuckled as Ben bashed his newly-constructed tower to the ground, and wondered whether this trial was going to be as hard as he had thought. He would have to review Gushue's previous evidence again before tomorrow but for now, he was content to enjoy a rare moment of peace with his family.

"I told you he was a southpaw," he remarked to Elizabeth, as Ben picked up a crayon in his left hand and started scribbling on the newspaper.

"You sure about that?" Elizabeth said with a laugh as Ben switched hands.

"You know, we should really start thinking about getting him a little playmate," Elizabeth said, leaning back across David's lap.

"Love to," David said, putting down his coffee and scooping her up.

"I didn't mean right this minute," she said laughing.

"I did. You won't mind if we disappear for a little while, will you Ben?" David dropped her back gently onto the couch and smiled as Ben looked on in puzzled amusement.

"No, I'm serious."

"Are you sure you can handle two rug rats by yourself?" David said, lying next to her. "In case you hadn't noticed, I'm hardly ever here."

"Well you're not going to be working like this forever are you?" she asked.

"I certainly hope not," he replied. But It's not going to get any better in the near future, that's for sure."

"They say two is easier than one anyway. The older sibling helps out."

"Is that what they say?" David asked sarcastically. "What do you say Ben? Ready to change some diapers?"

Ben giggled with delight at the sight of his parents laughing.

"I think that's a yes," Elizabeth said in triumph as the phone shattered their peace.

"Oh who's that," David groaned.

"It's probably for me—I'm the popular one," Elizabeth said, as she got up to get it and slapped him playfully on the leg.

A minute later, she was calling out from the kitchen.

"David, it's J.P. Gallant."

"I'll take it upstairs," he said, wondering why Gallant would be calling him at home.

He closed the door to his small study and picked up the receiver.

"J.P.?"

"David. Sorry to bother you at home."

"No problem. What can I do for you?"

"Something has come to my attention that I felt I needed to discuss with you personally before court tomorrow," Gallant said seriously.

"And what's that."

"There's some evidence in the police file that you didn't get in the disclosure package."

"Do you mean new evidence?"

"No, actually it's not. But it was news to me. It came up in a meeting I just had with Pat Gushue. I wasn't previously aware of it and it seems to have slipped though the cracks."

David's senses were buzzing by now.

"What sort of evidence?"

"Well, there are some phone records from the victim's hotel room, and a DNA test."

"You've got to be kidding!" David said, feeling a surge of indignation. "What DNA test?" He added quickly. Even though the murder weapon was covered in both Tom's prints and the victim's blood, David knew that the lack of any of Tom's DNA in the vicinity of the victim's body was a key factor in Lane's initial strategy.

"A hair sample, found on the victim's jacket."

"And whose DNA is it?" David asked abruptly.

"We don't know. Look, I'm going to send this over to you right now so you can see for yourself. The purpose of the call is to let you know two things, the first of which is that I knew nothing about any of this until tonight. The second is that this was an honest mistake by the RNC. There was no intention to conceal anything. They just didn't know they…"

"You've got to be kidding J.P. You call me up after the trial has start-ed and tell me there's all this shit out there that you haven't disclosed. What else does the RNC have that it doesn't feel like disclosing?" he said sarcastically. David's heart was pumping now. "I'll be looking for a mistrial first thing tomorrow morning, I can tell you that."

"You'll never get it," Gallant replied coolly. "Where's the prejudice to your client? You're defence is that he did it, but he's not responsible. This evidence changes nothing."

"That's crap and you know it."

"Look, go ahead and do the research, but you'll find I'm right. In the meantime, do you want this sent to your office or home?"

"Send it here," David said in an annoyed tone, giving him the address.

"It'll be there in fifteen minutes." Gallant paused. "I know you're pissed off and maybe you have a right to be, but I'm just trying to do the right thing here."

"Sure, whatever," David hung up.

He walked back and forth from the phone to the window a few times before taking a deep breath. His head was swimming. The DNA test meant that someone else's hair had been found on Bruce's body, or else it would have been part of the Crown's evidence. Its significance to any defence was debatable, since it could have been from any number of people who came into contact with the victim's coat in the hours or days preceding the murder. On the other hand, it was not Tom's, so as long as it was unidentified, it remained possible evidence of another murderer. The only problem with this theory, as Gallant had correctly pointed out, was that David had abandoned the concept of another murderer when he went for automatism. And what the hell was in those phone records? He paced the floor anxiously until he heard the doorbell. Racing downstairs, he passed Elizabeth and Ben in the kitchen.

"What's wrong?" Elizabeth asked, immediately recognizing the anger in her husband's eyes.

"Gallant's been holding out on me," he said, continuing on to the front door.

"What do you mean?" she asked, as David returned to the kitchen and ripped open the envelope.

"He held back evidence. I don't know what it all means yet. Sorry hon, I've got to look at this stuff right away."

"Say goodnight to your son first," she said holding the toddler up to him.

"Goodnight buddy," David said kissing him on the cheek as the little boy pulled on his father's ear.

"Tell me about it later," Elizabeth said, pecking David's cheek before he bounded back up the stairs.

Five minutes later he had scanned the papers and was trying to put them into place. The DNA test was self-explanatory—it wasn't Tom's, or anyone else's that they could identify. As for the phone records, there was an incoming call to Stuart Bruce's room at ten-thirty from a number that had been identified as a payphone at a shopping centre on the other side of town. He tried to consider the possibilities logically. It could easily have been the murderer calling. Who else would be calling from a payphone at that hour? It would explain why Bruce had left his hotel room at eleven on a miserable night to go for a walk in the park. On the other hand, the call could just as easily have been a wrong number, and there was likely no way to ever know for sure.

David sat back, ran his hands through his hair and tried to think clearly. He had to determine whether he had enough for a mistrial. Even if he did, it would not end the matter for Tom, since Gallant would likely be given another opportunity to try the case with a different judge and jury. If there was not enough evidence, David had a very difficult decision to make, between staying the course on the one hand, or relying on this new evidence, together with what he already knew, to create the possibility of a third person—the mystery man—having committed the murder on the other. He looked at his watch. It was eight o'clock. He had to get to his office and hit the books. He was in for a long night.

chapter twenty-eight

D avid and Gallant sat at their respective tables and waited for Hutton to emerge from the door behind the bench, neither looking at the other or speaking a word. It was two-thirty in the afternoon and the judge had summoned them to hear his verdict on David's hotly contested motion for mistrial. He had been up half the night researching the law and the other half trying to decide what to do. The key to a mistrial was prejudice to the accused, which was David's dilemma. If on the one hand he stuck with his original defence, the new evidence was not really that relevant. On the other hand, if the new evidence was enough to make him reconsider his whole defence strategy, it might be very prejudicial indeed. The question for David was really whether to change anything at all. But the new evidence had a very unnerving effect on him, since it teased him with the possibility that there might just be enough evidence out there to get an acquittal on the basis that a third person had committed the murder. He had talked himself into changing the defence, then around three a.m. he had reversed that decision when he had reviewed the concrete evidence of the crime scene again.

During the morning's proceedings, which were held without the jury, Gallant had been very careful to offer to accommodate any adjournments David might require to change defences, in order to appear reasonable, knowing that such a change would be a very difficult choice at this stage. Gallant had also done his homework well, and cited some key decisions in his favour on the issue of what constituted enough prejudice to the accused to warrant a mistrial. For his part, David was operating on just under two hours' sleep and, burdened with the weight of having to question his defence strategy all over again, he almost hoped that his motion would fail so that he could get on with the automatism defence. As the door opened and the clerk called the room to its feet, Hutton took his seat and shuffled some papers before clearing his throat.

"Mr. Gallant," he began in a gruff voice. Gallant seemed to tense in anticipation of what was to come. "I have been on the bench for over fifteen years, and never in that time have I seen such utter incompetence on the part of the prosecution," Hutton let this preface sink in before continuing. "In case you hadn't noticed, this is a murder trial. I've seen better preparation for traffic court."

David enjoyed Gallant's discomfort as the lambasting continued for a few more minutes, but he then sensed a sharp turn in Hutton's speech.

"Having said that," Hutton turned towards David now. "I fail to see that there is real and significant prejudice to your client in this case." David tuned out the rest of Hutton's speech, knowing the conclusion that came a few minutes later. "Your motion for a mistrial is denied, Mr. Hall."

David nodded in acknowledgement.

"You may have whatever time you require to review this new evidence," he added.

"Thank you, My Lord," David said respectfully. "An adjournment to tomorrow morning will be fine." He had already reviewed the material thoroughly and there was little point in delaying things unnecessarily.

"Granted. As for you, Mr. Gallant, I assume you will convey my remarks to your colleagues in the RNC," he said, staring at Gushue and the other police officers seated behind Gallant.

"Yes, My Lord," Gallant said sheepishly, as Hutton grunted and rose to leave.

Having lost the first legal battle in the trial, David could at least claim a moral victory, and perhaps a little sympathy from the judge, for however long that might last. After a quick chat with Tom, he gathered his papers and headed for the office, to take advantage of a rare opportunity to catch up with the rest of his practice and to try and get some sleep before resuming trial the next day.

chapter twenty-nine

The trial had been running for over two weeks now, and the Crown was approaching the end of its case. With each day of testimony David was growing increasingly anxious to present his side of the story. Because of his unusual defence, David was forced to listen quietly as Gallant paraded witness after witness before the court. He was also forced to forego cross-examination on most of the testimony, even when he knew that a witness had left himself open to attack, since it was not part of his overall plan. The one exception was his cross-examination of Inspector Gushue, during which David had forced him to admit that Tom had some of his own blood on his head on the morning he was discovered. David had smiled politely at Gushue after eliciting this information, and closed his cross-examination. Returning to his seat with a look of contentment, he stole a glance in Gallant's direction and thought he saw a slightly puzzled look on his adversary's face. This fact, even more than Gushue's testimony, had buoyed David's spirits, and he had permitted himself a wink of encouragement in Tom's direction as his client seemed just as confused.

David watched as the victim's older brother, James Bruce, took the stand and was sworn in. With the legal part of his case established, Gallant was after the jury's moral outrage. The only problem was that his victim gave him little to work with. Although Stuart Bruce had been married, he had divorced a long time ago, and with no children or widow to offer, James Bruce was the best Gallant could do. An engineer in his late fifties, James Bruce was a very respectable-looking witness. With the preliminary questions out of the way, Gallant had him describe his brother's career, from his education at the University of Toronto and then Osgoode Hall, to his practice as a commercial and securities lawyer. He mentioned his younger brother's numerous appearances before the Supreme Court of Canada and the obvious pleasure he had derived from practising law. He described him as a man totally devoted to his work, who had accepted a certain degree of loneliness as part of the bargain. As David watched him testify, he couldn't help feeling a little uneasy whenever Bruce looked his way.

After Gallant had obtained what he wanted, David wisely declined any cross-examination and was a little surprised to hear Gallant rise and state for the record:

"The Crown rests its case."

Hutton looked at his watch.

"It's four-thirty Mr. Hall. Do you want to start this afternoon or wait until tomorrow?"

"I think tomorrow would be better, My Lord," David replied quickly, suddenly realizing he didn't know where his star witness was. Although Dr. Clark had flown in a couple of days prior, and the two had already met to go over his testimony, David had told him he wouldn't be needed until later in the week.

"Any objections, Mr. Gallant?" It had been several days after the mistrial motion before Hutton had resumed addressing the prosecution by name, as opposed to by an angry nod or grunt. That he would even ask Gallant for his input, albeit rhetorically, was a sign that his anger had faded.

"Not at all, My Lord," Gallant said with a wide smile.

"Very well. Adjourned until tomorrow at nine."

David arranged his notes on the table in front of him as the clerk finished swearing in the defence's main witness. What Dr. Felix Clark had to say, and how he said it, would make or break Tom's defence and David knew it. He took a deep breath as judge Hutton looked to him.

"Mr. Hall."

"Thank you, My Lord," David said, getting to his feet. "Could you state your name for the record?" he asked Clark. He couldn't help thinking that Clark couldn't look the part any better if he had tried. His steel grey hair and neatly trimmed beard, combined with spectacles, a bow tie and a finely-tailored suit gave him an aura of intelligence and class. But David knew the best was yet to come. Clark was more than just a pretty face.

"Dr. Felix Clark," he replied in a confident voice that matched his appearance.

"And what is your occupation, Dr. Clark?"

"I am a clinical psychiatrist and a member of the faculty at the University of Toronto."

"Can you provide the court with your educational background?" David asked.

"Certainly. I have a degree in biology from the University of Toronto, a PhD in microbiology from Princeton University, and an M.D. from Harvard."

"And how many years have you been practicing psychiatry?"

"I've maintained a clinical practice for twenty-five years."

"And what about teaching?"

"I was a professor at Harvard for eight years, and I've been at U of T for the past ten."

David let this information sink in as he returned to his table and picked up a ten-page document.

"This," he said, waving the document in the direction of the jury, before turning to Hutton, "is Dr. Clark's curriculum vitae, which has been provided to this court and the prosecution. I am prepared to take the witness through it in detail, including the ninety-five publications to his credit, but in the interest of time, I wonder if we can have Dr. Clark declared an expert witness in the field of psychiatry?"

"I'm prepared to declare Dr. Clark an expert Mr. Hall," Hutton said, smiling at Clark. "Unless you have some basis for objection, Mr. Gallant…"

"No, My Lord," Gallant said. There was little else he could say.

"Thank you, My Lord."

David returned to his table and glanced at his notes.

"Have you ever had occasion to consult with the accused, Dr. Clark?"

"Yes, actually I have," Clark said, as Hutton, the jury and Gallant all inched a little further ahead in their seats. "About fifteen years ago, I spent a couple of months as a visiting lecturer at Memorial University. A classmate and friend from my undergraduate days was the Dean of the medical school here at the time—Dr. Rolf—and he convinced me to come and see Newfoundland, and do a little teaching at the University. At the time, I was working on a paper on criminal psychology and I had the occasion to see several inmates at the Penitentiary here in St. John's, and at the Whitbourne juvenile facility. That is where I first met Mr. Fitzgerald."

"So your visit with Mr. Fitzgerald was for research purposes?"

"In part, yes, but it was also to conduct a clinical assessment of Mr. Fitzgerald."

"Was there anything in particular about Mr. Fitzgerald that made you assess him, over the other boys at the facility?"

"Yes, there was. Mr. Fitzgerald had been exhibiting signs of dissociative behaviour, which was one of the areas I was researching."

"Can you explain what you mean by dissociative behaviour—in layman's terms?"

"Certainly," Clark continued confidently, launching into a clear and understandable discussion of the principal characteristics of the dissociative state.

David could barely contain his excitement at Clark's impeccable performance as a witness. He also noticed that every one of the jurors, and Hutton himself, seemed to hang on his every word.

"And what was it about Tom that made him worth looking into, from the point of view of your research?" David said, awaiting the crucial point of Dr. Clark's testimony.

"Staff at the Whitbourne facility had reported two incidents of somnambulism," Clark paused and then added "or sleepwalking, as it is commonly known."

"And how was that relevant to your research?"

"Somnambulism, combined with certain other behaviour, is sometimes indicative of a predisposition to dissociative episodes."

"But surely not everyone who sleepwalks has such a predisposition," David said, as they came to the crucial part of Clark's testimony.

"Certainly not. Somnambulism is not in and of itself an indication that a person is predisposed to experiencing a dissociative episode. But combined with other factors, it has proven to be a very reliable indicator indeed. In fact, that was the conclusion of the paper that resulted from my interview with Mr. Fitzgerald—and a number of other subjects over the course of about two years."

"And what are some of those other factors?" David inquired easily as Hutton leaned even further forward in his chair.

"Psychological trauma, most often as a result of childhood physical or sexual abuse. Or in the more immediate context, an event that causes a psychological blow, such as losing one's job, or marital breakdown."

"Are there any other factors?"

"Yes, physical trauma to the head, such as a concussion."

Gallant quietly leaned over to the junior lawyer seated next to him and whispered something. He probably knew where this was leading, but there was nothing he could do for now. David pressed on as the jurors sat, virtually transfixed by Clark's confident, soothing voice.

"So when you saw Tom back in the mid 1980s, was there any evidence of any of these other factors?"

"Yes, Tom suffered physical abuse at the hands of a foster father for a number of years."

"Would it be reasonable to assume that the effects of that abuse would stay with Tom forever?" David said, seeing Gallant rise.

"Objection your Honour. Counsel is not supposed to be testifying."

"Let me rephrase the question," David offered quickly, before Hutton ruled. "What sort of effect does childhood abuse have on the victim?"

"I don't think there is much question that it remains with the victim, to some degree, forever," Clark said, as Gallant was forced to sit down.

"And what were your conclusions about Tom following the 1987 assessment?"

"I concluded that Tom's sleepwalking was most likely a manifestation of a transient psychological disturbance. In other words, Tom's sleepwalking was probably caused by an emotional flare-up."

"Was he mentally ill in your opinion?"

"No, not at all. Transient disturbances alone are rarely indicative of mental illness. Tom's performance on a wide range of psychological tests was well within normal limits. My research—which I might add has been confirmed by some eminent researchers and writers in this field of psychiatry—revealed that without a clinical basis for mental illness, transient disturbances such as sleepwalking are most often the result of external, rather than internal forces."

"And what role does a history of abuse play in these disturbances?"

"It can make a subject more vulnerable to their effects, though it is important to distinguish between vulnerability or predisposition on the one hand and clinical mental illness, such as schizophrenia, on the other."

"So, a subject with such a background is predisposed to these transient disturbances…"

"Objection," Gallant rose again. "He's leading the witness My Lord."

"I'll withdraw the question," David said.

"The jury will disregard that last question," Hutton ruled.

"Dr. Clark," David continued, "is a person who suffers from these transient disturbances mentally ill?"

"Not at all. And I might add that I found no evidence of mental illness whatsoever in my assessment of Mr. Fitzgerald."

Glancing at the jury and noting that they seemed transfixed by Clark's testimony, David decided to go in for the kill.

"Can you give a medical description of what happens to a person who experiences somnambulism?"

"Certainly," Dr. Clark said, apparently enjoying his time on the stand as much as his audience. "The subject enjoys the usual command over bodily functions, but they are essentially divorced from his consciousness. The functional aspect of the link between the brain and the body is there, but not the conscious one. The most common analogy is that of a robot, which can perform fine motor skills, but with no awareness of doing so."

"Can a person in a state of automatism control their actions?"

"No, they are oblivious to external communication, at least on a cognitive level."

"Can you explain that?"

"The subject might respond, for example to being pushed. They will not, however respond to verbal communication."

"So is it impossible to reason with a person in such a state?"

"Yes, since they for all intents and purposes cannot hear you."

"Can they understand the consequences of their actions?"

"Objection, My Lord!" Gallant jumped to his feet. His whole case was on the line and he knew it. "That is for the jury to decide, not this witness, regardless of his qualifications."

"I disagree, My Lord, this is precisely the area of the witness' expertise," David said firmly, knowing that even if the objection were sustained, he had done more than enough damage to the Crown's case. This was evident from the thoughtful expressions on the faces of the jurors as Hutton considered the issue.

"I'm going to allow it, provided that the jury is clear that we are talking about the witness' opinion in general, not with respect to the accused specifically."

"Thank you, My Lord," David said, nodding to Clark.

"No, a person in a state of automatism in my opinion cannot understand the nature of their actions, or foresee their consequences."

"Thank you, Dr. Clark," David said with a smile. Gallant could only hold his tongue while his blood boiled.

David pretended to look for something in his notes to give the jury time to consider the full weight of the last point in the deathly silence of the courtroom.

Hutton looked at his watch and then at David.

"Mr. Hall," he began.

"I have only one more question for this witness, M'Lord," David said with a smile.

"Very well," Hutton grumbled.

"Dr. Clark, you've seen the transcript of Dr. MacDonald's testimony before this court, have you not?"

"Yes, I have."

"If it please the court I would like to read from that testimony now." David had copies of the excerpt for the judge and Gallant, who had his own copy anyway and had a pretty good idea of which page David was about to read from.

"At page 7 of his testimony," David continued, "I asked him whether the physical evidence was consistent with Tom Fitzgerald having suffered a blow to the head and he answered, and I quote: 'Yes, there was evidence that he suffered a blow to the head. There was a laceration and a significant contusion.' I then asked...," David started to say.

"M'Lord, I hope it is not my learned friend's intent to re-read Dr. MacDonald's evidence in its entirety," Gallant said, rising to his feet. "The jury was here for his testimony," he added sarcastically, his frustration showing.

"One line, M'lord, that's all I intend to quote," David replied innocently. "I would be happy to give my own summary of the witness' testimony instead, though I'm not sure the Crown would be any happier with that," David added, looking towards Gallant, who was trying unsuccessfully not to look annoyed.

"Go ahead Mr. Hall," Hutton said. "But get to the point."

"Thank you, M'Lord. I then asked Dr. MacDonald whether it would be possible to describe the injury as a concussion, to which he responded as follows: 'It could, due to the significant bruising over the skull'."

David placed the transcript back on the table and walked towards the jury.

"I have just one last question for you Dr. Clark," David said, leaning on the front rail of the jury box. "In light of Dr. MacDonald's testimony with respect to Tom's physical state, your own testimony this morning on the factors that go into a diagnosis—if I can call it that—of automatism, and your personal knowledge of his psychological background, is it in your expert opinion possible that Tom Fitzgerald was in an automatic state on the night of May 12th?"

"My opinion," Clark said, cutting through the unearthly silence that had followed the question, "is not only that it is possible, but that it is most probable."

David surveyed the faces of the jurors as he let Clark's final statement sink in. There were mutterings and movement from the back of the courtroom as people whispered and scribbled notes.

"Thank you, Dr. Clark," David said, returning to his seat while Hutton adjourned for lunch.

chapter thirty

"How's he doing?" Tom asked as soon as David arrived in the interview room of the lock-up, located in the basement of the courthouse.

"Are you kidding, he's awesome. He's got the jury eating out of his hand. If he told them the moon was made of green cheese, they'd probably believe him now," David couldn't contain a broad grin.

On hearing this good news, Tom exhibited a rare smile too.

"So it's lookin' alright huh?"

"We're still a long way from being out of the woods Tom, but we'd be hard-pressed to ask for better testimony from anyone," David was trying not to sound too excited himself. "Don't forget, he hasn't been cross-examined yet either. Gallant will be coming at him with everything he's got. He has to."

Tom nodded soberly. Then looked at David thoughtfully before speaking again.

"Why's he doing this anyway? A big shot like him…"

"Because he believes you're innocent Tom."

Tom chuckled.

"What?" David asked, puzzled by his client's reaction.

"I don't know. This whole friggin' thing seems crazy. This guy with a dozen degrees standing up there and tellin' a room fulla people I turned into a robot and slit this poor fucker's throat—and the best part is they're believin' it!"

David was taken aback.

"I thought the reason they could believe it was because it was the truth, Tom?"

David noticed a fleeting and unfamiliar expression on Tom's face, almost like that of a poker player who has just picked up the fourth ace. It had gone just as quickly as it had appeared, and Tom simply nodded.

"Yeah, I s'pose it is."

David sat in the holding cell at the lock-up with his client, who was looking at his hands. After Hutton's instructions to the jury were completed, David had spent an hour or so with Tom, before returning to the office to try and get some work done. He had soon discovered it was pointless, and had decided to return to see how Tom was coping with the pressure. Though David's reputation and career as a criminal lawyer were certainly on the line, his freedom was not, and he could only imagine what his client was going through. It had been only four hours since the jury had begun their deliberations, but already it felt like days.

After David had finished with Clark three days prior, Gallant had taken his best shot at undoing the damage to the prosecution's case, but Clark hadn't wavered. Every time Gallant tried to dilute his opinion, Clark had countered with something even more damaging and in the end, Gallant had given up. Wanting to maximize the impact of Dr. Clark's testimony, David had not called any further evidence, and had closed the defence. Gallant had called his own psychiatrist and poked some holes in the defence, but his testimony and credentials had been far less impressive. David had spent a great deal of time on his summation and he felt he had been successful in conveying what he wanted to the jury, but from the moment he had finished and Hutton's instructions to the jury had begun, his heart had been in his throat. He knew the trial had gone as well as he could have hoped, but David had not dared to let himself believe he might actually have won Tom's freedom.

"So how long do you think it'll take 'em?" Tom asked, breaking the anxious silence.

"I don't know Tom, but the fact that they're taking their time is probably a good thing," he replied, knowing it was impossible to tell what it really meant. The silence returned for a few more minutes before they were jolted to their feet by the clang of the metal door opening.

"We're gonna transport you back to the Pen in five," said a burly guard, who closed the door again just as quickly, as the two men sighed in disappointment.

"At least I can have a smoke there," Tom said with a grin.

David nodded with a smile. He considered having one himself.

"Well, I'm gonna head home for a while," David said, patting Tom on the shoulder. "I'll drop in on you later at the Pen."

"You'll let me know…"

"Of course. The minute I hear anything, you'll be the first to know, okay?"

Tom nodded as David glanced through the Plexiglas window at a guard who was holding a phone to his ear. David watched as he said something to the other guard, who unlocked the door.

"Hang on," the second guard said, entering the room. "The jury's back…"

"What?" David asked quickly.

"You're due upstairs in ten. I'll take him up in five," he said, motioning to Tom.

"Okay, thanks," David said, as the guard closed the door again.

"So what do you make of it?" Tom asked.

"I don't know, Tom."

"It's bad, isn't it? The longer the better, that's what they told me at the Pen…"

"That doesn't mean anything Tom," David said with a wave of his hand, although he generally subscribed to the same theory. "It could just as easily be a quick acquittal as a quick conviction."

"So this is it, huh?"

"This is it Tom. It'll all be over soon."

David picked up his briefcase and knocked on the glass.

"Whatever happens," Tom began, pausing to clear his throat. David waited as his client appeared to be struggling with the rest. "You done a good job for me…I mean it."

"Thanks Tom, I appreciate that," David said, patting him on the shoulder. "I'll see you upstairs."

The door slammed behind him as David left the lock-up and was met by a cool evening breeze coming in through the Narrows. Somewhere out there in the waters beyond Signal Hill lay the first of the season's icebergs. He took a deep breath of the sea breeze and began walking up the stairs on the side of the courthouse that led back up from Water Street, preferring to be alone outside with his thoughts. Tom was right—this really was it; the culmination of months of work and a number of serious gambles on David's part. What happened in the next fifteen minutes would have a significant impact on his career either way, and as he reached Duckworth Street and noticed the reporters buzzing around the front door of the courthouse, he collected himself for the final act in Tom's play.

Passing through the cameras and microphones, David made his way deliberately to the courtroom, where he found his client and Gallant already waiting. He gave an encouraging nod to Tom as he took his seat. A moment later, Hutton appeared and summoned the jury. Tom watched every face for a tell-tale sign but noticed nothing. His heart was racing as Hutton asked for the verdict and the foreman stood to read it out. The words echoed in his ears and his mind closed itself to every other sound in the room. Unable to move, he closed his eyes and repeated the verdict to himself silently.

"Not Guilty."

A moment later, he was on his feet, wrapping his arms around Tom, who looked stunned. As they embraced, David caught sight of Gallant, who was looking down as he shuffled some papers.

"Thank you…thank you…," was all David could hear, as the court adjourned and he felt the warmth of his client's tears on his neck.

chapter thirty-one

It had been almost a month since the jury had returned its verdict, a day that changed David's life forever. After all the hard work he had put into Tom's case, not to mention the stress of gambling on the defence itself, the victory had been all the more satisfying. David had given countless interviews for local and national media outlets in the frenzy that followed the trial. He had even gotten calls from as far away as Australia for his comments on the verdict.

And while the whole experience had been thrilling, his initial elation had been tempered by the Crown's repeated assurances of an appeal. David had tried not to become preoccupied with the appeal. He decided instead to take a couple of days off with Elizabeth and Ben, once the media blitz was over, before returning to the office to try and restore the rest of his practice. He had been in touch with Tom regularly, and though his client was enjoying his newfound freedom immensely, he feared the prospect of losing it on appeal all the more.

"Here you go," Elizabeth said, handing David a coffee. He put down the letter he was reading and took the mug.

"Asleep already?"

"Yes, he's been really good about going to bed lately," she said, joining him on the couch. "He likes it when you're here to kiss him goodnight."

"So do I," he said. "Let's go outside, it looks beautiful out there."

They went out and sat on the deck, which although tiny, gave them a nice view of the harbour. It was one of those relatively rare summer evenings in St. John's when the warmth stayed in the air even after the sun had gone down.

"I've been thinking," David began, leaning on the rail. "Maybe I'm spending too much time at work."

"But I thought this is what you wanted—winning a trial like Tom's."

"It is. It's the rest of it that I can't stand. The stuff I have to do in order to get a case like that. I wonder if it's really necessary."

"You mean you should go out on your own?"

"I don't know," he sighed. "Maybe."

"Well now's the time. Every criminal in the city must know your name by now."

"Yeah, but they all want me to work for free," he laughed. "Besides, after tomorrow, that could all change."

"When will you know?" she asked.

"Gallant has until five o'clock tomorrow, and it looks like he's going to use all his time."

"Do you think he might not appeal?"

"That's a tougher question than most people think. Obviously he's under a lot of political pressure to appeal, but that doesn't mean he's got good grounds. I've been through the transcript over and over and I can't find an error in law. Hutton was very careful not to make any mistakes in his charge to the jury. And as for the rest, the verdict is really based on a finding of fact. They believed Dr. Clark—and you can't appeal that."

"Are you going to see Tom tomorrow?"

"Yeah, I told him I'd drop by his girlfriend's place and wait it out with him."

"God, it must be horrible for him," she said, shaking her head. "To know you're innocent, but that your freedom is so fragile…"

"Hmm," David mumbled over his coffee.

"What is it?"

"Nothing. My mind was just wandering. You're right—it must be horrible, but hopefully it will all be over tomorrow."

They sat on the deck and enjoyed the warm evening breeze.

David let out a sigh of exasperation as he came to a stop at the bottom of the hill and saw the gridlock on Duckworth Street. The Friday afternoon rush was starting already and it wasn't even four o'clock yet. Glancing in the rear view mirror and seeing nothing behind him, David slammed the car in reverse, spun back up the hill and sped off down a side street. He would have to chart a relatively complicated route through the downtown's maze of one-way streets and make a few illegal turns, but if it got him up to Rawlins Cross ahead of the snarl of traffic coming up Prescott and New Gower Streets, it was worth it. He had to get across town and break the news to Tom, before it hit the radio.

Gallant had called less than ten minutes prior and advised David that there would be no appeal. And though it made objective sense that Gallant had been unable to construct the type of technical argument required for an appeal based on Hutton's judgment, David had still been floored. Gallant had even been gracious in defeat, offering grudging congratulations. David had called Tom's number but gotten a busy signal, so he was out the door and in his car within minutes.

As the uncertainty he had felt over the last month melted away and he knew he really had won the trial for good, David felt a rush of excitement. This would silence his critics, which included Kelly Lane, and secure a reputation he could build a criminal law practice on. Darting precariously between a thick line of traffic, David crossed New Gower and sped up Long's Hill. With any luck, he would be at Tom's girlfriend's apartment in a few minutes.

Pulling into the parking lot, he spotted Tom sitting in a lawn chair, on a second-floor balcony. He got out of the car and called out. Tom looked down and waved.

"What?"

"It's over."

chapter thirty-two

When Tom's girlfriend had gotten home, she had insisted on David staying for supper. Not wanting to be rude, he had accepted their invitation to stay for a drink with some friends they had hastily invited for an impromptu celebration. That was several hours and drinks ago and David had lost track of the time, caught up as he was in the triumphant little gathering. Near midnight and feeling no pain, he and Tom found themselves alone on the balcony.

"Wanna smoke?" Tom said, offering his pack.

"Sure," David said, accepting a cigarette and a light.

"Well, you really did it didn't ya?" Tom said with a smile and a slap on the shoulder.

"We did it, Tom. And let's not forget Dr. Clark," David said, raising his drink.

"Yup," Tom nodded, doing the same. He sat back in a chair and blew out a long trail of smoke. He shook his head and let out a laugh.

"What?" David said, smiling along.

"Ah nothin', you wouldn't believe it anyways," Tom shook his head.

"Try me," David said, still smiling. "You can tell me anything. I'm your lawyer remember?"

Tom got up and leaned on the balcony, taking another drag of his cigarette.

"I'll tell ya somethin' funny," he said, a wry grin on his face. "All that sleepwalkin' shit—I made it up."

David shook his head and let out a short laugh.

"Yeah, sure Tom."

"No, I mean it. It's all bullshit."

"What do you mean?" David's smile was fading.

"I mean I fuckin' made it up."

"But it was in your records from when you were a kid. How could you…"

"It was just for attention, that's all," Tom said with a wicked grin. "It got me attention from the social workers when I was in foster care, and it worked at Whitbourne too. But I didn't know it'd save me from a life sentence."

Tom took a sip of his drink and continued.

"You know what else?"

"What?"

"I never got in a scrap on the way to the park that night either—more bullshit," he chuckled.

David shook his head in disbelief.

"But what about the bump on your head?"

"I don't know how it got there—that's the real truth."

Tom looked at David and noticed his shocked expression.

"You're pissed off at me now aren't ya? 'Cause I never told you."

"I...I'm just surprised Tom, that's all."

"Well whad'ya expect me to do. You came up with this whole automatism thing all on your own. Jesus, I didn't have the heart to tell you the difference."

David sat back in the chair and let out a sigh. The two men just stared into the starry night for a while before Tom spoke again.

"So you think I did it now, right?"

"I didn't say that, Tom."

"You wanna know the truth?" Tom asked, leaning towards him unsteadily.

"Yeah, I do Tom."

"I don't know what the fuck happened that night. That's the God's truth. Anyways, it's all history now."

David stood up slowly, "I'd better get going Tom," he said distractedly, "it's late."

David awoke to the high-pitched laughter of his son downstairs. He glanced at the clock radio and realized his wife must have given him the rare opportunity to sleep in. She had been asleep when he got home last night, around one a.m. He lay back and thought of what he had learned last night, and the uneasiness he had felt on first hearing it returned. There was a certain amount of humiliation at having been duped by his own client, but there was also a distinct moral unease that went with the possibility of his having set a guilty man free. But what was it Tom had really admitted anyway? He had lied about his sleep-walking, which didn't make him a murderer. More disturbing to David was his client's admission about the events of that May evening over a year ago. He tried to place Tom's words in context. He was drunk when he confessed all this, that was for certain. David wished he had just left after dinner, then he could have savoured his victory in good conscience.

Returning to Tom's exact words, David wondered why he hadn't just come out and said he had done it if he really had. And Tom's not remembering anything of the fateful night was really nothing new. Then again, Clark would never have testified if he had been given all this information, which meant Tom would be sitting in jail at this particular moment, instead of sleeping off a victory celebration. Even if David knew Tom had murdered Stuart Bruce—which he didn't—what Tom told him was privileged, so there was really nothing David could do. But it kept gnawing at him anyway. Perhaps it was because he had always believed Tom was innocent, before the automatism defence had even entered his mind. And though it was technically irrelevant whether David believed his client was innocent or not, it had certainly fuelled his desire to get an acquittal for an innocent man. With the possibility that David's belief had been an illusion came great disappointment, made worse by the fact that Tom had played him like a fiddle. Suddenly David's enthusiasm seemed naïve, even foolish. Perhaps this was why so many of the senior criminal lawyers seemed so jaded, and why none of them had believed in Tom's innocence from the beginning.

For better or for worse though, David had done his job and done it well. It was time to put Tom Fitzgerald behind him now and get on with his life. He got up and opened the curtains to find a beautiful Saturday morning waiting for him outside. Thinking it was a great day for a picnic, he walked towards the stairs and followed the laughter coming from the kitchen below.

chapter thirty-three
—july

David was cursing under his breath as he lugged his overloaded briefcase to the top of the stairs inside the courthouse. The muggy mid-summer heat had done nothing for him on the brief walk over from the office, and it was only accentuated inside the old building. Lacking air conditioning, it felt like a sauna on days like this, when the sun beat down on the copper roof and warm air festered in the main lobby. Luckily, the requirement for the heavy black court clothes was relaxed in summer sittings, and David was relieved to feel a little breeze from an open window as he entered the motions court upstairs. He exchanged a few hellos with some of the other lawyers who were sitting around chatting, awaiting the arrival of the chambers judge. A moment later, Mr. Justice Cooper entered the room and took his seat, followed by Phil Morgan, who just made it in before the clerk closed the door. Having stood to greet the judge, the lawyers all took their seats; Phil sat next to David.

"If I'd known you were here I could have dumped this on you," he whispered, showing him a thick pile of documents.

"Nice try," David whispered back. "What is that anyway?"

"It's his application for solicitor and client costs against us," Phil said, gesturing to the back of Andrew Royal, Q.C., a senior member of the bar who was seated front and centre.

"Well, at least you get to go first," David replied. The Supreme Court of Newfoundland was long on tradition, and there was an unspoken but immovable pecking order in motions court.

"Mr. Royal?" Judge Cooper smiled from the bench as the clerk shuffled through the papers to find Royal's motion.

"Thank you, M'Lord," he said, getting to his feet as Phil arranged his papers. "I appear for Great Northern Insurance M'Lord, in the application before you."

"And who is counsel for the Respondent?" Cooper said, the smile gone from his face, along with any other trace of humanity.

"Philip Morgan, M'Lord."

"I see. Well, Mr. Royal, I'll hear from you first," His Honour's smile had returned.

"Good luck," David said under his breath as Phil sat back down.

Having gone down in flames in less than five minutes, and with no great desire to rush back to the office and tell McGrath he had lost his motion, Phil had decided to wait through the half-dozen other routine motions before David's. Being an uncontested motion, it was done in two minutes.

"Come on, you deserve a coffee after that lambasting," David said with a laugh as they closed the courtroom door behind them.

"That's 0 for 2 this week on McGrath's files," Phil said with a grim chuckle. "If I keep this up, I'll be looking for a new job."

They emerged from the lower entrance of the stifling courthouse into a warm breeze off the harbour. Crossing Water Street, they headed to

Atlantic Place and were soon enjoying the air-conditioned comfort of the food court.

"So, since when are you McGrath's motion man anyway?" David said as he returned to their table with coffees.

"It's not him, it's his lackey—Lane," Phil said, shaking his head. "She runs McGrath's personal injury practice for him when he's away, but as soon as she smells trouble on a file, she passes it off to a junior so she won't look bad."

"Like this morning's motion…"

"Exactly. I could have told her we'd get hammered—but she knew the damage was done, that's why she gave me the file."

"That's bullshit," David said, sipping his coffee. They had both come to accept the politics as a fact of life at the firm, but that didn't stop them from complaining about them from time to time.

"She's tricky," Phil continued. "She waits until she thinks she's fucked something up, but before the other side has called her on it. Then she makes up some reason for passing the file on, and whoever gets it doesn't know there's a problem until its too late."

"I know what you mean," David nodded his head. "Although she's stayed away from me lately."

"That's because she knows she can't mess with you now— Mr. Automatism," Phil grinned. "I bet it just eats her up inside, that she passed on that case."

"Yeah, but that'll wear thin eventually, and I've got a real bad feeling about Lane. I wouldn't put anything past her."

"Neither would I."

"Speaking of bad feelings…," David said, noticing J.P. Gallant over at the counter ordering a coffee. "I never told you about Tom."

"What about him?" Phil said, instantly interested.

David leaned in closer and lowered his voice.

"I think he did it."

"I thought you said he was innocent?" Phil said quietly.

"I did. But he said something to me when we'd both had a few drinks, and well…"

"What did he say?"

"He said he didn't really remember what happened that night."

"So what," Phil said dismissively. "That was your defence wasn't it? Now you're upset because he's confirming it?"

"It's not what he said Phil, it was the way he said it. The look in his eye."

"Ah," Phil said, shaking his head. "I could never understand why you ever thought he was innocent anyway. I mean with all that evidence at the crime scene—Jesus. Which makes your winning his case all the more incredible. You did a great job. There's no point questioning it now."

"I know, it's just that I really did believe he was innocent. I know the evidence didn't support it but it was a gut feeling. To win the freedom of someone I thought was truly innocent was such a high, but that makes the reality all the more unpleasant."

"Boy, you sure are hard to please," Phil said with a chuckle. "You do the unthinkable and win the murder trial of the year, with something as crazy as automatism. Now you're a freakin' celebrity and you're unhappy."

David laughed.

"I guess I shouldn't complain."

"I guess you shouldn't," Phil said in mock indignation. "You should try out my practice for a week, representing deadbeat dads on legal aid certificates—that'll change your perspective, I'll tell you."

"Maddie told me about your custody trial. She said you did a hell of a job getting the mother sole custody."

"I got lucky. Dad put his foot in his mouth one too many times on the stand and I was able to beat him up a bit on cross—messy business though."

"Your client must have been happy," David said, draining his cup.

"Yeah so was I, until I got back to the office."

"What do you mean?"

"Turns out the dad was a friend of McGrath's sister."

"Who told you that?"

"Lane. Who else? She said McGrath was pissed off."

"What were you supposed to do, drop the file? Half the town knows McGrath in one way or another."

"Might not have been a bad idea," Phil laughed.

"Did McGrath say anything to you?"

"No."

David gave a dismissive wave, "Lane's so full of shit she probably made the whole thing up."

"Yeah, maybe. To tell you the truth, I'm getting a little tired of all the politics. Having to take files you don't want and dump the ones you do. It's no way to practice law," Phil sighed.

"All part of the master plan, I guess."

"Hmm," Phil said, looking over David's shoulder before whispering, "Don't look now, but here comes Mr. Law himself."

"Who?" David's question was interrupted by an unfamiliar voice from behind him, calling his name. David turned to see Francis Sullivan Q.C. approaching from the direction of the escalators.

"Hello," Sullivan said, extending his hand.

"Mr. Sullivan," David nodded, shaking his hand. "You know Phil Morgan I think," he added, gesturing to Phil.

"Yes, of course. I remember you from the Law Society formal." Sullivan shook Phil's hand. "I was wondering if I could talk to you for a moment David, a Law Society matter...," he tailed off, indicating the end of his interest in Phil's presence. Apart from being the managing partner of the largest firm in St. John's, Sullivan was a Law Society bencher with a seat on a number of committees, from finance to discipline.

"I've gotta run," Phil said, looking at his watch and patting David on the arm. "I'll see you back at the office. He nodded to Sullivan before he left. "Nice to see you again."

"Likewise," Sullivan smiled, setting his soft leather briefcase carefully down on a chair. "Have a seat," he gestured and David obliged, unsure of why. Sullivan didn't practice criminal law, and as far as he knew, none of David's personal injury files were against insurers represented by Sullivan's firm.

"First of all, I wanted to congratulate you on the Fitzgerald trial," Sullivan said, adjusting the cuffs of his shirt so the requisite half-inch protruded beyond the sleeves of his immaculate blue pinstripe. Apart from his legal acumen, Sullivan was known for his expensive tastes, especially for sharp clothes.

"Thanks," David said, still unsure where Sullivan was headed.

"Fine work, David. You really took a lot of people by surprise, including most of the defence bar," he added the last bit with a conspiratorial grin.

"Well, I have to admit I was pleasantly surprised myself at the outcome. I'm sure luck had something to do with it."

"You're being too modest," Sullivan shook his head. "It took a lot of guts to go with automatism, not to mention skill to pull it off. I'd hate to be in the RNC's shoes now," he added with a wink.

"I'm sure they'll find the killer in time," David said, feeling a little uncomfortable in saying so.

"Oh you know as well as I do they aren't going to go looking anywhere else, are they?"

Sullivan said it more as a statement than a question, leaving David to wonder whether he should answer.

"Of course not," Sullivan answered for him, with a flash of his pearly whites. "But I'm sure you'll be the first to know if they do."

"Who knows what the future will bring," David replied vaguely.

"Your future," Sullivan smiled again. "That's really what I wanted to talk to you about, not the Law Society."

"Oh," David raised an eyebrow. This was an unexpected turn.

"You're a rising star David, we can all see that. I'm sure Bill will want to keep you in the fold, and as firms go he's at the helm of one of the best," Sullivan's expression changed to convey his sincerity. "But you should make the most of your experience so far by surrounding yourself with the leaders in the field."

"I'm not sure what you mean," David said honestly. It certainly sounded like a job offer but as far as he knew there was only one person at Sullivan's firm doing criminal law.

"Bowring, Hallett is looking to expand its criminal practice group David, and as you probably know the merger means we're directly affiliated with some of the leading criminal lawyers not just here but in Halifax and Moncton as well."

David knew that the firm had recently merged its operation with several law firms in Atlantic Canada.

"I'm sure it's a first rate operation," he said, "but I'm pretty happy where I am."

"I'm sure you are," Sullivan nodded. "And trial work is the best there is—I've been there. But take some friendly advice from someone a little longer in the tooth."

David smiled, not sure what he meant.

"I've met your lovely wife, and I'm sure she's behind you one hundred per cent, but a trial lawyer's practice doesn't lend itself well to family life. Do you have kids?"

"We've got an eighteen month old—a boy."

Sullivan smiled.

"Ah, those are the times David. They really are. What's his name?"

"Ben."

"Nice name. Well, I'm just saying that there may come a day when you want a different kind of practice, maybe for his benefit if not for yours. And if that time does come in your life, it's always good to keep your options open. Just think about it, that's all I'm asking," Sullivan handed him an off-white business card, embossed with Sullivan's name in gold lettering. David accepted the card and nodded.

"I'm flattered," he said.

"Feel free to call me any time if you want to discuss it. Or talk to some of our junior guys. They'll tell you it's a great working environment, and the compensation packages are the best in town." After a moment, Sullivan stood and extended his hand, "I'd better get going. I hope to hear from you David, but I'll understand if I don't."

"Thanks," David said, shaking his hand and sitting back down as Sullivan departed. He retrieved the card from his jacket pocket and looked at it again. He was wary of Sullivan's reputation, given McGrath's warnings, and he had no intention of joining some boutique firm that did only white-collar crime, but he couldn't help feeling good about the offer nonetheless. That Sullivan had thought him worthy of a personal visit was all the more flattering. Things were really looking up for him. He smiled and tucked the card back in his pocket as he made his way towards the exit and the bright sunshine outside, a smile on his face.

chapter thirty-four
—august

The St. John's civic holiday known as the Regatta is billed as the oldest sporting event in North America, and although it had begun as a boat race up and down the often gusty Quidi Vidi Lake, it had grown into a day-long party over the years. The boat races were still the central attraction, but people had taken to hosting backyard parties and barbeques all over town. Phil Morgan had hosted his annual deck party at his and Judy's house on Forest Road, which offered the opportunity to see the races without ever having to stray too far from an ample supply of cold beer.

David and Elizabeth had pawned Ben off on her parents and made their way over just in time for the final race, and the beginning of the evening's festivities. Sitting at his desk at nine-thirty on the morning after, David drank his third glass of water and popped a couple of aspirin. He chuckled as he glanced out the window and noted Phil's furtive progress across Duckworth Street. David and Elizabeth had left at one and Phil was in full-flight at that point, so he was likely having a much tougher morning. The phone rang and ended his surveillance.

"There's a reporter from *The Telegraph* on the line," Joanne said. "Do you want to talk to him?"

"What about?"

"He didn't say."

"Put him through," he said finally, with a sigh. He supposed it was some follow-up piece on Tom. Before that trial, David had very little involvement with the media, but he had been besieged in the weeks that followed the verdict and again, although to a lesser degree, after the appeal period had elapsed.

"David Hall."

"It's John Nugent calling from *The Telegraph*. I was wondering if you'd care to comment on this morning's interview on VORW," Nugent said, referring to a popular local radio station.

"What interview?"

"Inspector Pat Gushue was discussing the RNC investigation into the murder of Stuart Bruce. You haven't heard it?"

"No, I haven't," David said, sitting up and taking more interest in the call.

"Inspector Gushue seemed to be implying that they might be returning their focus to Mr. Fitzgerald, and I was wondering if you had any comment?"

"That's absurd," David said quickly, before remembering he was talking to a reporter. "Well, I haven't heard the interview so I'm not prepared to comment at this time, other than to say that my client has been tried and acquitted."

"Maybe I could call you back when you've had a chance to review the transcript of the interview?"

"Sure. Yes, call me back later," he said, hanging up. His mind was racing. He knew that the general rule was that a person could only be tried once for one crime, but he also knew there were exceptions to every rule. He considered the possibility that the RNC had unearthed some pivotal new evidence but even then, it would be such a long shot from a technical point of view that it wasn't worth worrying about. He decided to find out what he was dealing with first.

An hour later, he had obtained the transcript from the Internet, and determined that Gushue's actual words had been a lot more vague than Nugent had suggested. When asked whether the RNC still suspected Tom was guilty, Gushue had simply replied that the RNC only ever had one suspect. Although not much of a vote of confidence for Tom, this was a far cry from saying he was a suspect in an ongoing investigation. Just to be sure, David was now calling J.P. Gallant.

"I thought you might be calling," Gallant said dryly.

"Can you blame me? I've got *The Telegraph* calling me for comment."

"Look, Gushue should have been a little more careful in his choice of words…," Gallant began.

"You can say that again. Am I going to get your assurance that he will provide a clarification of his statement before I do the defamation research?"

"Relax, David. It's already in the works. As for your comment to the paper, I can confirm that Tom is not a suspect in any active investigation."

David paused as Joanne came in and handed him a note indicating that Nugent was on the line.

"Alright, but promise me you'll keep the reins on Gushue. I don't want to be dealing with this kind of thing every time someone asks him why he hasn't got a suspect."

He hung up and nodded to Joanne, who returned to her desk and sent the call in.

Five minutes later, it was all taken care of, except for one thing. He had tried to call Tom earlier but had gotten no answer.

"Joanne," he called out through the open door. "Can you try Tom's number again?"

"No need," she called back. "He's downstairs."

"So, how have you been Tom?" David asked, shutting the door as Tom took a seat.

"Not too bad," he said in his usual, gruff manner. "'Til this morning anyway."

"I take it you heard Gushue on the radio," David said with a nod.

"Yeah, I heard. He can't…"

"Don't worry Tom, they can't come back at you now. And anyway, I called Gallant as soon as I heard and he confirmed Gushue was just shooting his mouth off. The radio station will be reading out a clarification from Gushue on tomorrow morning's show."

"Hmm," Tom said, apparently not totally appeased. "There's some legal thing about not goin' after me again isn't there?"

"Yes, there is. *Res judicata* is the legal principle—or double jeopardy."

"Yeah, yeah I think I heard of that," Tom said with a nod. He shifted in his seat and said nothing for a moment as David tried to guess what he was thinking.

"Listen," Tom began, "about that night at my place, what I said…"

"You had a fair bit to drink. I wouldn't worry about it," David said, not wanting to get into it.

"So if the cops called you to testify…"

"They're not going to ask me to testify and even if they did, whatever you tell me is protected by solicitor-client privilege."

Tom looked at him for a moment before speaking again.

"You think I done it though, don't you?"

"It doesn't matter what I think. You were tried and acquitted, that's all that matters. Do you think I'm going to go running to the cops just because you said something when you were half drunk? Is that why you're here?" David said, with a certain amount of indignation in his voice.

"I just don't like the fuckin' cops going on the radio sayin' I'm still their suspect," Tom replied.

"Well, like I said, there's no reason to be concerned."

"Alright then," Tom said, getting up and moving towards the door. Before leaving, he turned to David, "I never did it, you know."

"I didn't say you did. And anyway, it's all over now. Get on with your life Tom."

Tom looked at him, shook his head and then he was gone.

David sat back and crossed his arms. He couldn't help feeling a little unsettled by the meeting. Tom was clearly trying to minimize whatever damage he thought he had done with his revelation at the party. And even though David had been telling the truth when he said it was all over, it made Tom look even guiltier in David's mind, which bothered him even more. He looked at his watch and decided to go get a coffee. He had to get on with his own life as well.

chapter thirty-five
—september

David had always loved fall in Newfoundland. After a sumptuous Sunday brunch at the Fairmont Hotel, he and Elizabeth had taken Ben in his wagon for a stroll along Water Street, browsing in the stores and enjoying the brilliant sunshine that warmed the cool September air.

"So where do you see yourself in five years?" Elizabeth asked, putting her arm in his as they walked.

"How about walking down Water Street on a beautiful Sunday afternoon with my lovely wife?"

"Good answer," she said with a laugh. "But I meant work."

"I don't know. But I really should be spending more of my time doing this."

"And how do you do that?"

"That's a good question. First of all, I've got to change jobs."

"I've noticed you seem stressed out lately. But wouldn't that be the same anywhere if you're practicing criminal law?"

"Sit down, Ben," he said, noticing the little boy leaning precariously over the side of the wagon. "It doesn't have to be. If I could spend all my time on criminal files, I think I'd be happy. It's the politics that I don't like."

"But it must get better. As you get more experience, you must get to delegate more."

"That's what I used to think too. But look at Todd Davis," David said, referring to an intermediate partner at the firm. "He's a partner and a twelve-year lawyer and he can't take a crap without asking permission, let alone have control of his own practice."

"What about Tom's trial—surely that must have given you a boost?"

"Yeah, but that doesn't mean I'm suddenly free to run my own practice."

"Well, why don't you go out on your own?"

"It's not that simple. I'd need start-up money, and a bigger client base to make a go of it," he said with a sigh. "I'm not going anywhere for a while."

"Well, as long as you're at that firm, you have to try not to let it get the better of you. I hate it when you're unhappy."

"You're right—there are more important things in life," he said with a smile, scooping the little boy out of his wagon and hoisting him onto his shoulders.

David buttoned up the top of his overcoat and leaned into the fierce wind that whipped down Duckworth Street. He had once again underestimated how quickly the weather could change during the five minute walk from his office to the convention centre. He jaywalked across New Gower and hustled to his destination, cursing as the rain began to fall in icy sheets. He entered the lobby and shook off the rain, following the rich smell of freshly-brewed coffee to a large room outside where some familiar faces were gathered. He hung up his coat and headed for the coffee urn. With an injection of caffeine, he was ready for some socializing before the morning's session got under way.

The annual two-day symposium on criminal law was a must for all practitioners of the field, offering a chance to get up to speed on the latest developments in the law and to catch up on gossip.

Making his way into the room, David took a seat at the back next to Mark Bursey, a junior lawyer he knew casually.

"Well, if it isn't Mr. Automatism," said Bursey, mockingly.

"Very funny," David said with a grin.

"I still can't believe you pulled that off," Bursey said, shaking his head.

"I get that a lot," David said with a smile. "And I'm never sure it's a compliment."

"You know what I heard though…," Bursey said quietly.

"What did you hear?" David smiled.

"I heard they're looking at Fitzgerald again."

"What, that interview with Gushue? That was months ago…"

"No, no, this is recent. I heard they found new evidence."

David shook his head. "There have been rumours floating around for months, none with any truth to them."

"Well I hear this one's different. They went back over every scrap of evidence, and then some."

"Oh yeah," David said casually. "And what did they find?"

"Tom had someone doing research on psychological disorders for him while he was in the Pen."

David laughed. "Now I've heard it all."

"A client of mine overheard two cops talking. They said they checked his girlfriend's library records and discovered she had taken out a bunch of psychology texts in April."

David shook his head again. "It's time the RNC found something better to do with their time."

Bursey chuckled as the first speaker got started, and the shuffling and chatter gradually died out.

As he sat there listening, a feeling of unease crept over David as he considered Bursey's story and what it could mean. One possibility was that Tom really had pulled the wool over his lawyer's eyes, since the timing of his covert research coincided exactly with when he chose to divulge the story of the assault on the way to Bannerman Park on the night of the murder. Even though Tom couldn't have realized the story would be the deciding factor for Dr. Clark, it could certainly have been invented with the purpose of heightening David's resolve to fight for his client.

A second and more ominous possibility at this point, was that despite Gallant's assurances to the contrary after Gushue's comments over a month ago, the RNC had kept its file on Tom open.

Though he tried to concentrate on the lecture, David couldn't avoid the uncomfortable feeling in the pit of his stomach. When he got back to the office, he would have to do some research of his own.

chapter thirty-six

David's research had led him to a couple of conclusions. The first was that it was very rare for an accused to be re-tried on the same offence. The second was that contrary to popular belief, even among lawyers, such a re-trial was not impossible. As David made his way through the cases in which it had been permitted, trying to distill a hard and fast list of necessary criteria, he began to feel more and more uncomfortable with the whole idea. There were certainly significant obstacles in the Crown's path if it chose such a route, but these could be easily lowered or removed altogether with the introduction of significant new evidence. He began to imagine what the RNC might have uncovered since the trial, and in light of Tom's comments during that time period, nothing was beyond the realm of possibility. Without any idea of what the Crown might or might not have in the way of new evidence, David had gone as far as he could in his efforts to assess his client's position. What he needed now was advice.

David poked his head around Bill McGrath's door and noticed he was in one of his usual positions, with his feet up on the desk and the phone at his ear. Noticing David, McGrath waved him in as he wrapped up his conversation.

"What's up?" he said, putting down the receiver. Before David had uttered his first word, McGrath's secretary was at the door.

"Don't forget the luncheon at twelve-thirty," she said.

"Right." McGrath looked at his watch. "Friggin' Law Society luncheons. I can't stand them, but I'm accepting an award."

"I can come back…"

"I've got five minutes. Why don't you shut the door."

David did and returned to his seat.

"I wanted your advice on Tom Fitzgerald," he began.

"What about him?"

"You remember the comments a few months ago on the radio about Tom being a suspect?"

"Yeah, they were retracted weren't they?"

"Yes, they were, and Gallant assured me there was nothing to them. But I've been hearing rumours again, rumours I don't like."

"Hmm," McGrath said, taking his feet down and putting his elbows on the desk. "You think they might be looking at taking another run at him?"

"I don't know. Like I said, all I've heard so far are rumours. But I did some research and I don't like what I found."

"Yeah, I remember looking at the issue a couple of years back and being surprised," McGrath said, rubbing his upper lip with an index finger.

"I'm wondering if I should talk to Gallant and give him whatever exculpatory evidence I've got that I didn't use at trial because of the automatism defence."

"You didn't have that much did you?"

"Not really, but there was that preliminary forensics report that Lane had done, that suggested the possibility of a right-handed killer. And some other stuff that helped Tom out."

"You've got to be careful though," McGrath said, shaking his head. "You don't want to look like you're trying to throw them off the scent."

"That's true, but if it helps them to direct their efforts elsewhere, there's got to be some value in providing it."

They discussed the possible ramifications for a few more minutes.

"You haven't discussed this with anyone else have you?" McGrath asked.

"No."

"Good. Keep it that way and let me think about it. In the meantime, have a good hard look at your evidence and see if it's really worth the risk."

McGrath rose and reached for the suit jacket slung across the back of his chair. "I've got to go. I'll talk to you later."

"Thanks Bill."

"You bet. By the way, are you interested in the charity pro-am tomorrow? I've got an opening." McGrath said, leading the way out of his office.

"Sure," David said quickly, not wanting to miss a round of golf at the best course in town. He would have to double-check but he didn't think he had anything on tomorrow that would prevent him from playing.

"Maybe we can talk some more then," McGrath said, following David out of his office.

chapter thirty-seven

There was barely a sound, apart from the flutter of a bird's wings or the whoosh of a distant car. Although the morning air was cool, there was only enough wind to cause the slightest rustle in the tops of the golden trees. The silence was broken by the metallic ping of a titanium driver as it connected with a golf ball, sending it sailing into the distance.

"Nice shot," David said as McGrath stooped to get his tee and returned to the cart.

"Beats the office, doesn't it?"

"Sure does."

"They must have had a late night chasing skirts," McGrath said with a chuckle, referring to the other half of their foursome, who had missed the shotgun start. Whatever their reason, David didn't mind. It wasn't often he got to spend any time one on one with McGrath, especially in such a relaxed atmosphere. The firm paid for a couple of teams in the annual fall classic, which was a charity event played by local business people and players for the local American Hockey League team.

"Come on, they'll probably catch up with us at thirteen."

David started the cart and headed off down the path towards the fairway.

"I was talking to a couple of law school buddies when I was in Toronto last weekend," McGrath said as they bounced along in the brisk morning air. "They're criminal lawyers with big Bay Street firms, and they were pretty impressed with your work on the Fitzgerald trial."

"Really?" David couldn't help having a feeling of pride.

"You really made a mark for yourself, and it took a lot of guts."

"Thanks, but I couldn't have done it without your support."

"Ah," McGrath said with a wave of his hand. "We've got to help each other out, that's the good thing about being in a firm."

"Yeah, I guess it is."

"Some of the guys have been talking about making you a junior partner, how's that make you feel?"

"It makes me feel pretty good, actually," David said, shocked and flattered at once.

"That's good," McGrath said with a smile. "But partnership means sacrifice you know, and putting differences behind you for the good of the team."

As he pulled up next to his ball, a good fifty yards short of McGrath's, David waited for the rest. He knew McGrath's opening remarks had been too good to be true.

"I know you and Kelly had your differences over the Fitzgerald case, and I know you had no intention of betraying her…"

"Bill, I didn't…"

"Let me finish. It doesn't matter who did what or who said what. The point is, we need to work as a unit, or we all lose. I know you think she's been hard on you but she's trying to help you in her own way."

David held his tongue and selected a three-iron.

"You're a good young lawyer with a bright future David. And I see your future at the firm, but you need to be able to respect the other partners."

"I don't have a problem with Kelly, it's the other way around."

"Now see, that's what I mean. You each blame the other instead of working it out."

"So what do you want me to do?" David asked.

"Like I said, I want you to bury the hatchet with Kelly. Promise me you'll make it work."

David nodded, after only a brief pause. As unpleasant as it was, he could tolerate Lane in return for an early entry into the partnership.

"Good," McGrath said as David got into his stance. "Now straighten up that front arm or you're going to slice."

David and McGrath had been joined by the goalie and the star centre at the fourteenth hole and had enjoyed an entertaining round listening to the players' stories about life on the road. Following the round, there had been drinks and a barbeque at the clubhouse, and before he knew it, David was looking at his watch and realizing it was after midnight. Tired and slightly drunk, he decided to call it a night, but not before thanking McGrath, who was holding court at the bar, surrounded by a mixture of lawyers and hockey players. He was always at the centre of everything, and he seemed at home there.

"Thanks for the game," David shouted over the noise as McGrath waved back.

Twenty minutes later, a cab pulled up outside David's door. As he emerged from the back seat, a couple appeared in the glow of the streetlight a few feet from his house and passed by, arm in arm. He greeted them with a smile and made his way gingerly up the front steps and unlocked his front door.

As he closed the door behind him, the engine of a dark sedan came to life as it pulled away from the curb twenty yards down the street. It passed slowly by the house before turning on its lights and disappearing into the night.

chapter thirty-eight
—october

David read the letter once more on-screen before hitting the print key and getting up for a stretch. As the printer whirred into action, he looked at his watch. It was eleven-thirty and he was tired. He looked out his office window and noticed the trees swaying in the dark, windy night. Added to the steady stream of rain that he heard whipping against his window for the past hour, it would not make for an enjoyable walk up to his car. He sat back in his chair and went through his e-mails one more time, satisfied that he had attended to everything urgent. A pile of phone messages sat on the corner of his desk, but these could wait for tomorrow morning. In fact, he realized with some satisfaction, his practice seemed under control, probably for the first time since the start of the Fitzgerald trial almost six months before.

It had been a week since McGrath had called him into his office and advised against contacting the police. David had followed this advice, since the upside was questionable and the downside potentially dangerous. He had heard no fresh rumours about any new efforts focused on Tom and he was trying to forget about the whole thing. It had also been ten days since his golf game with McGrath and he had been doing some serious thinking. While the prospect of a partnership this early in his career excited him, he had been less than thrilled by McGrath's other comments. If sucking up to Lane was part of the package, it lost a lot of its lustre. And besides, he thought, the fact that he had made a mark for himself with Tom's defence made him less eager to jump at an offer with nasty strings attached, even if it was a partnership offer. Francis Sullivan's offer to jump ship to Bowring, Hallett was proof of this, even though David had little interest in working in the stuffy environment of the city's "premier" firm, as its partners liked it to be known as. On the other hand, he was still quite junior to be even considering such a prospect, and didn't relish the idea of hanging out a shingle and trying to fend for himself right now. Not with the overhead he would need to run even a small office. Apart from anything else, a lot of his current clients were long on needs and short on cash. While most paid their accounts in full, they usually required long-term repayment plans to do so.

So for now, David had decided to stay where he was, which wasn't so bad. He had gotten a small raise and the partners had generally allowed him to concentrate on criminal files, though he did have the odd dog file that flowed down from the third floor. But when he compared his situation with that of his peers, he felt a lot more fortunate. Phil Morgan had been complaining about having hopeless personal injury files dumped on him from upstairs, especially by Kelly Lane. And as for David's relationship with Lane, he had to admit it had improved somewhat recently. They weren't friends and they never would be, but at least she had been staying out of David's face.

David started packing his briefcase and then abandoned it, realizing he wouldn't be doing much more than sleeping when he got home, and decided to leave it all for the morning. He switched off his computer and turned off the light. The office was quiet, with whoever had been stomping around on the third floor long gone. He set the alarm and locked the front door behind him as he stepped out into a gale. He squinted to shield his eyes from the cold pellets of rain and zipped his coat all the way up. Duckworth Street was quiet as he crossed and began his ascent up Church Hill towards the side street where he always parked. As he reached it, he turned side on to shelter himself from the sleet and reached in his pocket for his car keys. He made his way along the cul de sac lined with row houses on either side and bound at the far end by a vacant lot. David was fiddling around looking for the right key under the glow of the streetlight when he thought he heard the sound of something over the howl of the wind. Hearing the sudden roar of an engine and making out a large black form coming at him, he just had enough time to jump onto the hood of his car as the vehicle grazed his back and careened past, before turning up the hill in a squeal of tires.

David lay on his back on the hood of his car, his heart pounding and his mind searching for some explanation other than the obvious—someone had just tried to kill him.

chapter thirty-nine

"Wow," Phil said, shaking his head in disbelief on hearing David's harrowing tale over his morning coffee.

He paused to think while David sat in front of his desk, looking worried.

"Are you sure it wasn't just some drunk?"

"Drunk or not, you don't speed up when you're about to hit someone unless it's intentional, and you don't drive around with your lights off, unless you don't want to be seen. Besides, you know where I park. The only reason you'd be on that street is if you lived there, or you were waiting for someone…"

"Maybe you stumbled onto a drug deal and they thought…"

"Come on Phil, give me a break."

"Okay, okay, I'm just saying don't jump to conclusions, that's all."

"What do you expect me to do? Besides, there aren't that many possible conclusions." David said.

"Are you saying it was Tom?"

"Who else would it be? I told you what happened at his victory party. And with Gushue on the radio over the summer and the rumours going around lately, maybe he heard them too, and he thinks I'm going to turn on him."

"Did you get a good look at the car?" Phil asked.

"Not really. Like I said, the lights were off, and anyway I was too busy trying to get the hell out of the way. All I know is that it was a big dark thing, probably a clunker."

"What does Tom drive?"

"I have no idea. I don't even know if he owns a car."

"Hmm," Phil said, rubbing his lip. "So what are you going to do?"

"Well I can't really go to the cops now can I?"

"Why not?"

"And tell them what? That I think my former client tried to run me over? Jesus," he shook his head. "Besides, I have no proof, and what if I'm wrong?"

"Did you tell Elizabeth?"

"God no. She'd be completely freaked out."

"Well, you've got to do something."

"What though?" David said, looking at his watch. "I've got to go, I've got a peace bond hearing at nine. I'll catch up with you later."

As David sat in the courtroom waiting for the other side to show up, his mind was still on the previous night, when someone tapped him on the shoulder.

"She's not going to show. Don't waste your time."

David turned around to see the familiar face of inspector Pat Gushue smiling at him. "I didn't know you were involved in this," David said.

"I know the complainant. And I know her husband too—your client's a mean friggin' drunk, but he must have convinced her to take him back. I was talking to the officer working the file down at the station this morning. I'm here on another matter so I said I'd pass it on to you."

"Well thanks," David said.

"No problem," Gushue replied, making his way out.

David waited for the Justice of the Peace and explained his understanding that the complaint had been withdrawn. Since there was no lawyer or applicant present, he asked to have the peace bond application struck and after giving a few minutes' grace to the applicant while a couple of other matters were heard, the JP dismissed the bond application. As he walked out the courtroom and crossed the lobby, David spotted Gushue, waiting outside another courtroom with a coffee in his hand.

"Thanks again for the info," he said, as Gushue nodded.

"Can I ask you something off the record?" David said, as Gushue finished his coffee and tossed the cup in the trash can nearby.

"Shoot."

"I've been hearing rumours about your investigation," David began.

"What investigation?"

"Come on, you know which investigation."

"Oh you mean the Bruce murder?" Gushue said with a wink. "And what rumours have you heard?"

"That you're considering taking another run at Tom."

"Well you of all people should know we can't do that."

"I was hoping to forget about the law on the subject and just get a straight answer from you—are you targeting Tom or not?"

"Why, are the rumours making you nervous?"

"No, but I would hate to see my client dragged into another unnecessary legal battle."

"Why? You'd still get paid. That's the beauty of being a lawyer isn't it?" Gushue said with a grin.

"Come on, just tell me whether he's still a suspect that's all, off the record."

"Off the record hey?" Gushue said, nodding. "Alright, I'll tell you if you'll answer one question for me, off the record."

"What's that?"

"Do you still think he's innocent?"

"We both know that's irrelevant, but for what it's worth, yes I do," David lied.

Gushue shook his head and laughed. "You friggin' lawyers, you're all the same."

"That's why we're so popular," David said sarcastically, resigned to the fact that Gushue wasn't going to confirm or deny anything.

"Tom Fitzgerald is as guilty as sin," Gushue said, just as David was about to leave.

"And you won't find a cop in St. John's who doesn't think so, but we had our shot at him and he walked, so now we've got to look elsewhere."

David nodded.

"I've got to admit," Gushue said with a wink, "that was some fucking rabbit you pulled out of the hat with Tom's defence. But don't get too cocky, they won't all work out like that."

"I'll try to remember that," David said as he headed for the escalator.

As he made his way out of Atlantic Place and across Water Street, he thought about the previous night's events. Maybe Phil was right. What if he had just stumbled across a drug deal, or a drunken nutcase? Neither were beyond imagining late at night downtown. And as for Tom being involved, it didn't make any sense. As David reached the top of Purdy's Lane, the sun broke through the clouds and took the edge off the cool fall wind that blew down Duckworth Street. Turning east towards his office, he drew a deep breath of crisp ocean air and decided to forget whatever had happened the previous night—and Tom's case as well for that matter.

chapter**forty**

"I'm just saying, I won't be responsible for my actions if I have to spend two weeks with your asshole brother-in-law, that's all," David said as he came into the living room with two cups of coffee and handed Elizabeth hers.

"It's a big condo, and it's not like we'll be hanging out with them every day…"

"It's not big enough and you know it, Liz."

"But what will I tell my parents? They'll be so disappointed."

"Tell them we don't want to impose with Ben. Say he's developed a sleeping disorder that keeps him awake all night, I don't know."

"They're his grandparents for God's sake," Elizabeth sighed and put her cup down on the sofa table. "I know how much you hate Sean. Believe me I can't stand him either, and I never would have committed to this if…"

"What do you mean committed. Did you say we were going?"

She just sipped her coffee.

"Elizabeth?"

"I sort of said we'd be going, before I knew Janet and Sean were going. You said your folks would be in Nova Scotia so I thought…"

"Well that's just great. It's bad enough we've got to spend Christmas in Florida, but with those two," he shook his head.

"I'm sorry honey, I should have discussed it with you but I thought you'd like the idea."

"Why?" David said. "Why would you think that? And since when are you into a green Christmas? I thought you were all gung ho for sleigh rides, tobogganing and hot toddies."

"I am, I just thought it would be nice for a change."

David drank his coffee in silence as she looked at him, gauging his reaction.

"You're a real piece of work you know that?" he said, breaking into a smile.

"It'll be nice for Ben," she said, slipping beside him on the loveseat.

"Oh sure, play that angle. Like Ben cares whether it's winter or summer, as long as Santa comes."

"You're so cynical," she said with a mock frown.

He put his arm around her as she leaned into him.

"Promise me we won't be sitting around the dinner table at the condo every night. I can't bear the thought…"

"Of course not. And if Sean starts yapping, ask him how the business is doing."

"Why?"

"Guess."

"You mean he's run it into the ground already?"

"I don't think it's doing well. Mom said she was talking to Janet and apparently Sean's got a lot on his mind, if you know what I mean."

"But he's only been in control for a year. Even I thought he would last longer than that," David said with a chuckle.

"Be nice," she scolded. "The point is, he's probably not going to be his cocky self. That doesn't mean you have to rub his nose in it."

"I'd never do that honey," David said sarcastically.

"Did you hear that?" Elizabeth said, sitting up and cocking her head.

"Probably one of the damn cats again," David replied. "Did I tell you they got into the garbage last week? What a mess."

"Isn't it garbage day tomorrow?" she asked.

"Thanks for reminding me," he said with a sigh.

"Well I know you hate doing it in the morning."

"Yeah, I suppose I'd better do it now, before I get too comfortable."

"Thank you David."

"For what?" he said, getting up.

"You know. The Christmas thing means a lot to me."

"I know."

David shivered as he hurried to tie the bags and stuff them into the garbage cans. There was a cold mist in the air and the foghorn was going full tilt, cutting though the damp air. He lugged the garbage cans out of the bin and dragged them over the grass until he reached the driveway at the side of the house. Between the dark and the fog, he could barely see two feet in front of him, and he tried to anticipate the pothole he knew was coming up somewhere on the left. As he reached the front of the house and entered the light from the nearby streetlamp, someone cut into its grainy beam, causing him to jump back.

"Whassup?" said a voice. David smelled a mixture of alcohol and cigarettes.

"Tom?" he said, recognizing the gruff voice.

"Yeah, it's your old buddy Tom come to see ya."

Tom's backlit figure loomed over David in the fog. He squinted to look at him and noticed Tom had something in his left hand.

"Jesus, you scared the shit out of me," David said, with an edge on his voice that reflected his fear.

"Can't I drop by to see an old friend?"

Neither man moved.

David instinctively tried to put some distance between them and angled his way towards the curb.

"If you don't mind, I'm going to dump these," he said.

"Go ahead."

With the garbage cans on the curb, David stayed where he was, causally glancing around to see if there was anyone else around. There wasn't.

"So what can I do for you, Tom?" David asked, watching Tom's left hand. When it moved and caught the light, David realized it was a beer bottle he was holding.

"I wanna get somethin' straight," Tom said, draining the beer and keeping the bottle.

"You ever hear of a phone?" David was starting to feel angered by the discomfort Tom was causing him.

"Am I interruptin' an important meeting?" Tom asked, his voice dripping with sarcasm, making an obvious reference to David's failure to return a recent phone call for two days.

"No, but you can't just stroll out of the fog like that…"

"I never did it."

"You never did what Tom?"

"Don't fuck around. You know exactly what I'm talkin' about."

David was alarmed by his tone. He had never heard it directed at him before.

"Look Tom, I thought we'd been through all this."

"I'm not talkin' about all that legal shit. Can't say nothin' 'cause of whatever privilege…"

"So what are you talking about then?"

"I was down at the bar and I was thinkin' I need to clear the air…"

"What do you want from me?" David asked. He noticed Tom stagger a little. It was obvious he was on a bender.

"I want you to say you don't think…I want you to say you believe me."

"Do you really want to get into this now, out here in the middle of the night?"

"Yeah, yeah I do."

"Tom, I'm going inside and I'm going to bed. Call me tomorrow at the office if you want and we can chat okay?"

"Don't you turn your fucking back on me," Tom snarled.

David turned and watched as Tom inched closer, the beer bottle still in his hand.

"Tom, you're drunk," he said, his heart beginning to race. "Go home and call me in the morning."

Tom kept coming.

"Do you want me to call the cops?" David asked.

Tom stopped dead in his tracks and a second later the light came on over a neighbour's door. "You'd turn me in to the fucking cops wouldn't you?" Tom said, "After all we been through."

David watched as his neighbour appeared at the door.

"What's going on out there?" the man called out from his front step.

"It's okay," David called back, as Tom retreated.

"Call me tomorrow, Tom."

"Fuckin' lawyers. I thought we were friends," he said as he crossed the street and disappeared into the shadows.

"What took you so long?" Elizabeth asked, as David walked past the living room where she was still sitting on the couch.

"One of the bags burst," he said quietly. She got up and made her way to the bottom of the stairs.

"Coming to bed?" she called after him.

"I'll be right up," David replied from the kitchen, where he was pouring water into a glass that shook in his hand. The cold night air had made him sweat, too.

chapter forty-one

David had stayed up half the night thinking about his confrontation with Tom and had come up with only one certainty. He was scared. He had tried to immerse himself in work on arriving at the office, but he couldn't concentrate. Was he in danger? Having the person you defended on a murder charge show up at your house in the middle of the night was bad enough. But when you knew, or at least thought, he was guilty, it was even worse.

On the other hand, he couldn't help thinking of the expression on Tom's face when he threatened to call the police. He had looked...hurt, was the only word that came to mind. It seemed almost silly that a guy like Tom would react like that. With his background, and his manner, you would hardly expect him to be the sensitive type. But that look on his face was etched in David's mind and he couldn't help feeling guilt, or even betrayal.

David spent the morning thinking about it and then pulled Phil away from his desk by offering him lunch. As they sat over their chicken salad sandwiches and soup, he described the previous evening's events, with Phil looking more and more alarmed as David related the story.

"This is getting too weird," he said, unconsciously wiping the corner of his mouth with his sleeve. "First, you're almost mowed down in the street and now this. You've got to do something."

"I don't know," David replied, shaking his head. "You should have seen his face when I said I'd call the cops."

"Oh, I'm sure he went home and cried his eyes out. Give me a break…"

"You don't know him…"

"Don't start with that again. Like you really know him. You know he's been feeding you a line from the start. Now that he's told you he did it, he's obviously uncomfortable and he wants to convince you he's innocent again."

"Yeah, but…"

"But nothing," Phil interrupted, waving his sandwich. "It's basic criminal psychology. But the fact that he showed up at your house. That's not good."

"But what if it wasn't anything more than the booze talking? And I go to the cops…"

"You don't have to tell them he's a murderer," Phil protested. "Just say you had a dispute over something unrelated to the case."

"They're not going to buy that."

"Well what are they going to do? Re-try him for murder because he threatened you?"

"That's what I'm saying, though. He didn't even threaten me, really."

Phil brushed the crumbs off his jacket and shook his head.

"You do whatever you like, but I think you're taking a risk not saying anything." He looked at his watch. "I'm in Family Court in twenty minutes."

Arriving back at the office, David hadn't made it to his seat before the phone started ringing. Joanne was still at lunch, so he took it himself.

"David Hall."

"David, I'm so scared. Please come home."

It was Elizabeth, and she sounded frantic.

"What's the matter," he said as his heart leapt to his throat. "Are you alright? Is Ben…"

"There's a letter saying someone's going to kill us."

"What are you talking about? A letter from who?"

"I don't know…," she broke into tears. "He's going to kill us all David."

"Alright, lock the doors, I'll be right there."

"Hurry."

He slammed the phone down and bolted down the stairs and out into the street.

chapter forty-two

"Thanks for coming over," David said as he closed the door behind Inspector Pat Gushue. Finding Elizabeth in tears on the couch when he got home, David had seen no alternative. Something had to be done. Not wanting to alarm her even further, he had convinced her to take Ben to her parents' house while David dealt with the police.

"This the letter?" Gushue said, noticing the single sheet of paper on the coffee table.

"That's it."

"Did you touch it?"

"Well…yeah, just to read it. My wife opened it, and I guess she touched it too."

"Probably won't get anything off it anyway, but you never know," he said, donning a latex glove and turning the letter around to read it. It was short and to the point, composed of large, colourful letters cut from magazine pages and glued to a sheet of plain white paper. It read, "LEAVE THE CASE ALONE OR YOUR FUCKING DEAD—ALL OF YOU."

"No spelling bee winner here," Gushue said, shaking his head. "And you say your wife opened it?"

He flipped the opened envelope over and read the address.

"Yeah," David sighed. "She's upset—obviously. I took her to her mother's."

Gushue nodded.

"It's like something out of a bad movie," David said, sitting down and running his hands through his hair. "Have you ever seen this type of thing before?"

"You'd be surprised," Gushue said. "Most of the time it's a crank."

"Most of the time...," David looked at him as Gushue took a seat across from him.

"Any idea who might have sent you this?"

David leaned forward and put his head in his hands while Gushue waited patiently.

"There's more to it than just the letter."

"Oh yeah?" Gushue leaned forward on the sofa.

"A couple of weeks ago, I was at the office working late. I left around eleven and walked up to Montague Street, where I park my car."

"Off Church Hill?"

"Yeah. It was a shitty night. Cold, rainy and windy."

"I remember that night," Gushue said with a grin.

"Anyway, I'm by my car, fumbling for the keys, when all of a sudden, I hear the noise of an engine and I look up just in time to jump out of the way of an oncoming car."

"Are you saying someone tried to run you over?"

"It looked that way. It came out of nowhere, without any lights on and just took off after missing me."

"And you didn't report this?"

"No."

"Why not?"

"I don't know. After sleeping on it, I wondered if it was intentional."

"It sounds pretty intentional to me."

"There's another reason I didn't want to say anything."

Gushue waited silently.

"This incident happened not long after a meeting with Tom Fitzgerald."

"Did something happen at the meeting?"

"Let's just say that by the end of our discussion, Tom was offended."

"Offended?" Gushue raised an eyebrow. "Or angry?"

"That's just it. He wasn't angry, or threatening in any way."

Gushue nodded.

"Alright. So how long was it after this meeting that you were almost run over?"

"Couple of days."

"So maybe the two incidents are unrelated," Gushue paused, adding innocently, "...unless there's something about your meeting with Tom that you're not telling me."

"There's more," David said.

Gushue sat back.

"Last night, Tom paid me a visit here, outside the house."

"Did he threaten you?"

"Not really. Well, sort of."

"What did he say?"

"He said he was upset, and…at one point he told me not to turn my back on him."

"Hmm," Gushue muttered.

"I told him if he didn't leave I was going to call the cops."

"Did you ask him about the drive-by?"

"No."

"So what did he do when you said you'd call the police?"

"He left. It might have been because the neighbour's light came on, too."

Gushue nodded. "So he shows up in the middle of the night threatening you, and the next day you get this," he said pointing to the letter. "That's not a very smart move. He would have to have mailed it before…"

"He was drunk, too."

"Ah, good old alcohol. You can always rely on it to make people do the dumbest things."

"I don't know what to make of it, to be honest," David said. "But now my family's involved and that's where I draw the line. I haven't told my wife about last night, or the incident with the car. If she finds out, she'll freak."

"Well, at least we've got a pretty good idea who the first suspect is going to be."

"So what happens now?"

"Uttering threats is a criminal offence, you know that. I need you to give a statement and then I need to have a chat with Tom."

"He's my client, for Christ's sake!"

"Do you want to protect your family or not, David?"

David sighed and looked at his feet.

"Let's do the statement, and then we can take it from there," Gushue said.

chapter forty-three

Two days had passed since David had spilled the beans to Gushue and he had not been able to think straight since. Sitting at his desk, poring over a case he had printed off from a legal research site, he realized he was reading the same paragraph for the third time. Getting up in exasperation and heading to the coffee pot for a refill, he saw Kelly Lane coming down the stairs. Since McGrath's lecture on the links, David had been trying very hard to be amicable to Lane, who he had to admit seemed to be doing the same. But he still didn't trust her.

"Any news on the letter?" she asked. The story was all over the firm.

"No, nothing."

"They couldn't get any prints?"

"No. Whoever it was, he was careful," David said, filling his cup as Lane hovered on the second floor landing.

"You don't think it was Tom?"

"I don't know what to think any more."

"You're not blaming yourself for giving a statement to the cops are you? Come on, anyone in their right mind would have to think it was him. What does he expect anyway, pulling a stunt like that?" Lane patted him on the arm. "You did the right thing."

"Yeah, I guess."

"I'm in court in fifteen, I'll talk to you later."

"Yeah, thanks Kelly."

David returned to his office, followed a few seconds later by Phil, who came in and shut the door behind him.

"What's up?" David asked, puzzled by Phil's expression.

"I can't believe that two-faced wench," Phil said, motioning towards the stairs.

"What do you mean?"

"I heard a rumour…"

"What?"

"That McGrath's on the warpath because you went to the cops without talking to him first."

"Why's it any of his business?"

"He thinks going against a client gives the firm a bad name."

"Where did you hear this?"

"Greg Caines told me it came up at the partner's meeting yesterday. He also hinted that there was a difference of opinion."

"Meaning?" David inquired.

"Meaning most of the partners said they would have done the same thing, except for Lane…"

"That snake," David said.

"I can hear her teamwork bullshit now. I'm telling you David, since Tom's trial, she's been out for your blood, and for some reason McGrath listens to her."

"And if I'm wrong about Tom, she'll get as much mileage out of it as she can."

"But it's still five against two," Phil added.

"Like it matters. You're not going to tell me any of the others have a say if McGrath decides I screwed up, are you?"

As Phil thought of an answer, the phone rang. It was Joanne.

"Sorry to disturb you, but it's Inspector Gushue on the line."

"I'll take it."

"I've got to run. I'll catch up with you later," Phil said, heading out the door as David nodded and pressed the flashing button on his phone.

"Morning, David. I've got some news for you," Gushue said.

"Good or bad?"

"Maybe a bit of both. You said the drive-by was the night of the fifteenth, right?"

"Yeah, it was a Tuesday," David said, checking his desk calendar to confirm the date.

"Well, it wasn't Tom."

"How do you know?"

"Cause he was in the emergency room at the Health Sciences."

"Are you sure?" David sat down.

"I checked the ER records myself. He was there from nine until after midnight."

"What for?"

"Sprained his wrist moving furniture—so he says. Had to stick around for an x-ray and it was a busy night. It's all there in the hospital records."

David's mind was racing, trying to fit this information into place.

"You still there?" Gushue asked.

"So, what does that mean?"

"Well, for starters it means he didn't try to run you over."

"What about the letter?"

"Good question. All we know for sure is it was dropped off at a mailbox downtown the day before Tom showed up at your place. We didn't get anything in the way of prints."

"So it's looking more like someone other than Tom."

"I didn't say that…"

"Well, why the hell would he show up at my house, the day after he'd mailed me a letter telling me he was going to take out my whole family, and threaten me some more?"

"You said yourself he was drunk."

"I said he was drunk, not brain-dead. Jesus," David threw his head back in exasperation. "I should never have made that statement."

"You did the right thing. If it's not Tom, we have to find out who it was."

"I've got to go," David sighed.

"I'll keep in touch."

David hung up the phone and looked out the window. This was becoming a nightmare. Not only had he betrayed his own client and possibly damaged his future at the firm, he was further than ever from determining who was behind all this, or why.

chapter forty-four

"So what do we do now?" Elizabeth said, her hand over her mouth as she paced the floor of her parents' living room.

"I don't know. I don't even know where to start," David replied, as he got up and put his arms around her. "It'll be alright, I promise you."

Elizabeth's mother entered the room with a tray of tea.

"Here you are," she said, setting it down on the side table and passing David a cup and saucer.

"Thanks…"

She looked out the big picture window at the rain and tut-tutted.

"I can't remember a fall this wet. But still so cold."

"Yes, it's awful," Elizabeth agreed as David sipped his tea silently. The events of the past few days had been difficult for David and Elizabeth, but also for her parents. David's were on holiday for another week and he hadn't told them, so as not to ruin their trip. Elizabeth's parents had been gravely concerned by it all, and though her mother had been as understanding as could be expected in the circumstances—David didn't blame her for being upset—her father had been quick to blame it all on David's choice of career.

"Any news from the police, David?" Elizabeth's mother asked.

"No, I'm afraid not," David replied.

"Your father spoke to the travel agent this morning," she said, turning to Elizabeth. "He's booked two open-return tickets to Tampa."

"I thought we agreed we'd talk about that," Elizabeth said. "David can't just up and leave, you know."

"Maybe you should go with Ben," David said. "I'm sure it's just a prank, but you can't be too careful."

"I'm not going to Florida without you," she said, shaking her head. "I feel safer here."

"Why don't I come along, if David can't go?" her mother offered.

"This is ridiculous," Elizabeth said. "I'm not having my life hijacked by some lunatic."

"The RNC has offered to put an unmarked car outside the house at night," David said.

"There, that settles it. We'll stay here until this blows over."

David looked to Elizabeth's mother for a reaction. She and Elizabeth were both very strong-willed women when they wanted to be. And though it sometimes drove him crazy, David had to admire Elizabeth's spirit.

"Very well," her mother said with a sigh. "But your father is not going to like it."

As if on cue, a beam of light crossed the front window as Dr. Lloyd Furlong's car pulled into the driveway.

"Here he is now. I'll tell him myself," Elizabeth said, with a wink to David.

Later, as he lay awake in bed in the guest room, with Elizabeth asleep at his side, David racked his brain for some explanation of the mysterious series of recent events. Despite his assurances to Elizabeth and her family to the contrary, David was worried. He had not told them about his encounters with Tom or the unidentified car for fear of sending them into a panic, and while he felt uneasy about withholding this information from his wife, he didn't know what good it would do her. He went back over everything Gushue had said and decided that for all intents and purposes, the police investigation was at an end. With no evidence worth anything from the letter, there was really very little they could do other than watch and wait. In any case, regardless of Tom's alibi for the night of the drive-by, David was sure Gushue thought the letter was Tom's doing. In fact, although Gushue refused to admit it, David suspected the RNC's real focus now was using his statement to reopen the murder case against Tom.

For his part, David felt nothing but shame whenever he thought of his statement to Gushue. It had been a very short jump indeed to the conclusion that it was all Tom's fault. In a matter of minutes, he had swept away a bond of trust that had taken him over a year to earn. As he lay awake staring at the ceiling, he knew two things for certain. The first was that whoever had sent that letter was Stuart Bruce's murderer. The second was that David was going to find out who it was, not only for his own sake, but to set things right with Tom Fitzgerald.

chapter forty-five

For the past few days and nights, David had been reviewing Tom
Fitzgerald's file, and there was lots of it to review. Over the course
of a year, thousands of pages of reports, transcripts, research and
other documents had been compiled, and as he flipped through
a transcript of testimony of one of the Crown witnesses, David
wondered whether there was any point in continuing. It was getting
late but he decided before calling it a night, to take a quick peek at
the growing pile in his in-tray that he had been ignoring all week.
Joanne usually did a good job of alerting him to the urgent mail,
so he didn't really expect any ticking time bombs, but he couldn't be
too sure.

David scanned a couple of routine letters and flipped through a Bar
Association newsletter, stopping at a picture in the middle. It was a
photo taken at a dinner party for a class reunion, which didn't interest him nearly as much as the attractive blonde sitting in the centre.
He had seen her in chambers the other morning and had been
impressed with her courtroom skills, as well as her more obvious

attributes. Phil had also mentioned her as being the centre of attention at Unified Family Court among the male segment of the family
law bar. He scanned the fine print under the photo and located her
name. Now he remembered the name—Sharon Cates. He recognized
a few of the other smiling faces and noticed they were all looking
towards someone seated to the right, represented only by an arm in
the right foreground of the picture, holding out a glass of wine. The
man's cufflink caught David's eye and he decided he would have to
get himself a shirt with French cuffs one of these days. It really did
look classy.

David tossed the newsletter into the recycling box under his desk and
switched off his computer. Leaving the office, he discovered a fresh
blanket of snow on the ground and big, fat flakes falling in the still
night air. The snow dampened the noise of the passing cars and as he
crossed Duckworth Street and headed up Church Hill, the scene
reminded him of a Christmas card. He loved Christmas, and his
spirits were buoyed by the knowledge that it was just around the
corner—until he remembered their trip to Florida. If it had seemed
unappealing before, David knew it would be a nightmare now, on the
heels of the events of this past week. The last thing he needed was to
be at close quarters with Elizabeth's extended family, so they could
scold him for endangering Elizabeth and Ben.

As he reached his car, something occurred to him that stopped him
in his tracks. He stood there with the wet flakes gathering on his head
for a moment before retracing his steps back down Church Hill and
to the firm. Reaching his office, he switched on the light and headed
straight for the side table. He picked up one of the accordion folders
and pulled out the crime scene photos, flipping through them one by
one as he stood over his desk, melted snow dripping from his hair.
The picture in the newsletter had struck a chord. The evidence at the
crime scene included a cufflink with the school crest of Osgoode Hall
Law School, the victim's alma mater. As he found the photo he was
looking for, his suspicion was confirmed. He was looking at a picture

of Stuart Bruce's body laying on the grass in Bannerman Park. The picture was quite clear and one of the victim's shirt cuffs was visible, peeking out from the sleeve of his jacket. There could be no doubt that Stuart Bruce was not wearing cufflinks on the night he died.

chapter forty-six

David had lain awake practically all night thinking about the cufflink at the crime scene. It had never occurred to him before that it might not belong to the victim, since it was inscribed with his law school's logo. Trying to revive himself with a long, hot shower while Elizabeth and Ben slept, David stood under the warm jet of the shower, mulling over the possible significance of his discovery. On the one hand, it was entirely possible that the cufflink had fallen out of Stuart Bruce's pocket in the midst of his murder. But the evidence was not consistent with much of a struggle, tending to indicate the killer had taken advantage of the element of surprise. It might also have already been at the scene, but that seemed too much of a coincidence. One other possibility remained: that it belonged to the killer.

David turned off the shower and reached through the steam for a fluffy towel. Within fifteen minutes, he had dressed, kissed his bleary-eyed wife and sleeping son good-bye and rushed off to work without so much as a bagel, promising himself he would get something to eat later. Arriving at the office, he fired up his computer and poured a coffee. He wasn't due in court and Joanne would be another half an hour, so he had at least that much time before having to deal with the morning's emergencies. Logging on to the Internet, he did a search and was soon connecting to the website for Osgoode Hall Law School. He clicked around for another five minutes before he found what he was looking for. He clicked on it and scrolled down through the school's alumni list and swore under his breath when he realized they only had the past five years online. Undeterred, he clicked his way back to the home page and found a phone number for the administrative office. Realizing he had an hour and a half on Ontario, he printed off the page with the phone number and clicked around some more before abandoning his inquiries until he could get in touch with someone by phone.

David sipped some coffee and went over to his side table, gathering up the file he had left the previous evening. He brought it over to his desk and read through the summary of the crime scene evidence again, focusing on the subheading entitled, "Personal Effects." Skimming down through the list, he noticed an entry and a date at the bottom, indicating who had eventually taken possession of the listed items—James Bruce. He remembered the victim's brother from the trial. What had been his reaction on finding the cufflink among his brother's personal effects, he wondered? He wasn't about to call him up and ask him, but from the evidence at trial, the brothers did not appear to have been close. Would he have even known whether his brother wore French cuffs? Probably not, but as he considered it, David knew his first order of business, other than getting that alumni list, would be to find out as much about Stuart Bruce as he possibly could.

At two-thirty in the afternoon, David got in touch with someone in the office of alumni affairs at Osgoode Hall who promised to fax him the class list for 1968. While he waited impatiently, he tried to concentrate on some work, but it was pointless. He was only half-listening to an insurance adjuster's warnings on the phone when Joanne walked in with what looked like the fax.

"I think you'd better pass the file on to your lawyers," David said, nodding to Joanne before hanging up. He grabbed the fax from his in tray.

"Thanks, Jo."

He flipped the cover page over and scanned the class list, recognizing Stuart Bruce's name, but no other.

"Do you have the legal directory out there?" he called out, referring to the annual list of North American lawyers, which appeared in Joanne's hand a few seconds later.

"Thanks. Could you close the door please?"

He picked a name from the alumni list and looked it up. Jane Taylor, now a Q.C. in a big Toronto firm. He called the number and asked for Taylor, and was soon speaking with her secretary.

"Ms. Taylor-Wynn's in a meeting. Would you like to leave a message for her?"

"Uh, no thanks," David said, hanging up. What was he supposed to say? He was the lawyer who had successfully defended the man accused of murdering this woman's classmate, and since there was no official reason for the call, he could hardly expect much cooperation. He sat back and thought for a few minutes. An idea occurred to him, and without thinking too much about it, he picked the next name from the list and looked it up. This one wasn't a Q.C., so maybe there was a chance he would actually get through directly. He dialed the number, another with the 416 area code. After a couple of rings, someone answered.

"Mr. Randall Bryce please," he said.

"Speaking."

Picking a name off a letter on his desk, David replied quickly.

"My name is Scott Jenkins, I'm with the Osgoode Alumni association. I'm doing a piece on the late Stuart Bruce for an upcoming newsletter and I'm trying to contact his former classmates for some background information."

"Oh, I see. Yes, I heard about poor Stuart. What a terrible thing."

"Yes, it was. Did you know him well?"

"Not especially. We weren't really in the same social circle."

"Well, what can you tell me about him?" David continued hopefully, ignoring the propriety of this little charade.

"He certainly was very bright. Always had the last word with the professors, moot champion, that sort of thing."

"Was he a popular student?"

"He was certainly well-known," Bryce answered diplomatically, without adding more.

"What about after law school? Did you cross paths at all?"

"Not really. I went out west for a few years before coming back to do criminal work. Stuart went straight to Bay Street. Securities and commercial litigation I think, and very good at it by all accounts."

"Yes, I've heard," David lied.

"So when is this article going to be published?"

"We're not exactly sure yet. Probably some time in the new year," David said, sensing the need to end the conversation. He asked a few more routine questions before thanking Bryce for his time and politely wrapping it up.

David hung up the phone and looked at his watch. He still had lots of time before business hours came to a close in the eastern time zone. He quickly looked up another name and dialed the number, feeling his heart rate quicken a little.

chapter forty-seven
—november

"Are you out of your mind?" Phil said, practically choking on his coffee as the two sat in the Duckworth Street Deli, a favourite among St. John's lawyers.

"Calm down," David said, hushing him. "It's not that bad…"

"Not that bad? You're impersonating someone else—you could be disbarred for stuff like that."

David shook his head.

"Nobody's going to disbar me Phil. Besides, it's not like I'm using my real name."

"This is the 21st century," Phil protested. "Have you ever heard of caller ID?"

David knew he was right but tried to downplay the danger.

"I'm just trying to get some information…unofficially."

"And what are you going to do if someone calls your bluff? These are lawyers you're talking to, not the most trusting people in the world."

"I don't know what else to do. I've got to start somewhere."

"Why?"

"You know why, Phil. For my own sake, and for Tom's, I need to know who killed Stuart Bruce, and since I don't know who the murderer is, I'm trying to find out as much as I can about the victim."

"Surely the police can do a better job."

"Gushue's convinced, along with the rest of the RNC, that they've already got their man. He's not going to follow up on anything, unless it incriminates Tom."

"Well you're not going to be much use to yourself or Tom if you get busted for obtaining information under false pretences," Phil said.

"So what do you suggest?"

"I've got an uncle in Toronto. Used to be a cop, now he's a private eye."

"Really?"

"Yeah. Spends a lot of time getting dirt on cheating spouses—that kind of thing. Last time I was there, he took me out for a beer and he showed me his personal favourites. It's amazing what you can get with a telephoto lens...," he shook his head. "Anyway, the point is, I did some legal work for him and he owes me a favour. If you get me the numbers I'm sure he'd make a couple of calls for you."

"Are you sure? I can..."

"Get me the numbers and I'll call him tonight."

David was sitting at his desk, reviewing the judgment on one of his recent civil trials. By the second page, he experienced a sinking feeling as he realized the line of reasoning the judge was laying out was not looking good for his client. Unable to maintain his focus, he skipped to the last page and read the conclusion. He sighed and tossed the decision onto the desk. Having found the defendant liable for the motor vehicle accident that had caused David's client—Gerry Burden—to sustain injuries, Judge Edward O'Reilly had decided not to believe any of the evidence David had put before him as to its severity. Burden's testimony, as well as that of his family doctor, an orthopaedic surgeon, and a chiropractor had all described a significant injury to the lower back as a result of being rear-ended while sitting in traffic. But O'Reilly would have none of it, preferring to rely on the insurance company's expert witness. An orthopaedic surgeon from Halifax, he had been flown in for a one-hour assessment and summarily decided that there was nothing wrong with Burden's back, and furthermore, that he was a malingerer. David had attacked on his cross-examination, pointing out that in the dozens of cases the good doctor had assessed for this particular insurance company, he had never found anyone to have a compensable injury. He thought he had scored points on the cross, but apparently, O'Reilly had not been impressed.

David put his feet up on the desk and rubbed his eyes. It was only mid-morning and he was exhausted already. It had been almost a week since Phil had contacted his uncle and asked to check out the alumni list, and David was hopeful he would soon have some news. There had been nothing from Gushue, which wasn't surprising. David longed for a good night's sleep in his own bed but Elizabeth insisted on them staying at her parents' house for the time being, and the lack of sleep, combined with the invisible but constant tension whenever her father was in the house, was beginning to wear him down. Now, he had the Burden decision to deal with.

Gerry Burden had originally been McGrath's client, but upon reviewing the file and seeing that it was a straightforward winner on liability and not a particularly lucrative injury, McGrath had passed it off to David. But its relative unimportance didn't make McGrath's expectations any less demanding, and the result was definitely not good news. This was only David's third personal injury trial and his first defeat, having obtained a reasonable level of damages for his clients in the first two, and he couldn't help feeling crushed at the result this time around. David looked out the window, but the grey morning offered no comfort. The previous night's snowfall had been pounded since dawn with a cold, heavy rain that had turned it into a sloppy mess of slush. He rose from his chair, ignoring the ringing phone and trying to decide whether to face the music from his client or his boss first. He wondered which would be worse.

chapter forty-eight

"Dada," said Ben as he saw his father come through the front door, dripping wet from the rain outside.

"Come here," David said, scooping him up and tickling him until he giggled and squirmed.

"You're home early," Elizabeth said, appearing in the front hall. "How was your day?"

"Don't ask," he replied, putting Ben down and taking off his coat.

"That bad?" Elizabeth said, cocking her head.

"Worse."

"Well," she said, pecking him on the cheek and putting her arm around his waist. "Come into the kitchen and have a glass of wine and tell me all about it."

"Where is everyone?"

"Dad got called in for surgery and Mom is at Janet's helping her pick out wallpaper."

"Oh," David said, suppressing a smile.

"And don't pretend you're disappointed," she said, slapping his arm playfully.

"Where's that wine?" he said, as they made their way back to the kitchen, while Ben ran through their legs, waving a toy plane around.

"So, what is it?" she asked, handing him his wine.

"I lost a case."

"You're probably not the only lawyer in the world to suffer that fate, are you?"

"It was one of McGrath's," he added, as though he need say nothing more.

"So did you give it any less effort because it was McGrath's?"

"Of course not."

"Then you either accept it and move on, or you appeal."

"It's not quite as simple as that," he said shaking his head.

"Why not?"

"I can only appeal on certain grounds, and anyway to a certain extent the damage is done."

"Why?"

"Because McGrath gave me the file and I blew it, that's why."

Elizabeth put the wooden spoon back in the pot and picked up her wine glass.

"If McGrath is so concerned about winning all of his client's cases, maybe he should try them all himself," she said, sipping her wine.

"But this was such a slam dunk, I still can't believe we didn't get anything for damages. I just seem to be in a bad place right now, what with the whole Tom thing, and the letter."

"You're just having a bad day, that's all. Everyone has them."

"Bad month you mean," he sighed.

"People have those too, and this weather isn't helping," she said, looking out the kitchen window. "I've had a pretty good day but every time I look outside or hear that fog horn I feel a suicidal urge coming on."

She put down her glass and approached David, putting her arms around him and planting a kiss on his lips.

"Maybe it's time we went back to our own home," she said, looking up at him.

"Really?" David smiled.

"The more I think of it, the more the letter seems like a hoax."

David nodded.

"And your father?"

"You let me worry about Dad. I can handle him."

"Oh, I know you can handle him," David said with a chuckle.

"And what do you mean by that?" she said in mock indignation.

"Oh nothing," he said, kissing her until they were both jolted by an ear-splitting crash from the dining room.

"What the hell...," David rushed into the adjoining room, with Elizabeth right behind him. The two just stared in silence at their son, who was standing on the dining room table, toy airplane in hand, surrounded by the shattered crystal that had once been a chandelier.

"I think now would be an excellent time to go back to our house," David said flatly, a smile on his face.

"Benjamin Hall," Elizabeth said, putting her hand over her mouth.

chapter forty-nine

David was hit by a rush of warm air as he stamped his feet and the firm's heavy front door swung shut behind him. Another dusting of snow had fallen overnight and as he shook off a chill, it felt as though winter might be here to stay. He slipped off his overshoes and made his way into the reception area, where the phones were ringing and the support staff were buzzing, even at this early hour. November was always a busy month at the firm, and this year was no exception. He climbed the stairs and said his customary good mornings on arriving at the second floor. Joanne was on the phone and nodded acknowledgement as he entered his office, noting the fresh stack of files in his in-tray. He took off his coat, choosing to keep his suit jacket on until he warmed up, and switched on his computer.

Frowning with disapproval at his brown-ringed cup, David made for the coffee machine by the stairs and was pouring his morning salvation into a clean mug when Joanne hung up the phone.

"Morning, David."

"Morning, Jo. Nice looking pile you dropped on the corner of my desk."

"That's just for starters. I'm working on another pile over here," she said pointing to a stack on her side table.

David pulled a face.

"I took a call for you from John Pearcey earlier," Joanne added, trying to prioritize his day. "He said it was important."

"Hmm," David muttered, tossing some sugar in his murky brew. "Wonder what he wants."

"Beware the Reaper," Phil Morgan said, emerging from his office with a smirk.

"Very funny," David said.

Apart from being a prominent member of the St. John's criminal bar, John Pearcey was the chair of the Law Society's Discipline Committee.

"I'm kidding," Phil said, noting David's glum expression. "I'm sure he's calling about a file."

"How was the West Coast?" David asked, referring to Phil's trip to Corner Brook on a family law trial.

"Just grand," Phil said, pouring himself a coffee and following David into his office. "Talk about a hostile atmosphere."

"So they really do hate St. John's lawyers out there, do they?"

"Apparently so," Phil shook his head. "So, how did it go with McGrath?"

"Oh, he was thrilled," David said sarcastically. "You know, he complimented me on losing the case. And as for Burden, well, he was a really happy camper too."

"He can't blame you. He had a lot of pre-existing back problems didn't he?"

"He was entitled to something, though."

"Maybe."

"Either way, McGrath's less than impressed."

"Don't worry about it," Phil said. "By the way, have you heard anything from my uncle?"

"No," David said as Joanne came in with a list of phone messages.

"I think he left a message on the service last night," she said, pointing to one of the messages.

"Well, there you go," David smiled. "I'll give him a call right after I find out what Pearcey wants with me."

"Yeah, do that," Phil said. "I've got a pre-trial I've got to go finish preparing for. I'll catch up with you later."

David stood staring at the menu behind the counter at the Duckworth Street Deli. He was vaguely aware of a dull noise all around him as he fixated on the menu. It seemed to be getting bigger and brighter before his eyes. His reverie was interrupted by a terse voice.

"Sir?"

"Yes?" he snapped back to reality as the young girl behind the counter came into focus.

"Dollar fifty please."

"Oh," he said awkwardly, realizing he had been daydreaming in the line-up. He quickly paid for his coffee and headed for the door, bumping into Phil on the way out.

"There you are. I've been looking for you all afternoon. My uncle's trying to get in touch with you."

"I'm in shit, Phil," he said quietly.

"What are you talking about?"

"The call from Pearcey this morning. You were right; somebody filed a complaint with the Law Society."

Phil looked surprised.

"It's one of the people I called for information about Stuart Bruce," David added.

"You mean…"

"They must have checked with the law school and discovered I was lying."

"But how would they know who you were?"

"Probably call display, just like you said. The point is, they know. And now the Law Society knows too."

"Ah," Phil shook his head. "They're not going to do anything…"

"They're looking into whether it warrants a hearing."

The news seemed to catch Phil off-guard, but he recovered quickly. "Why don't you call the guy up and apologize," he suggested.

"Even if I do, I don't know if they can drop a complaint once it's filed. I have to check the rules but I think a hearing is automatic."

"Who else is on the committee?" Phil asked, considering the options.

"Bunch of old boys I think. No one who's going to give me a break."

"Well, what does a hearing really mean anyway?"

"It's pretty formal actually. A panel of three, witnesses, legal counsel for both sides in some cases…"

"Forget that," Phil said quickly, pulling him towards the door. "You check out the procedural rules. See if there's any discretion to toss a complaint. I'll make a few calls and see who's on the committee. Maybe someone can help."

David followed him back outside reluctantly.

———————

Sitting in his office with the door closed poring over the procedural rules of the Law Society's Discipline Committee, David wondered how he could have been so careless. And he could only shudder at the thought of what would happen if McGrath got wind of this prank. David was already in his black books for turning on his former client, and blowing the Burden case. This would be the final straw. As he scanned the rules, looking for an out, the phone rang. Recognizing the Toronto area code he picked it up.

"David Hall."

"Hi David, Marty Brown calling. Phil's uncle."

"Hello. I'm sorry I didn't get back to you earlier. It's been one of those days."

"No problem. You got a minute?"

"Yes, sure. I want to thank you for helping out," David said.

"Well don't thank me yet. I didn't really find out much. I got in touch with some former classmates and people the victim worked with and didn't discover anything unusual."

"I see."

"Seems like a real go-getter. Smart guy, top of his class, worked in a big Toronto firm for ten years or so and then set up his own shop and made a shitload of money in the process."

"Go on."

"He was your typical class A-type workaholic. His main focus was securities law, but he also represented a lot of multinational insurance companies."

"I imagine that didn't leave much time for a life outside work though," David said.

"Nope. Failed marriage early on and no time for much else after that. He died a bachelor. He did have one brother, not very close though."

David remembered James Bruce from the trial.

"Enemies?" David asked.

"Lots of 'em. And so much for respecting the dead. Jeez, you'd be surprised at the emotions his name brought out. He was known as quite a hard-ass. Do anything to win."

"Don't suppose anyone confessed to killing him, did they?" David asked hopefully.

"I'm afraid not. I located most of the people on the class list—I'll fax you my notes—but there are a few MIAs. You want me to check them out?"

"Don't bother. You've done enough already. What do I owe you?"

"It's a favour for my nephew. On the house."

"Thanks again," David said. He was a little disappointed that nothing had turned up, but at this point, he was more interested in trying to preserve what was left of his career. And in his frustration, he felt like forgetting he had ever come across the name Tom Fitzgerald. It had brought him nothing but trouble.

As the grey November sky turned to black outside, and the rush hour traffic on Duckworth Street picked up, David sought solace from the desktop picture of Elizabeth and Ben taken under the statue in Bowring Park, before returning gloomily to his research.

chapter fifty

It was just after nine the next morning when McGrath appeared at David's door. He didn't bother to knock, preferring to enter and close the door behind him, which David knew was a bad sign.

"What's all this about a Law Society complaint?" he said, leaning on the closed door.

"How did you…"

"So it's true. You were calling people pretending to be with Alumni Affairs—that's true too, I suppose?"

David acknowledged him with a slight nod of his head and braced himself. This was not going to be pleasant.

"Do you know what they could do to you, David?"

Not giving much time for a reply, McGrath answered his own question. "They could suspend your licence for this."

"It was a stupid thing to do, but I felt there was no other choice."

"What the hell are you talking about?" McGrath asked, shaking his head and pacing back and forth in silence before continuing. "Look David, I can understand this threatening letter rattling you but I just don't know what you're going to do next. First, you give a statement to the cops about your own client, and now you're impersonating people to find out about his alleged victim. What in God's name were you thinking?"

"The statement was an error in judgment, I admit that. But in the circumstances, I'm a little surprised at the firm's reaction…"

"You're lucky I didn't throw your ass out on the street," McGrath ranted. "This firm has a reputation to uphold, David. How do you think it makes us look, as a unit, when one of us turns on his own client? Jesus Christ, we were considering making you a partner and you go and do something like that on your own, without so much as a warning to me, or anyone else."

"I was concerned about the safety of my family—I still am!"

"Fine, but you're not working alone here. You should have come to me for help. You can't just do whatever the hell you want and expect everyone else to just nod and smile."

David kept his eyes on the desk in front of him, while McGrath paced. Joanne knocked on the door and peeked inside, about to ask David something, but seeing McGrath and noting the expression on his face, she opted for a hushed apology instead, quickly closing the door again.

"With the statement, even though I think you should have had the courtesy to talk to me about it first, at least I can understand your motives. But the Law Society complaint…that I can't understand."

"The letter wasn't sent by Tom, I'm convinced of that, but the RNC has its blinders on and they won't look anywhere else. Gushue's busy trying to take another run at Tom, so the letter is great for him. And yes, the statement was stupid of me, Gushue used me and now that he's got what he wants, he doesn't give a shit about who really wrote that letter or what it means."

"But the case is over David, you have to move on. Take a holiday with your family."

"You know what Bill? I want to drop it—I really do—but I can't. I can't because I don't think it is over. Gushue sure as hell doesn't think so."

"Never mind Gushue," McGrath said with a wave of his hand. "The Crown's never going to try and take another run at Tom. I know there are exceptions to double jeopardy, but he's got to be in the clear on this one."

"I'm not so sure," David said, shaking his head. "In fact, I'm starting to wonder if Gallant had this in mind the whole time."

"What do you mean?" McGrath looked puzzled.

"You don't think it was strange the Crown didn't appeal?"

"I think they realized it was a fairly tight legal judgment that left little or no technical grounds for an appeal," McGrath replied, shrugging his shoulders.

"Exactly, so officially they throw in the towel, and instead of wasting time on an appeal they can't win, they devote their time and energy to taking another shot on a different charge—like manslaughter."

"That sounds pretty far-fetched," McGrath said, sitting down for the first time and considering the possibility.

"Not if you look at the way Gushue's acting. And the worse thing is I've probably given him exactly what he wants with my statement."

McGrath sat silently for a moment.

"Even if they were considering it," he said, "why not wait for them to lay a charge, instead of sneaking around like some cut-rate gumshoe trying to get information?"

"You know as well as I do that it'll be too late once they start the legal process all over—they'll never drop it. Another trial would mean another year or more of Tom's life in limbo, and having been acquitted based on a defence like automatism on the first charge, what do you think his chances of another acquittal would be?"

McGrath got up and started pacing again, apparently considering David's arguments.

"So what about this complaint. How do you plan to handle it?"

"I've checked out the rules of the discipline committee and basically there has to be an automatic hearing every time a complaint of fraud is filed. But there is one out."

"What's that?"

"If the person making the compaint withdraws it, but even then the chair still has discretion to proceed, so I'd have to convince Pearcey…"

"Never mind Pearcey, I can handle him," McGrath said sitting down again, and leaning forward in the chair. "What you need to do is work on the complainant."

David nodded slowly, surprised to be thrown a line.

"Can you do that?"

"I have no choice," David said quietly.

"And when the complaint's out of the way, we'll discuss the rest," he said, getting up to leave and stopping at the door.

"And don't believe every rumour you hear, David. We're still a team around here you know."

David nodded as McGrath disappeared out the door. He was just beginning to regain his composure when Joanne appeared at the door, looking worried.

"Come in Jo."

"You're late…," she said, looking at her watch.

"For what?" he asked.

"Provincial Court—the White sentencing, remember?"

It took a few seconds to register in his mind that he had been preparing for the sentencing as McGrath had walked in.

"Shit!" he said, grabbing the file and reaching for his jacket.

"I tried to interrupt your meeting but it seemed…" She stopped in mid-sentence as her boss was already halfway down the stairs, with his suit jacket half on and no overcoat, despite the frigid weather that awaited him outside.

chapter fifty-one

It was almost six p.m. and it had been a very long day. The morning's run in with McGrath, combined with a busy day, had left him exhausted. He was putting on his jacket when the phone rang. He had no intention of answering it but glanced at the phone anyway, out of habit. He noticed the number was from an area code he did not recognize and his curiosity overcame his fatigue. He didn't recognize the voice at the other end at all.

"David Hall."

"Mr. Hall, my name is Erin Hay. I'm returning your call about Stuart Bruce."

David paused for a moment, realizing that in the confusion of the past few days, he had forgotten leaving a message with one person on the Osgoode alumni list other than Randall Bryce—a lawyer in Chicago.

"I realize you're probably near the end of your day there," she said, "but if you wanted to talk about Stuart…"

"Actually, Ms. Hay, I should tell you…," David began, not wanting to provide grounds for another complaint to the Law Society.

"How is Stuart anyway?" she interrupted.

"You didn't know?"

"Didn't know what?"

"He was killed, about a year and a half ago."

"Oh my God. I had no idea."

"I'm afraid so."

"I moved to the States twenty years ago and lost touch with most of the old law school gang. I just assumed you were calling about some sort of class reunion. But this is awful—poor Stuart."

"Look, Ms. Hay. I have to be honest with you. I'm not really with Alumni Affairs at Osgoode."

"I don't understand."

"I'm the lawyer for the man accused of Stuart Bruce's murder."

"Why would you…"

"I was just trying to find out some background information about Mr. Bruce, but I shouldn't have bothered you."

"When is the trial?"

"My client was acquitted several months ago."

"So why the need for more information. Is there an appeal?"

"No, I was just doing some follow-up work."

She paused at the other end as David prepared to thank her again for her trouble and hang up.

"What sort of information were you looking for?" she asked.

David was surprised she still wanted to talk.

"Anything, nothing—I don't know. What kind of a student was he? What kind of a person? Very general I suppose."

"He was very bright, and the kind of guy you couldn't help but admire."

"So you liked him?"

"He could certainly be charming, engaging, and I couldn't help but admire his ruthlessness when he showed it."

"Really," David took out a pad and sat at his chair, scribbling her name at the top of the page.

"How was he ruthless?"

"Maybe that's not the right word. He was just so full of self-confidence. I think he expected it to come naturally to everyone else. He just sort of said whatever was on his mind, without necessarily intending to hurt anyone else."

"But he did?"

"Sometimes," she said, pausing. "I'd be interested to know how our classmates described him."

"I really didn't get very far in my inquiries…"

"I see," she replied, seeming unsure of whether to continue. "Well, like I said, I really haven't been in touch so I'm not sure I'm the best person to give you current information."

"I understand," David said. "Before you go, do you have any idea how I can get in touch with Laura Berkley or Bill Stanley? They're the only two left on the alumni list that are unaccounted for."

"You're not going to pull your Alumni Affairs stunt again are you?"

"No, of course not. That was a mistake. All I want to do is touch base with them. And whether they want to talk to me once I tell them who I am is entirely up to them."

"I'm pretty sure Laura got married while we were articling and changed her name, though I can't remember what it was. As for Will, I doubt you'll track him down."

"Why do you say that?" David asked.

"He went through a bit of a rough time while I was still working in Toronto…maybe it's not appropriate for me to be discussing it…anyway, it's been thirty years."

"I understand," David said, wondering what she was leaving out, though whatever it was had to be irrelevant after all that time—as was this whole conversation the more he thought about it.

"Well, I appreciate your time Ms. Hay."

"You're welcome," she said, hanging up.

David put the receiver down, his eyes lingering over Stanley's name before he tossed the alumni list into his desk drawer. He got up and put on his coat, and had gotten to the landing before his curiosity got the better of him. Returning to his office, he dug around underneath his side table and pulled out a box that contained part of Tom's file. He retrieved a file folder and sat behind his desk, flipping through it until he found what he was looking for—the inventory of evidence from Stuart Bruce's hotel room, taken the morning following the murder. Scanning the list of items that had been catalogued, he stopped at a piece of hotel stationary that had been found on the desk by the phone in Bruce's room. The notes confirmed his memory of what was written on the pad. His curiosity satisfied, he considered the words for a moment longer, then tossed the file onto his desk and headed for home.

chapter fifty-two

"So what's up with the complaint?" Phil asked as he and David left the counter at the Supreme Court registry, having filed some court papers after finishing their respective morning appearances in chambers.

"I spoke to Randall Bryce this morning and explained why I did it. He seemed to accept my apology but he said he'd have to think about withdrawing the complaint."

As they neared the Water Street exit, they stopped to button up their overcoats against the cold November wind blowing outside.

"What does your gut say?" Phil asked.

"I don't know, but whether it goes ahead or not, the damage is done."

"You mean with McGrath?"

"I feel like I'm doomed at that firm, like it's only a matter of time."

"Don't be so hard on yourself. And as for McGrath, he'll get over it."

"He should never have found out—that's the other thing."

"Still no idea who told him?"

"No. There aren't that many people who would have known…"

"Probably someone on the Law Society staff mentioned it over a coffee to the wrong person. You know how easily it can happen in this town."

"So much for confidentiality."

"You know what?" David said, as Phil opened the door and they braced themselves for the cold. "If I get out of this complaint in one piece, I'm going to forget about this whole mess. I've wasted enough time and energy on it already, and where's it gotten me?"

"You're probably right."

"The letter must have been a crank, and I haven't heard anything since. As for the car, it could have been anything really—probably a drunk driver."

Just as they were about to leave, Inspector Gushue bounded up the steps and in through the open door.

"Jesus it's enough to freeze you out there…Hello gentlemen," Gushue said as he rubbed his hands together and blew into them.

"Got a minute?" he asked, looking at David.

"I was just leaving actually," David said.

"I can see that, but this won't take long," Gushue persisted.

"I'll catch up with you back at the office," David said to Phil, who nodded and headed out the door.

"What's up?" David asked.

"Let's take a load off," Gushue said, leading the way from the doorway to a bench at the foot of the stairs leading down from the courtrooms above. "I wanted to talk to you about the Bruce case."

"What about it?" David asked, immediately on the defensive.

"Now don't go into your shell before you hear what I've got to say. I know you think we're still after your client—your former client, I guess."

"Are you going to tell me you're not?"

"I'm a practical guy David, and I know that pursuing him any further is a waste of time."

David said nothing, waiting for the catch.

"Which leaves me with a dead man and no one to answer for it."

"So what do you want from me?"

"I've been thinking about your defence a lot lately—how you switched to automatism so late in the game."

David looked puzzled.

"So?"

"Let's cut the shit David. You know I don't really believe in this automatism thing, and maybe you don't either but that's none of my business and you've got your job to do."

"Are we talking officially here?"

"No. This is strictly off the record."

David nodded.

"Now I know you must have considered a conventional defence for Tom; that someone else did it. But because you didn't end up going down that road, none of that evidence ever made it into the record, or anywhere beyond your firm's front door."

"Are you saying you're actually going to start considering a suspect other than Tom?"

"I'm telling you that I've got to start all over again on this case, and I'm asking for any evidence you have that could help me."

David considered it for a moment as a group of lawyers came down the stairs toward them. "Hello," he said to Francis Sullivan, who led the passing group, which included Andrew Royal, Q.C. and another senior lawyer he didn't recognize, all of whom were taking part in a big commercial trial that had been in the news. David hadn't spoken to Sullivan since his thinly veiled job offer several months ago and he sensed a distinct chill as Sullivan passed by now, ignoring David's greeting.

"Friend of yours huh?" Gushue remarked after the group had passed, recognizing the brush off as well.

David ignored the jab.

"Did you guys ever check out Signal Investments?" he asked, returning his attention to Gushue. "It was written on a notepad found in Bruce's hotel room," he added, noticing the puzzled expression on the inspector's face.

"I'm not sure," Gushue shook his head.

"Well, I'll take that as a no."

"Don't forget we found Tom within a hundred yards of Bruce's body with the murder weapon in his hand, and all of Bruce's cash and plastic. We didn't think we had to look much further."

"Alright," David said, holding up his hands. "Point taken. In the circumstances, I can see why it might not have been a high priority."

"So you think it could be something?"

"I don't know. But it's worth checking out."

Gushue nodded, writing the name in his notebook.

"As for any evidence developed for Tom's original defence, I'll have to think about that—carefully."

"Fair enough," Gushue said, before taking a booklet out of his jacket pocket.

"Now," he said "Before I let you go, how about buying a ticket on the RNC raffle?"

David rolled his eyes.

"Those have made the rounds at work already. You guys are going to put me in the poor house."

"Oh come on, a rich lawyer like you."

"Oh yeah, I'm loaded," David said sarcastically. "You see those guys over there?" he whispered, motioning to Sullivan and the other two lawyers now chatting quietly by the entrance to the Registry. "Those are the guys you should be hitting up, not the lowly associates like me."

"Thanks for the tip; I'll get to them later," Gushue said with a smile. "Come on, they're only five bucks each and you could win a cruise."

"Give me two," David sighed, opening his wallet.

chapter fifty-three

David pulled up to the curb outside his house and knew immediately that something was wrong. The presence of Elizabeth's father's spotless Volvo itself was unusual, since Dr. Furlong rarely slummed it in David's neighborhood, whether his daughter lived there or not. But the way it was carelessly parked—half in and half out of the driveway—exposed to passing traffic, was evidence that David's father-in-law had been extremely distracted upon his arrival.

David climbed the steps to the front door and before he could reach it, Elizabeth swung it open and lunged into his arms, crying.

"What's the matter?" David asked, alarmed.

Hearing nothing but muffled sobs, David cradled her face in his hands and asked her again.

"What is it Elizabeth? Where's Ben?"

"Come inside," Elizabeth's father said gruffly from inside the front porch.

David put his arm around Elizabeth and gently directed her inside.

"Please, Elizabeth," he said as he closed the front door behind her. "Tell me what's wrong."

"It's your Goddamn murdering client again—that's what's wrong," Elizabeth's father said with his arms crossed.

"What are you talking about?"

"Someone called here, David…," Elizabeth said, dabbing her eyes with a handkerchief.

"Who called?"

"I don't know. He said…," she took a deep breath. "He said if you ever talk to the police again about the Bruce case, he'd…," she burst into tears.

"What?"

"He said he'd kill us all, starting with Ben."

"Don't you worry honey," her father said, rubbing her shoulder.

David pulled her to him.

"It's okay. We're going to…"

"I hope you're happy David," her father began. "This is what you get for…"

"That's enough Daddy," she interrupted, wiping her eyes. "Can you check on Ben for me?"

"Hmm," he grumbled, before reluctantly heading upstairs.

"When did this happen?" David asked, leading her to the couch and sitting beside her.

"About an hour ago. I called you at the office but you…"

"I came straight from court. I was planning on going back to the office tonight." David said, shaking his head. "I can't believe this is happening—it doesn't make any sense."

"Have you been talking to the police about Tom?"

"Not really, and even if I was, how would anyone know?" David put his hand on her shoulder and looked her in the eye. "Did it sound like Tom?"

"It was muffled, but it was definitely rough around the edges. It was so…so horribly eerie. I'm scared, David. He said if we told the police about the call he would know and he would…"

"This is insane."

"You think it's Tom?" she asked, blowing her nose.

"Why would he do this? He's the obvious suspect if I do tell the cops, so why put his head in the noose?"

"Why would anyone else do it?"

"I don't know. I really don't know."

"I can't stay here like this David, not in this house…"

"It's alright Elizabeth," he said calmly.

"It's not alright David, and you know it. You can't go to the police, and you don't know who's doing it, so how can you say it's alright?" She was angry now, her frustration taking hold.

"I'm sorry Liz. I know you're scared."

"Let's go down to Florida early. We'd be leaving in a couple of weeks anyway," she said plaintively.

"I can't just up and leave. I've got a trial in two days…"

"Well Ben and I are going down with Mom—tomorrow."

David said nothing, and nodded his head. He could hardly blame her.

"That's probably a good idea."

"Please come with us. I'm so afraid."

He kissed her on the cheek and pulled her to him.

"I'll stay at Phil's place until I can get away. It'll be alright, I promise."

chapter fifty-four
—december

"What are you going to do?" Phil said, sitting heavily in David's client chair the next morning.

"I called Charlie Whalen in Toronto to see what he could find out about Signal Investments."

"Your stockbroker friend," Phil nodded. "Where'd you come up with Signal anyway?"

"It was a name Bruce had scribbled on a notepad at the hotel—it's probably nothing. The truth is I don't know what to do, but I'd better think of something soon. If I leave Elizabeth down there too long with her parents, they'll have her talked into leaving me for a respectable doctor."

"And the death threat?"

"I don't think it's for real. I'm sure it's just to scare me off—but I still can't understand why."

"And what if it is for real?"

"I'm not doing anything with Tom's case, so I don't even know how to take it seriously."

The two sat in silence until Joanne knocked at David's door.

"Come in."

"I know you're in a meeting, but Mr. Pearcey is on the phone…"

"I'll take it."

Phil got up.

"I don't know about you but my day is blocked. Let's talk about this tonight—you're staying at my place until this blows over."

"Thanks, Phil."

"Don't mention it," he said, shutting the door behind him.

David picked up the phone.

"David, it's John Pearcey. How are you this morning?"

"Fine, thanks," David said, trying to interpret Pearcey's tone for a telltale sign of what was to come.

"I'm calling to let you know that the discipline committee will be holding a hearing into the complaint against you next week."

David felt his stomach churn. He had known that technically a hearing was a distinct possibility, but he had assumed that the committee would see no need after his apology to Randall Bryce had been accepted.

"I'm surprised," David began. "I mean, since the complaint has been withdrawn…"

"The complaint hasn't been withdrawn," Pearcey interrupted.

"I don't understand," David was taken aback. "After I apologized to

Mr. Bryce, he told me he saw no need to proceed with the complaint. I didn't even ask him to withdraw it."

"Well, I'm afraid he must have changed his mind since the complaint is still before the committee."

"There must be a misunderstanding. Perhaps if I spoke to Mr. Bryce…"

"I wouldn't do that if I were you. You'll be given every opportunity to defend yourself at the hearing," Pearcey said.

"When is this hearing?"

"Tuesday at 9:00 a.m., unless you'd prefer a later date. Mr. Bryce has declined the committee's offer to appear, but his written complaint will be the basis of questioning for the panel of three."

David sighed as he thought of the prospect of three crusty Law Society benchers grilling him over his embarrassing foray into investigative journalism.

"No, I'd rather get it over with as soon as possible. Where is it?" he asked, wondering whether the Law Society would be selling tickets for his public humiliation.

"Hearings are in camera at the Law Society's offices in Atlantic Place," Pearcey continued, as if sensing David's dread, before adding formally, "and you should consider being represented by counsel."

David contemplated this news in silence before it occurred to him to start thinking strategically.

"May I ask who's on the panel?"

"I will be chair. The other two members will be selected from among the benchers, in accordance with the rules."

David had met Pearcey on several occasions and he had always seemed a reasonable sort. Surely he could shed some light on what was really at stake here.

"Mr. Pearcey," he began tentatively. "I realize my actions may have been ill-advised, but I hardly think they warrant all of this. Am I facing serious consequences here?"

Pearcey paused before replying.

"My advice to you is to get counsel for this hearing and to treat it very seriously indeed."

For some time after Pearcey had hung up, David just sat there, the phone still at his ear as a feeling of doom crept over him like a cloud. What on earth had he done?

chapter fifty-five

David's reading was interrupted by the sound of footsteps downstairs in the firm's lobby. It was after nine o'clock and he was reaching the end of his attention span, and with any luck, a forgettable Thursday. After the morning's call from Pearcey, David had drifted through a much too busy schedule in somewhat of a trance, brought on by a mixture of disbelief at the impending hearing, and depression over his current state of general disarray. He needed Elizabeth and Ben now more than ever, to remind him of what was important in his life, but they were a thousand miles away in Florida. As if things weren't bad enough, he found himself stuck with having to prepare for a big discovery the next morning. His only objective was to get through the day tomorrow and try to re-group for next week. He had called Elizabeth at lunch and told her about the hearing, with the hope that her voice would buoy his spirits. But it had only made him long to see her all the more, to the point where he was seriously considering her suggestion of jumping on the first available flight to Tampa Friday afternoon and spending the weekend with her and Ben. But his fleeting hopes of even a brief reunion had been dashed upon remembering an important pre-trial motion on Monday morning that would require his attention on Sunday. Returning to the transcript he was reading, he tried to ignore the footsteps as they made their way up the first landing.

"Working late?"

David looked up to see McGrath standing there, a grim look on his face.

"Yes," David nodded, wondering whether he should mention his upcoming date with a discipline panel. He had only told Phil so far but he knew McGrath would find out from other sources. Bad news always traveled fast. "I've got a discovery tomorrow morning."

"Oh," McGrath nodded. His eyes flickered as he took a swig from a soda can. "Who's on the other side?" he asked.

"Warren," David said, referring to a regular in the rotation of lawyers that acted for one of the big automobile insurers.

"Hmm," McGrath nodded, helping himself to a chair. "Listen, David, I got a call from John Pearcey today about this Law Society thing," he began.

"Oh yeah?" What else was he supposed to say.

"I thought you said the guy was withdrawing his complaint?"

"He was. At least that's what he told me," David sighed. "Now it looks like he's changed his mind."

"Yeah," McGrath nodded. "I s'pose that's not unheard of." McGrath seemed unconvinced. Changing course, he leaned back in the chair. "You got any files against Frank Sullivan?"

David was surprised to hear the name. He had never mentioned Sullivan's overtures to McGrath, and even though he had never considered them, David felt guilty now.

"No, why?"

"Let's just say he's showing a lot of interest in your hearing."

"What do you mean?"

"John Pearcey's a good guy," McGrath continued. "He was good enough to give me the head's up. For whatever reason, Sullivan's got it out for you. He practically invited himself to sit on your panel, and John says he gets the feeling he wants to make an example out of you."

David rolled his eyes and sighed. Now it all made sense. David's lack of response to Sullivan's offer had obviously made him angry. He had heard Sullivan could be petty, and this was a perfect opportunity for him to get back at David for daring to slight him.

"I can't believe this," David said, shaking his head. McGrath waited patiently for him to elaborate.

David sighed again, before spilling the beans.

"Sullivan offered me a job a couple of months ago," he began. McGrath's expression didn't change.

"I said I was flattered but I wasn't planning on going anywhere."

"Uh-huh," McGrath nodded, his finger at his top lip.

"Sullivan said he'd understand if I didn't take the offer, but I guess that wasn't really true."

"I told you, he's a fucking blade. He'll smile right at your face as he's sticking the knife in your back," McGrath grimaced. "I wouldn't be surprised if he called up the complainant and egged him on—that'd be just his style."

"And I'm sure he'll be leaning on whoever's third on the panel to throw the book at me," David said, realizing Sullivan's influence in Law Society matters would be considerable.

"Yes, they all think the sun shines out of his arse over there," McGrath smiled. "He made the Law Society so much money on their investments they were ready to change the rules to let him stay on after his maximum five year term as Treasurer was over."

David's concern was evident in the ashen expression on his face. McGrath looked at him before getting up from the chair and taking a step towards the doorway.

"Yes, you can bet Sullivan will be putting the screws to the rest of the panel to crucify you," he said as a little grin crept over his face. For his part, David saw nothing to laugh at.

"But don't worry about it too much," McGrath drained his soda and tossed it into the wastebasket in the far corner for a three-pointer. "I'll have a talk to John—see if there's anything I can do," he said on his way out.

"Thanks, Bill," David said, trying to remain positive, though given his deteriorating circumstances, there really was little objective cause for optimism.

chapter fifty-six

L ate Friday afternoon, Joanne called in to say Charlie Whalen was on the line.

"Charlie?" David said, picking up the phone.

"No, it's Santa Claus," Charlie dead-panned, in his usual sarcastic fashion.

"Very funny. What have you got?"

"Well, nothing official, but lots off the record from the OSC," Charlie said, referring to a drinking buddy he had at the Ontario Securities Commission.

"What do you mean?"

"Signal Investments was the subject of a lot of complaints going back a few years, regarding a public offering that went bad."

"How bad?"

"About $3.5 million worth of bad. Everyone who bought in lost their shirts."

"But there was no official investigation?"

"No. Several different investors wanted a forensic audit, but because there was no evidence of any wrongdoing, nothing was done—officially."

"And unofficially?"

"Signal was looked at, but inquiries about its majority shareholder got tied up in red tape."

"How?"

"It's a privately-held offshore, domiciled in the Channel Islands—Guernsey I think."

"So?"

"So they ran into a disclosure problem. More like a brick wall actually. Those guys are worse than the Swiss when it comes to giving up information."

"There must be some way to find out who owned the shares though, isn't there?"

"Not always. And whoever it was took great pains to keep their identity secret."

"And if it were part of a criminal investigation?"

"Still no guarantee you'd find out, but at least you'd have a shot," Charlie said. "But I did find out something else that might interest you."

"Oh yeah?"

"My contact tells me someone fairly high up at the OSC had some informal discussions with legal counsel about whether there was anything the Commission could do to get to the bottom of the Signal deal. The lawyer's name was Stuart Bruce—isn't that the dead guy?"

David was speechless.

"You there?"

"Yeah, I'm here. If Bruce was investigating Signal and found out something…"

"But he hadn't even been retained," Charlie said. "They were just preliminary discussions."

"Either way, that's a hell of a coincidence," David replied, convinced there was nothing coincidental about the whole business. "Listen Charlie, I owe you big time."

"No sweat. But if anyone wants to know, you didn't come by any of this information through me."

"Understood."

David thanked him again before they said their goodbyes. After he hung up the phone, he sat for a moment in silence, mulling over the information. On the one hand, it was a fresh trail of evidence suggesting a potential motive for someone to want to get rid of Stuart Bruce. On the other, it didn't seem very likely that whoever was behind Signal would be easy to identify, and the connection between a murder in Bannerman Park and an off-shore swindle seemed more than a little unlikely. Perhaps he was letting his imagination get the better of him. He looked at his watch and decided he'd had enough for the day. As if on cue, Phil popped his head around the door. He took one look at David's haggard face and decided brutal honesty was the best policy.

"You look like shit."

"Thanks."

"My pleasure. Come on, I'll buy you a drink."

"Best plan I've heard all day," David replied, switching off his computer and pulling on his jacket.

chapter fifty-seven

David stepped off the elevator and made his way to the Law Society's reception area, giving his name to the receptionist before taking a seat. He scanned the selection of magazines and decided to give them a pass, preferring to fidget nervously while he awaited his lambasting. He had spent an awful weekend, alternating between missing Elizabeth and Ben, and worrying about what Francis Sullivan was cooking up for him this morning. Phil and Judy had refused to let him wallow in negativity, insisting David join them for a night out on Saturday. And though he had protested at first, he was glad he had gone along. Who knew how low he might have sunk if he hadn't been forced to laugh a little. Thankfully, the latter part of Sunday and all day yesterday had been devoted to a hotly-contested motion that at least had forced him to concentrate on something other than his current personal woes.

As he sat there waiting for his hearing, he had to smile at the irony of his current predicament. For the next hour or so, he would face some very embarrassing questions from the same man who only a few months before had been offering him a job. But he took heart in the knowledge that while he would certainly not enjoy the process, the end result was not likely to be very damaging. Late in the day on Monday, McGrath had dropped in to mention that he'd "had a chat" with Pearcey and was confidant that David would survive the hearing with his professional qualifications intact. David's chief remaining concern was the identity of the third member of the panel. He cringed at the thought it could be one of the senior crown prosecutors he would have to deal with on a regular basis.

He looked at his watch and sighed quietly, adjusting his tie and trying his best at a genuine smile for the benefit of the receptionist as she looked his way. Just then, the electronic ping of the elevator sounded and David heard the sound of approaching footsteps. As he turned to see who it was, he was surprised to see Bill McGrath waving a greeting his way before approaching the receptionist.

"They're waiting for you in there, Mr. McGrath," she said, pointing to a boardroom down the hall. McGrath smiled and turned to David, now standing in the reception area, a puzzled expression on his face.

"What are you doing here Bill?"

McGrath flashed him a grin and patted him on the shoulder.

"I'm here to sit on your panel—I'm the third," he said.

"But I thought…"

"Let's just say Sullivan's not the only one with pull around here," McGrath said quietly, as he leaned towards him. "Just tell the truth and you'll be fine. I'll see you in there."

With that, McGrath disappeared into the boardroom, leaving David agape in surprise. He sat back down and collected himself, a smile unconsciously appearing on his face.

"I don't know what to say Bill," David said as the elevator doors closed on the Law Society offices and they began their descent. The hearing had lasted only thirty minutes, and though it had indeed been an uncomfortable experience, the decision of the panel was not to punish David for his masquerade beyond a warning and an undertaking from him never to engage in similar conduct again.

"You should have seen the face on him when I walked in," McGrath said, laughing out loud. Sullivan's apparent plan to use the hearing to inflict career damage on David had actually gone out the window the night before, when John Pearcey had called to let him know who would be the third member of the panel. The sheer force of Sullivan's protest to McGrath's selection—despite the fact that the latter was as qualified as any of Sullivan's other recommendations under the Law Society rules—was ample proof to Pearcey that Sullivan had no intention of being objective in David's case, and made the selection all the easier to justify to himself.

"I've said it before, and I'll say it again to you now David—watch your back with that guy."

"I don't know what his problem is," David shook his head.

"Ah, he's been like that ever since he got here," McGrath gave a dismissive wave.

"What do you mean, when he got here—I thought he was from St. John's?"

"Naw, he's a mainlander—Toronto I think. Came around the time I started practicing. Even then, he had this attitude that he owns the friggin' place, and it's only gotten worse over the years."

"Well at least I know what to expect from him from here on in," David said as the elevator doors opened on the lobby. He put out his hand and McGrath took it in a firm shake.

"Thanks again, Bill. I've got to say I've never been so happy to see your face in all my life."

"My pleasure," McGrath smiled. "Just pissin' him off was worth it anyway."

As they walked towards the main entrance, onto Water Street, McGrath slowed and turned to face him.

"I know you've had a lousy couple of weeks, David, but now that this complaint's out of the way, maybe you should take some time and catch up with your family."

"I was thinking of going down this weekend, now that you mention it."

"Why wait? I'm sure you can get someone to cover whatever's on your plate for the rest of the week. Sometimes you need to get away for a while just to clear your head."

David nodded.

"Anyway, I've got a meeting up on Kenmount Road," McGrath said, looking at his watch. "You need a ride?"

"No, I'm good thanks," David replied. "I'm going to grab a coffee before I head back to the office. Maybe I'll stop into the travel agent and check out the flights to Florida."

"Do that," McGrath said with a wave, as he disappeared through the front doors.

———

Having done a quick mental assessment of his obligations for the rest of the week, and the time it might take to find and brief someone, David had decided the earliest he could leave for Florida was Thursday. He had dropped into the travel agent on the ground floor of Atlantic Place and now, armed with printouts of several possible flight options, he followed the fragrant smell of coffee to the food court, and bought himself a large dose of caffeine. As he was making his way back to the lobby, he heard his name from one of the tables off to his right. Following the voice, he saw Inspector Pat Gushue sitting at a table, from which a uniformed officer was taking his leave. Gushue waved him over.

"David, come have a seat."

"What's up?" David replied, remaining on his feet. All he could think of was the recent caller's threatened response to his talking to the police. "Not more raffle tickets I hope."

Gushue laughed.

"No, I figure I cleaned you out by now," he said with a grin. "Come on, sit down. I won't bite."

David looked around at the relatively thin crowd. Morning coffee break had long since passed and only the stragglers remained.

"Thing is," he said, sitting tentatively on the edge of the seat. "I'm kind of in a rush."

"Won't take long," Gushue said. "I was going to give you a call this morning, but since you're here I thought I'd tell you now."

"Tell me what?" David said, taking a sip of his coffee.

"It's about the death threat you received."

"The letter?"

"Is there another one?" Gushue asked. David wasn't sure if he was joking or not.

"No," he laughed uneasily. "Of course not."

Gushue appraised him a moment before continuing.

"I told you I had the envelope dusted for prints right?"

"Yeah, and you said you got nothing, other than Elizabeth's."

Gushue nodded.

"But," he said, "I may have caught a break. The lab boys found a hair in the envelope, and determined it was from a male."

David raised his eyebrows.

"I'm not really seeing why that's such a break. There are a lot of males around."

Gushue smiled.

"You remember the DNA sample we got from the crime scene? The one that got left out of the disclosure package?"

David grinned.

"You mean the one you withheld until the last minute because it wasn't Tom's?"

"Ah Jesus, here we go again," Gushue threw up both hands in exasperation.

"Alright, alright," David said, curious now.

"Turns out the lab boys matched the DNA from the crime scene with the hair from the envelope."

"So you're finally going to accept that it wasn't Tom—either the murder or the letter. That is good news," David said, patting Gushue on the shoulder. The latter sat quietly, waiting for David's smile to evaporate as the other consequence of the news sank in. After a moment, David voiced the concern now evident in his eyes, and deep in his heart.

"And whoever sent me that letter murdered Stuart Bruce." He didn't mention the more recent phone call that had prompted Elizabeth's departure, nor of the peril David was now putting his whole family in by talking to Gushue in public.

"I thought you should know," Gushue said, without denying David's conclusion. David looked over his shoulder to re-assess the crowd. He noticed a couple of people looking their way and suddenly felt a chill run down his spine. For the first time, he had objective evidence that a murderer was threatening his family—and here he was doing exactly what he had been warned against.

"I've gotta go," he said, getting up suddenly, knocking over his coffee in his haste.

"Are you alright?" Gushue asked, righting the coffee cup.

"I'm fine. I'm just late. Listen, thanks for the update. I'll be in touch."

Gushue watched as David hurried off towards the Water Street exit. Something was definitely not right.

chapter fifty-eight

"You've got to tell Gushue about the call. They can protect you," Phil said, biting into a piece of battered cod as he and David sat at the counter of a greasy spoon near the courthouse. They had decided to step out for lunch after David had recounted the details of the meeting with Gushue. David's food sat practically untouched in front of him. He said nothing.

"How?" David asked. "By putting me in the witness protection program. Come on Phil, this is real life here."

"That's just it—it's getting all too real. DNA evidence that whoever's threatening you killed Stuart Bruce. That's just plain scary in itself. But add to that what you know about Signal, and who's to say the threats aren't coming from someone with millions at stake?"

"What I really want to know," David said, pushing his plate away, "is where the hell is Bill Stanley?"

"The mystery Osgoode alumnus? I'll call my uncle Marty as soon as we get back," Phil said, looking at his watch.

"Somebody's got to talk to Erin Hay as well, officially," David said, as they got up to head back to the office. "There was something she wasn't saying about Stanley."

"What are you going to do about Elizabeth?"

"She doesn't know I was planning on coming down this week. I was waiting to confirm the flight." David sighed. "But she's going to be waiting for news of the hearing. She'll know something's wrong when I talk to her—even over the phone she can read me like a book."

"Why don't you just go? You're probably safer there anyway," Phil said. "Let me talk to Gushue."

David shook his head.

"I can't just run away from this. What am I supposed to move to Florida permanently?"

"Come on, I'll call my uncle," Phil said as they got up to leave. "We'll get to the bottom of it, don't worry."

He could tell by his friend's ashen features that David was less than convinced.

David sat at his desk on Wednesday morning, staring at the phone and tapping a business card he had pulled from his Rolodex against the receiver. He had spent the previous evening at Phil's, contemplating his situation and going over various parts of the Fitzgerald file before turning in just after midnight. It had been several hours later, as he lay in the spare room staring at the ceiling, before he had finally arrived at an inescapable conclusion. Now, wired on caffeine and stress, he picked up the phone and dialled the direct number on the card. A moment later he was anxiously awaiting the reply at the other end.

"Hi, it's David Hall. Listen, I need to talk to you and it's important. Actually it's urgent," he paused and looked at his watch. "Can I buy you lunch? Say Nellie's, at noon?"

He awaited the reply, and when it came, he sighed in relief and hung up the phone. He extracted a piece of paper from the file and headed out to the photocopier. He didn't have much time to assemble his case.

chapter fifty-nine

"Hello David," J.P. Gallant said as he approached the table where David was already seated.

"Thanks for coming, J.P."

"You're buying, aren't you?" he said with a grin. "So, what's this all about?"

"Tom Fitzgerald," David said in a low voice.

"Oh Jesus," Gallant said, rolling his eyes. "For the last time, there is no investig..."

"It's not that," David interrupted, hushing him. "My wife got a threatening phone call last week from someone."

Gallant's expression changed to one of concern.

"Whoever it was wanted me to stay away from the Bruce case," David continued. "Problem is, I've had nothing to do with it for ages, so

I don't know what I'm supposed to do."

"Did you talk to the RNC?"

"No, the caller threatened to kill us if we did."

Gallant nodded quietly. "There's got to be a way to get them involved. I'll do whatever…"

"I think I know who made the call, and who sent the letter."

"I'm listening…"

"It's the same person that killed Stuart Bruce."

"David," Gallant said softly, holding up his hand.

"I know what you're thinking J.P., but just hear me out. First of all, Tom's been tried and acquitted so I'm not here advocating on his behalf."

"That's good," Gallant nodded. "Because I still think he did it."

"You're wrong."

"Why are you so sure?"

"Because I know who did."

"And that would be?"

"Bill Stanley."

"Bill Stanley," Gallant repeated. "Who the hell is Bill Stanley?"

"I don't know—yet, but I'm getting closer to finding out."

David pulled out a thin file folder with some photocopies inside and laid it on the table between them.

"And this is?"

"Proof," David said, opening the folder and passing the papers to Gallant. "Inventory of evidence, and photos from the crime scene."

Gallant looked puzzled.

"Do you recall anything about a cufflink at the crime scene?" David asked.

"Not really, but I imagine you're going to point to one on this list," Gallant said, tapping the sheet of paper with his index finger.

"Correct. One gold cufflink inscribed with the coat of arms of Osgoode Hall Law School, as well as the year 1968."

"Gallant nodded his head. Yeah, I vaguely remember seeing it on the list. The victim went to Osgoode didn't he?"

"Yes, he did," David confirmed. "And he graduated in 1968."

"So, what's the problem?"

"The problem is the victim's not wearing French cuffs."

Gallant squinted to look more closely at the photo of Stuart Bruce lying in Bannerman Park.

"That doesn't mean anything...," Gallant said, shaking his head. "It might have fallen out of his pocket."

"That was my first thought too. But what about this?" David showed him a picture taken of Stuart Bruce's closet. The police had been very thorough in documenting both the crime scene and the victim's hotel room with photographic records.

"This guy's got a half dozen dress shirts hung up in his closet and not one has French cuffs. Don't you think that's odd?"

"I don't know," Gallant scratched his chin as the waitress arrived. "Can you give us a few minutes?" he said, covering the photograph with his hand.

"Whatever," she replied, rolling her eyes and disappearing again.

"Alright David, what are you getting at?"

David leaned forward in his chair and lowered his voice even further.

"Suppose the cufflink fell off someone else's shirt, or out of someone else's pocket—say it was the murderer's."

"Okay, say it was."

"That would mean the murderer was a former classmate, which would explain a lot of things."

"Like?" Gallant said, leaning ever so slightly forward in his own chair.

"Like why the victim would have met up with his killer in the middle of the night, and why there was little or no evidence of a struggle—both of which suggest he knew his killer."

Gallant said nothing.

"Then there's this," David said, pointing to another item on the list. "A piece of hotel stationary from the victim's room with 'Will' written on it, followed by the word "Signal Investments" further down on the same page. Innocent enough, right? After all the guy was a lawyer. He was probably making notes on estate planning for a client, or for himself, right?"

"You have another theory?"

"The notepad was found right next to the phone. There were several sheets removed that were found in the garbage can under the desk with names and numbers in the victim's handwriting, that corresponded with phone calls made or received by him earlier that evening and afternoon."

"So?"

"As you know, Bruce received a phone call around ten-thirty on the night of the murder. Suppose I told you I knew the following two things…"

Gallant said nothing.

"First," David continued, "that Signal Investments was involved in a $3.5 million swindle, and that the Ontario Securities Commission brass had been in touch with Stuart Bruce to find out who was behind a numbered offshore company that held the majority of the shares in Signal," David paused to take a sip of water. "And second, that I believe the word 'Will' was in fact a name—the name of the person who made that call at ten-thirty on the night of the murder."

Gallant had to be interested, but he was giving nothing away for now.

"Which brings me to Bill Stanley," David carried on, "...who according to one of his former classmates was also known as 'Will' at law school."

"How do you know that?" Gallant asked, breaking his silence.

"This is where you come in. I got a call yesterday from one of his former classmates—a woman named Erin Hay—who referred to him as 'Will'."

"Go on," Gallant was having trouble concealing his interest now.

"She wouldn't say much for fear of incriminating Stanley, but there was definitely something she wanted to tell me."

"And what about Signal, can you confirm any of what you've told me?"

"Not officially, but I can tell you the source is reliable."

"And this Erin, she didn't say anything specific?"

"No, like I said, she was afraid. But if you could ask her—officially I mean—she'd have no choice..."

Gallant sat back and considered it before speaking.

"I don't know..."

"I'm asking you to take a shot at it. My wife has had to leave town with my son because she's too afraid to stay in our house. I'm staying at Morgan's place," David shook his head. "This whole thing is getting out of…"

"Alright, I hear you. Let me make a few calls and see what I can do to get a statement from Erin…"

"Erin Hay."

"Right," Gallant took out a pen and scribbled the name on a napkin.

"I already mentioned Signal to Gushue, before the threatening call, but I don't know if he's done anything with it."

"Leave it with me," Gallant said as the waitress returned.

"Can I take your order gentlemen?"

"Actually," Gallant said, getting up. "I think I'd better get going."

"Thanks, J.P."

"Don't thank me yet," Gallant said, gathering up his coat and gloves. "I'll be in touch."

chapter sixty

"Do you think he'll help?" Elizabeth asked, as David sat at Phil's kitchen table, stretching the telephone cord from the wall-mounted base.

"I need a cordless," Phil said, stepping over the cord on his way to the living room with a plate of nachos and chicken wings.

"Yeah, Gallant's a good guy," David replied. "I think he'll do what he can. How's the weather down there?"

"It's alright, but I hate being here at this time of year. December and palm trees just don't mix for me."

"I wish you'd come back."

"You hurry up and get down here. Ben misses you."

"I should be able to get away by the middle of next week, but it's hard to manage my files while I'm dealing with all this other stuff," David paused before inquiring. "Does anyone else miss me besides Ben?"

"Oh you mean Daddy? He can't wait…," she said, bursting out in laughter.

"That's not exactly what I meant, Liz," David said.

"Seriously. Hurry up and get down here. We can go for nice strolls along the beach with Ben, and as for the evenings—I staked out a great little restaurant a few blocks from here, and with our live-in babysitters, we could even slip away for a night or two on our own…"

"Now you're talking."

"Well, I'd better go put Ben to bed. You be careful, okay?"

"Don't worry. I'll see you in a few days. I love you."

David hung up and joined Phil, who was sitting in the living room watching a hockey game. Judy was out of town on business for a couple of days.

"Everything okay?"

"Yeah," David said, taking a seat.

"So do you think you convinced Gallant?"

"I think he's pretty curious. He called me back this afternoon and said he had hit some red tape on Signal but he was working on a solution, and he had left a message with Erin Hay in Chicago."

"Well, that sounds like a good start."

"Yeah," David nodded.

"Are you going to the dinner tomorrow night?" Phil asked, referring to the Law Society formal Christmas dinner and dance, held on the first Friday in December each year.

"The firm bought a block of tickets," David said, nodding his head. "I'd feel bad if they went to waste."

"Or if we didn't take advantage of the open bar," Phil joked. "Where is it this year?"

"Murray's Pond I think," David replied, referring to the refurbished lodge located twenty minutes outside of St. John's.

"Oh yeah, the food's good out there," Phil said enthusiastically. That's it—no spouses, good food and free booze—we're going."

"Yeah, I could use a night out," David agreed.

chapter sixty-one

It was late on Friday afternoon and David was working furiously on finishing off a trial brief when Joanne called in.

"J.P. Gallant's on the line. Do you want to take it?"

"Yes, put him through please," he said, shutting the door and sitting in his chair to take the call. "J.P.?"

"Hi David. Sorry I didn't get back to you earlier."

"That's okay. Any luck?"

"I just got off the phone with Erin Hay."

"And?"

Gallant hesitated for a moment. "I'd rather talk to you about this in person. I've got a meeting that's going to tie me up for the next hour or so."

David looked at his watch—it was ten to five.

"Are you going to the dinner tonight?" Gallant asked.

"Yes, actually."

"Okay, we can talk there. You haven't discussed this with anyone else have you?"

"No. Well, apart from my wife and Phil."

"Alright, keep it that way."

"Can't you tell me what she said now? And what about Signal?"

"I'll tell you everything tonight."

"Alright," David said, hanging up, frustrated at the lack of details. He went to look for Phil and found him in a heated debate on the phone.

"What's up?" he asked his secretary.

"Someone's looking for an emergency injunction to stop their wife from taking the kids out of the province," she said.

"Uh oh," David said, pulling a frown.

"I think he's in for a long night," she added, switching off her computer and putting on her boots. "And I'm going to be late for happy hour."

"Have fun," David said, returning to his office and wishing Joanne a good weekend in the process.

"Don't forget the pre-trial on Billy Baker Monday morning."

"How could I forget that?" he said.

David clued up his files and cleaned out his e-mail inbox. Fifteen minutes later, he strolled over to Phil's office and peeked around the door. Phil was sitting in his chair, feet on his desk and staring out the window.

"What's up?"

"I'm screwed," he said with a sigh.

"Some kind of injunction?"

"Yeah, the kind that's going to have me working all night—so much for my free drunk."

"You want a hand?"

"No, there's nothing you can do. Besides, there's no need to ruin your evening too." He took a key off his keychain and tossed it to David.

"Here's the house key. I'm going to be here for a while doing research so you go on. Just leave the door unlocked when you leave for the dinner."

"You sure you don't want a hand, or some company?"

"Naw, just make sure you drink enough for the both of us."

David laughed.

"By the way, Gallant spoke with Erin Hay."

"And?"

"She obviously made an impression on him, but he didn't say much. He's going to talk to me tonight, at the dinner."

"Good. You can give me the scoop tomorrow."

David nodded and headed for the stairs.

chapter sixty-two

David straightened his tie and checked his watch. He would have to move it if he wanted to make the cocktail hour. He grabbed his keys and switched off the TV, leaving the front door unlocked on his way out. The snow from the previous day had long since melted in the unseasonably warm air which, combined with a cold offshore current had created a dense fog that would have made even the short walk to his car a challenge without the nearby streetlight. As he opened his car door, he heard the dull moan of the foghorn in the distance. It would not be a great night for a drive, but at least he wouldn't be driving home. He planned to cab it back and get a ride from Phil the next day to recover his car. He weaved his way through the light evening traffic and climbed out of the city towards the suburbs and beyond.

Twenty minutes later, he was parking his car at the edge of the fully occupied parking lot and practically groping his way through the fog to the lodge. Inside, the brightly lit hall was awash in tuxedos and evening gowns, and the laughter and bustle of the lively crowd was accompanied by soft classical music in the background. David checked his overcoat and made his way to the bar, chatting with acquaintances along the way. Fortified with a drink, he made his way into the fray, striking up a conversation with a couple of senior criminal lawyers he knew slightly. Before long, he spotted Gallant making his way through the crowd, with an attractive woman in a red gown. Taking advantage of a pause in the conversation, David introduced Gallant, who in turn introduced his wife to the group. After she had settled in with some of her friends, Gallant motioned for David to follow and made his way towards the large deck overlooking the pond, where a cluster of smokers were gathered. Gallant led David to the other end of the deck and leaned over the rail.

"Sorry to make you wait like this," he began.

"What did you find out?" David asked anxiously.

"You were right about Erin Hay. She did have something to say."

"Well?"

"Turns out Bill Stanley got himself in a bit of hot water not long after law school."

"How so?"

"Allegations of rape from the teenaged daughter of a client. He was never charged but the damage was done."

"That's not good, but what does it have to do with Stuart Bruce," David asked, a little disappointed.

"Maybe nothing. Except that Hay thinks Stanley may have changed his name before leaving town."

David considered the possibilities.

"So we don't know where he is, or what his new name is either," David said, shaking his head. "This is going from bad to worse."

"Not really. There are records when you change your name, so we'll find him eventually."

"Hmm," David frowned. Even if that were true, there was still no real link between Stanley, or whatever his new name was, and the murder. "And what about Signal?" he asked.

"Everything you told me checked out. I'm working with the RCMP, foreign affairs and the Department of Justice to try and get around the secrecy laws. I'm confident we'll get there but it will take a little time."

"As for the phone call your wife got, I'm having the number checked out—discreetly," Gallant said, laying his drink on the railing and putting his hands in his pockets.

"David, in light of all this, I think we should arrange for some protection for you until we've sorted all of this out. Where did you say your wife was?"

"She's in Florida at her parents' condo—and she's not going to be coming back any time soon unless the police have someone behind bars. I'm supposed to meet her there next week."

"That's probably not a bad idea," Gallant nodded.

The two just stood there for a while, gazing out at gloomy blackness.

"I knew it wasn't Tom," David said, a smile appearing on his face.

"Well, it's not exactly a closed case yet, but you've certainly given me something to think about," Gallant said.

"Who says we can't be on opposite sides of the fence and still see eye to eye," David said. "Well, you'd better get back to your wife."

The sumptuous dinner, accompanied by liberal servings of good wine, was followed by a series of speeches delivered by senior members of the bar and the Chief Justice. As these came to an end, so did the formal segment of the evening. The classical music was replaced with a live band playing a wide range of dance tunes. By 11:00 p.m., David was seated at a table with a group of young criminal lawyers and prosecutors, including Gallant, who were enjoying themselves with war stories in between dances.

As he reached for his drink, David felt a tap on his shoulder.

"Mr. Hall?"

"Yes?" David turned to see one of the waiters leaning towards him to be heard over the loud music.

"Do you have a blue Ford, licence number ASK 974?"

"Yes, I do. Is there a problem?"

"Your lights are on sir."

David looked puzzled. He was certain he had turned them off.

"Are you sure?"

"Yes sir."

"Alright. Thank you."

David got up and headed for the door, not bothering to get his coat. He crossed the parking lot through a thick fog to find that his car lights were indeed on. He also noticed that the doors were locked, which was stranger still since he rarely took this precaution. He patted his pockets and realized his keys were in his overcoat, and as he turned towards the lodge, he saw a dark shape off to his side. The last thing he remembered was a splitting sensation at the back of his head, before he was overcome by utter blackness.

At about eleven-fifteen, the phone rang at Phil Morgan's house. He had come home around nine-thirty with his research in hand and a plan to prepare the necessary court documents for his injunction. After four rings, the answering machine picked up, and after a few seconds a voice echoed through the kitchen where the machine was located.

"Phil, it's your uncle Marty. I've been trying you for a couple of hours now so I'm going to leave you this message and you can give me a call when you get it. I finally got a line on that Stanley character you asked me about. It turns out he changed his name in 1970, that's why your friend couldn't track him through the legal directory. Anyway, he should be pretty easy to find now—he's practicing law right there in St. John's. His name's…"

The voice was cut off by a long beep, indicating the end of the machine's allotted time. Phil didn't respond to the message, nor did he hear it, for at that moment he was lying on the floor of his kitchen in a puddle of his own blood.

chapter sixty-three

David felt himself lurch forward uncontrollably and opened his eyes, only to shut them again in response to the pain in his head. Feeling he was in motion and hearing the sound of an engine, he opened his eyes again to find himself lying across the back seat of a large truck or SUV. By the way he was bouncing around, it seemed the vehicle was traveling over a very bumpy road. He tried to feel his head, but realized his hands were tied behind his back. He looked into the front compartment of the vehicle but in the dim light, he could not make out the features of the driver. Feeling very disoriented and afraid, he opened his mouth slowly, before uttering a few words, having to repeat them again before the driver heard him.

"Wh...who are you?" he said.

The driver looked in the rear view mirror, but because of its angle, David could not see his face.

"So you're awake," he said, in a vaguely familiar voice.

"Where am I?"

"We're going for a little drive."

"Who are you?" David repeated, feeling behind him and touching with an index finger the duct tape that bound his wrists. He tried in vain to separate them.

"You should know, David. You're so fucking smart."

"You killed Stuart Bruce didn't you?"

"You tell me."

"You killed Stuart Bruce, and your former name is Bill Stanley."

"That's very impressive. You should have been a homicide cop instead of a lawyer then none of this would be happening."

David strained at the tape, trying in vain to free himself, as they bounced over a large pothole.

"Why did you kill him?"

"I'm sure you know by now, don't you?" the driver said, angry now. "You should have played it smart, David. God knows I gave you enough warnings."

"You're the majority shareholder in Signal," David said, feeling the cold metal of a seat belt buckle behind his back and trying to angle it between his wrists, "and Stuart Bruce knew it."

"That shows how little you know," the driver said with a chuckle. "I own all of the shares in an offshore company that used to own two-thirds of Signal, but nobody on this side of the Atlantic will ever know that."

"You don't think someone will get around the disclosure laws."

"No, I don't."

"If they're so airtight, then why did you have to kill Bruce?"

"I moved out here thirty years ago, and ever since, I've been building a career and a family. I'm a fucking pillar of society, but all it took was one meeting with that bastard Bruce to bring it all back."

"You mean the rape?" David said, recalling Gallant's revelation earlier that evening.

"There was no rape, but nobody believed it back then, just as nobody would now. And of course when Bruce showed up in town on an examination for discovery, he just had to make a snide remark about my leaving Toronto in a hurry so long ago. He couldn't have known I was involved, but when he mentioned he was looking into Signal...I lost it—I panicked."

David was trying to place the familiar voice, but without a face to go with it, it eluded him for the moment.

"He's got contacts all over," the driver continued. "The Channel Islands, the Caymans, Panama. Wherever there's a haven, he knows the territory—that's his practice. He'd have traced it to me eventually."

"And now that he's gone, you think you're in the clear?" David said.

"I was always in the clear. Like I said, I panicked. Luckily though, your friend was there to help me cover my mistake."

"Tom."

"I'll bet you're dying to know what really happened aren't you, after all that automatism bullshit?" the driver said. "I have to say, my hat is off to you for getting a jury to buy that—congratulations. As for Tom, the poor sap was in the wrong place at the wrong time. I had already dealt with Bruce before I came across him, passed out under a tree like the sad piece of shit that he is. I planted Stuart's cash and plastic on him, shoved the knife in his hands and that was it. It was perfect—until you screwed it all up, that is."

David's wrists slipped off the buckle again as he tried desperately to free himself. As he racked his brain trying to place the voice, something occurred to David for the first time.

"Were you involved in the case Bruce came to St. John's for?"

"It's a small world, isn't it?"

David tried to remember the names of the lawyers involved in the discovery that had prompted Bruce's trip to St. John's. There had been Tom Parsons and Roger Diamond of the local bar, and two lawyers from Halifax. But there was one other local. David strained his eyes to make out the profile that went with the voice, then it came to him.

"Francis Sullivan," he said aloud.

"Congratulations," Sullivan said with a snort. "And for your troubles, Sherlock, you're going to have a little high dive off Red Cliff."

David felt a chill run down his spine as he looked out the window into the blackness and realized the bumps he was feeling were on the remote and pot-holed road that led up to the top of Red Cliff. Only fifteen minutes outside of St. John's, it might as well have been in the middle of the Atlantic on a night like this. There would be no one to hear him shout. He worked even more furiously to position the metal prong of the seatbelt between his wrists and the other end against the seatback as he considered being thrown off the cliff into the frigid Atlantic. Even if by some miracle he wasn't dashed on the rocks before he hit water, he would freeze to death in minutes, if not seconds.

"The drive-by and the letters—that was you?" he managed to ask.

"McGrath asked one of my partners for advice on your plan to give the crown exculpatory evidence when you thought they were taking another shot at Tom. I used my son's car to give you a scare, and I was going to follow it up with a letter to make you think it was Tom who was out to get you, but I thought you had backed off. When you kept talking to Tom, and the police, and sticking your nose where it didn't belong, I sent the letter and then made the call. I gave you plenty of opportunities to back off—but you leave me no choice."

"So you overheard me talking to Gushue about Signal a couple of weeks ago at the courthouse," David said, as he leaned against the seatback, but the buckle slipped away before any pressure was exerted on the tape.

"And on the morning of your disciplinary hearing," Sullivan said. David groaned audibly—the hearing! So that was why Sullivan had gone after him, not because of the stupid job offer. "Bill McGrath should have stayed out of it. Little does he know he had a hand in signing your death warrant by showing up on that panel that morning."

"Don't make it worse," David said. "The cops already know you killed Bruce."

"Nice try," Sullivan said, "but I don't think Gushue would ever be convinced it was anyone but Tom."

"I've been talking to Gallant…"

"Good for you. There's nothing you could have told him that would stick against me. And don't forget he can never connect me to my stake in Signal."

David repositioned himself against the seatbelt buckle, but it slipped out uselessly from under him again.

"So why kill me? Like you said, I've got no proof."

"Because you're a pain in the ass, that's why," Sullivan said angrily. "And I'm not taking any chances."

"There's other evidence besides your interest in Signal," David persisted. "Like the DNA found at the scene…"

"What DNA evidence?" Sullivan replied.

"Gushue matched the hair from the crime scene with DNA from the envelope you sent me," David said quickly.

"You're bluffing," Sullivan scoffed, "and even if you're not, they'd have to have a reason to come looking for a DNA sample from me."

"And then there's the cufflink," David said, determined to keep Sullivan's attention away from his struggle to free his arms.

"What cufflink?"

"You left a cufflink at the scene."

Sullivan was silent for a moment. It was clear from his reaction that he did not know about this piece of evidence.

"You're full of shit. And even if there really is a cufflink, there's no way to prove it's mine."

"You're not going to get away with it Sullivan. I've already told Gallant everything I know. Why don't you give yourself…"

"Shut up!" Sullivan yelled, obviously annoyed.

"Anyway, don't you think my death is going to cause suspicion?" David said, re-positioning the buckle for another try at the tape.

"Not when they read the tearful suicide note I left at your lover's place."

"What are you talking about?"

"You know, the one where you explain you were confused by your feelings for Phil, and the damage your relationship would do to your marriages…"

"What in God's name are you talking about?" David said with a trace of fear in his voice, as the implications sank in. "What does Phil have to do with this?"

"I had to justify your death somehow, and I think I came up with a winner. It goes something like this—poor confused David kills his gay lover and then commits suicide in a fit of guilt by throwing himself over Red Cliff."

"You're out of your mind," David said, straining to separate his wrists and pushing back against the seat again. This time, the buckle stayed in place and he felt a tear in the tape.

"Ah, almost there," Sullivan said as they neared the end of the dirt road.

David leaned back on one arm and almost dislocated his shoulder trying to separate it from the other.

"At least it'll be quick for you, and your friend didn't really suffer—too much."

In a burst of energy fuelled by rage as much as the instinct to survive, David jumped up from the back seat and threw his arms around Sullivan's neck, causing him to lurch backwards and stomp on the accelerator in the process. As they struggled, David tightened his grip around Sullivan's neck, who seemed to be losing strength. But he slammed on the brakes and sent David flying over the front bench seat and smashing into the dashboard. As David got his bearings, Sullivan grabbed him in a headlock and started choking him, while trying to bring the vehicle to a stop without loosening his grip on David's neck. With his torso across the passenger side of the bench seat and his hands on the floor in front of the driver's side, David spotted the pedals in front of him. With a burst of energy, he broke free of the headlock and lunged desperately forward, slamming on the accelerator and sending the vehicle careening forward. Sullivan grabbed a fistful of David's hair and pulled fiercely with one hand, while trying to maintain control of the vehicle with the other. He stabbed at the brakes with his feet but made contact only with David's arm, and as their speed increased, he cried out in fear.

"The cliff, the cliff…Stop!"

At the last minute, Sullivan let go of David's hair and pulled frantically with both arms on the steering wheel, causing the SUV to lurch suddenly to the right. A split second later, David's wind was knocked out by a sickening jolt, accompanied by an ear-splitting crash of breaking glass and twisting metal. He lost consciousness momentarily, coming back to a throbbing and growing pain emanating from his ribs, and then his arm. He tried to move the arm and cried out in pain. He felt the pressure of the bench seat against his back, pinning him up under the dash on the passenger side, and tried to move his legs. Freeing one, he extended it out and felt the cold of the night air and began squirming his way backwards through the opening left by the broken passenger door. After what seemed like an eternity he had extracted himself from the vehicle and fallen out onto the hard ground. His arm was badly broken and his ribs felt like he'd been hit by a sledgehammer, but he was alive. As he took in the sight of the twisted vehicle in front of him, he wondered how that could be. It had slammed into a large rock, about four feet high and ten across. He struggled to his feet and made his way around the rear of the big SUV to the driver's side. As he approached the driver's door and looked beyond, he realized for the first time that the rock lay only a few feet back from the edge of Red Cliff itself. Even in the foggy darkness, David could see where the rocky ground gave way to the black void of a sheer drop that led straight down to the Atlantic, several hundred feet below. David shivered in horror as he looked back at the truck, and the gaping hole in the windshield through which Francis Sullivan's body had sailed before plunging over the cliff.

David stepped forward as far as he dared, peering out into the inky blackness for any sign of Sullivan. But there was nothing, only the sound of the swell below, punctuated by the slow, monotonous wail of the foghorn far off in the distance.

epilogue

David Hall sipped his coffee and read the morning paper, oblivious to the ringing phones outside his office door. Joanne had matters well in hand, as usual.

"Morning, David," came a familiar voice as David looked up from his paper and saw Phil Morgan in the doorway, waving his own copy of the morning paper.

"You read the article on the Wallace verdict?" Phil asked, referring to a client David had just defended—successfully—on an armed robbery charge.

"You bet."

"Couldn't ask for better PR for the firm," Phil said with a smile, referring to the law firm they had founded together three years prior.

After that terrible night at Red Cliff, David had returned to Phil's house to find a swarm of police cars, and he had entered the melee fearing the worst. As it turned out, Phil had been very lucky. The blow to his head had opened a huge gash on the back of his head, besides knocking him unconscious. But by a strange twist of fate, his wife, Judy, had arrived home unexpectedly shortly after eleven-thirty and had called an ambulance in time to get Phil to the hospital before his life had drained away along with all of his blood. And although there had been some post-traumatic memory loss, he had not suffered any lasting cognitive effects.

In the aftermath, it had been confirmed that one hundred per cent of the numbered company domiciled in Guernsey that had controlled Signal Investments was in fact owned by Francis Sullivan. And as Phil's uncle had already concluded, Sullivan and "Will" Stanley were the same person. The Bruce murder investigation had been revisited in depth, and further DNA testing confirmed Sullivan's genetic print matched the samples from both the crime scene and the envelope that had carried the threatening letter. More importantly, it cleared Tom Fitzgerald unequivocally of any involvement in Stuart Bruce's murder.

As for Francis Sullivan, the search by the RNC, the fire department and the Coast Guard of the waters off Red Cliff after that fateful night had uncovered no trace of him. Though the odds against surviving the impact with the windshield, let alone the fall itself, were impossible, David couldn't help but wonder from time to time whether Sullivan had managed to escape somehow, and was living somewhere in the tropics.

For David, the whole incident had given him a new perspective on things, and in the months that followed, he had made some important choices. The first was to shift his focus from work to his family. His brush with death had made him recognize that they were his first priority, and in talking with Phil, he had discovered his friend had come to the same conclusion. In light of that shift, the two had given their notice to McGrath, who after recognizing they had made up their minds, had wished them well and given them both a generous severance package to set themselves up with. Fittingly, David's last act at the firm was to settle William Baker's claim for a few thousand dollars, and a happier client David had never seen.

Once they were out on their own, David and Phil set about establishing a practice with a success that surprised even them. With David doing the criminal files and Phil handling the family law work, they had quickly built up an impressive practice. And while they both worked hard, neither was willing to take on more than he could handle for the sake of more money, and they had maintained a comfortable balance between home and work. Phil and Judy had begun a family two years prior, and with a new baby on the way, their young son would soon be getting a playmate. David and Elizabeth had added two girls to their family and Ben was enjoying his role as the big brother.

As for Tom, he had made good use of his freedom by cleaning himself up and starting a small office courier business, which happened to be the exclusive carrier for the law firm of Hall, Morgan, among others. He had married his girlfriend and seemed to be content in his new life. And though David's conscience would always be burdened by the way he had betrayed Tom, the experience had at least offered concrete proof of the need for the presumption of innocence—and faith in human nature—in the event David ever found himself in a situation where he needed reminding. And so, the terrible events of that foggy night in Bannerman Park had changed both of their lives in a positive way in the end.

acknowledgements

I'm grateful to my publisher, who took a chance on an unknown, as well as to my editor, Jocelyne Thomas, who provided valuable input at the editing stage (any errors are mine alone). My thanks also to all of the friends, colleagues and clients from East to North and in between, who contributed to this book in their own way. Special thanks to Paul Smith and Dreena Burton for their support early on, and to my sister Claire for her encouragement and advice.

Most of all, thanks to my parents, who will always be my compass.

nick **wilkshire**

is a lawyer with the federal Department of Justice in Ottawa. He was born and raised in St. John's, where he attended Memorial University (BA, 1990) and practiced law (LLB, Osgoode Hall, 1993) for several years with Williams, Roebothan, McKay & Marshall before leaving the province in 1996.